Simon Raven was born in London in 1927 ⟨
and King's College, Cambridge, where he read
in the King's Shropshire Light Infantry. In 195
and turned to book-reviewing. His first novel, *The Feathers of Death*, brought
instant recognition and his popular *First-born of Egypt* series encompasses
seven volumes. His TV and radio plays, of which *Royal Foundation* is the best
known, are classics. He also wrote the scripts for the *Pallisers* series and
Edward and Mrs Simpson.

C000173086

SIMON RAVEN

Shadows On the Grass

This edition published in 2001 by House of Stratus, an imprint of
House of Stratus Ltd, Thirsk Industrial Park, York Road, Thirsk, North Yorkshire, YO7 3BX, UK.

www.houseofstratus.com

Typeset, printed and bound by House of Stratus.

A catalogue record for this book is available from the British Library and the Library of Congress.

ISBN 1-84232-210-9

CONTENTS

AUTHOR'S NOTE

Everything in this memoir is essentially true. However, since I am tender about many of the dead and disposed to be civil to those yet living, I have occasionally made minor alterations in times, dates, names and places, in a word, in circumstance. Furthermore, some of the facts, in too readily memorable cases of treachery, cruelty or dishonesty, have been disguised, though not softened, by moral metaphor. This said, pray believe that what follows is what occurred.

SR

I

A SHROPSHIRE LAD

For several years, from 1966 to 1975, I used to play cricket for a small village called Worth on the Saxon shore. On the first Sunday of October we would play a match against Sandwich, the last match of the season. Although we had kind autumn weather, as often as not, warm enough yet agreeably brisk, the occasion was always melancholy. So many of us would not be there, for one reason or another, when the wicket was measured next April.

As one stood on the grass meditating on such matters, there would come a rumbling along the road which skirted our ground, a rumbling, a chugging and a clunking, from the direction of Deal. And soon, from behind the trees which stood on the Southern boundary, appeared huge lorries and traction engines, processing along the road to Sandwich, towing away the Fair. There went the swings and the roundabouts, the lions and the unicorns, the bumping cars, the high slide; there went the children's ponies and the lovers' boats: there, in a word, went the cortège of summer, one more summer going to its long home, as the wind over the salt marshes brought the first of the evening chill.

Then and for many hours afterwards I would think of other summers that had come and gone.

At much the same time of year in 1957 the last match of the season was drawing to a close on the ground of the King's Shropshire Light Infantry, with which Regiment I was then serving, at Copthorne Barracks, Shrewsbury. Our Regimental Depot was playing a team from somewhere out on the Marches. I was batting with a Sergeant Instructor in a fading light; we needed 21 runs in ten minutes, with two wickets still to fall. In those days there was no law

1

to enforce twenty overs in the last hour, and the marcher men were walking back and changing over as slowly as they could without actually marking time. Nevertheless, a few lucky hits from the Sergeant and myself brought us to a stage at which we required seven runs only to win, and would have one more over to play – if the over now in progress ended before 6.30. Since there was only one ball left of this and the time was 6.27, the next and vitally important over was virtually guaranteed.

Or so it seemed. But as the bowler started his run a telegram boy parked his bicycle against the pavilion and came strutting out on to the field, despite shouts from our supporters that he was to wait till the end of the over. The bowler took this as excuse to postpone the ball; the fieldsmen, delighted at this interruption, stood gazing at the wretched urchin as if he had been a messenger from heaven.

'Name of RAVEN?' said the boy.

'Captain Raven,' corrected the Sergeant.

'All it says is Raven,' said the boy.

I held out my hand. The boy gave me the yellow envelope and stood waiting.

'Right you are,' I called out to the bowler, stuffing the envelope into my pocket and waving the boy off the pitch. There was still just time to get the next ball bowled before 6.30 and so make sure of another over. But the boy stood his ground.

'Might be a reply,' he said.

'No reply.'

'How do you know if you haven't read it?'

'*Please wait by the pavilion.*'

'Haven't got all night to hang about.'

He stood there as firm as ever. If, as he well knew by now, he wasn't going to get a tip, he was getting full value from creating annoyance.

'Very well,' I said desperately.

I dragged the telegram from my pocket, took off one batting glove and tore the thing jaggedly open.

PLEASE PAY ONE HUNDRED SEVENTY OWING MONDAY LATEST OR COMPELLED TO INFORM COMMANDANT BEST RESPECTS
    THEWS JAMESON TURF ACCNT

A gust of wind took the red-hot missive from my hand and whirled it towards the pavilion. I gave chase. The clock struck the half-hour. The bowler waited patiently to bowl what must now be the last ball of the match. My telegram was fielded on the boundary by the friendly Commandant, who waved me back to the wicket. The Sergeant hit the last ball for six, but we were one short of victory, and I had lost £25 to the Adjutant, having laid him an even pony against a draw (draws being very rare on West Salopian wickets). My only consolation was that the Commandant had been too much of a gentleman to read my telegram before giving it back to me.

The shadows were crowding in on my military career that autumn, and close of play was imminent. Yet there were still a few laughs to be had before the game was absolutely up.

On the day after the match which I have just been describing, our cricket pavilion was converted into a 'Liaison Centre' for a theoretical operation in Emergency Civic Control. The premise was that Birmingham had been laid flat by a nuclear bomb and that such of the population as survived was ramping through Wolverhampton and towards Shrewsbury in an orgy of looting and rapine which had been inspired by the mob's apprehension that most of it would be dead of gamma ray poisoning (or whatever) within a very few days. The exercise comprised the Army (Regular and Territorial), the Royal Air Force, the Constabulary, the Civil Defence Force, the Fire Brigade, St John's Ambulance, representatives of the Churches and Unions, and also a number of Army Cadets, Boy Scouts and Girl Guides (Messengers). This combination was entrusted with the task of halting the rush of nuclear-crazed humanity, confining it, feeding it, going through the motions of trying to cure it, and finally burning it.

The affair started with a meeting of the Commanders and Seconds in Command of the various services in the Pavilion or Liaison Centre. I was present as Aide to my Commandant. He himself was present as Chief Umpire under the local General, who now treated the meeting to a description, distinguished by evident personal relish, of the situation which I have outlined above. Very well; what were we to do about it? We were, of course, to follow the official plan, which had been drawn up against such contingency by the Civil Defence authorities in Whitehall many years before. The plan was a prototype: all we had to do was to work out a version applicable in our immediate terrain.

What then was the Whitehall plan, on the basis of which our own must now be formulated?

1) A Defensive Line must be set up (in our case North-South, guarding the Eastern approaches to Shrewsbury).

2) Ambulance men in special anti-radiation suits (imaginary, for the purposes of this exercise) would detain all 'arrivals' from the bombed area and take them to decontamination centres. Any reluctance on the part of any

'arrival' would result in his arrest by units of Police or Army who would be deployed (also wearing theoretical anti-radiation suits) in support of the ambulance men. Any person who resisted arrest was to be shot *instanter* –

– Uproar from the representatives of the Churches and the Unions. Did the General mean that these poor human creatures (Churches) or deprived fellow-workers (Unions) were to be denied the compassionate welcome and succour of their brethren in Shrewsbury (Churches), were to be murdered in cold blood to spare inconvenience to the bourgeois householders of the suburbs (Unions)?

The General retorted that the exercise was about control and decontamination. If people refused to submit, then they were endangering their lives – But why, interrupted the senior representative of the Unions, had not all citizens of Birmingham been issued with anti-radiation suits before the war began, instead of being abandoned to hideous suffering by a cruel and ruthless capitalist regime – It might be, pointed out the Chief Fire Officer, that a distribution of such suits would be somewhat too complicated and expensive. As it was, there were, so far as he knew, no actual anti-radiation suits in the entire area. The ones to be worn by troops, police and ambulance men for the operation were, let us remember, imaginary. Very well, said the Unionist: as a matter of equality let all the refugees from Birmingham be equipped with imaginary suits too.

But if everyone had anti-radiation suits, said the Chief Constable, it would make rubbish of the exercise. Nonsense, said the Bishop: it would merely rule out the need for decontamination centres and the brutal methods attendant; there would still be all the problems of feeding, accommodating and tending the refugees. Furthermore, said his Chaplain, since they would all be in anti-radiation suits there would be no need, he was happy to say, to posit any rape in transit from Birmingham, as it would clearly be next to impossible to – er – Not in the least, said the Chief Constable: anti-radiation suits were equipped with zippers through which – er – masculinity might be asserted, and in any case the probability of looting still remained.

The Head of the Civil Defence Force, who had so far said nothing, enquired whether the refugees as well as their suits were to be imaginary. No, he was told by the Unionist; a token force of refugees had been assembled from the local leather works at double time and a half, payable by the War Office; each leather worker would represent a hundred fugitives.

While the Chief of the St John's Ambulance was enquiring whether segregation of sexes was desirable, and if so whether each leather worker represented a hundred of one sex or fifty of both, my Commandant opened a haversack and took out a plate, a cold roast partridge stuffed with chestnut, and a bottle of Claret.

4

'Lunchtime, General,' he announced, 'I've got a bird for you too.'

It was now my job to see everyone else fed. The rank and file of the various services were being entertained in the Men's Cookhouse, while those of approximately 'commissioned' status would accompany me to the Officers' Mess. The Bishop and his Chaplain insisted on humbling themselves and going to the Cookhouse (whither they were reluctantly accompanied by our own Padre); the Trade Unionists rancorously declined an offer of refreshment in the Sergeants' Mess ('more congenial') and insisted on accompanying the Officers; and the Girl Guide, our 'Messenger', was so heavily engaged in masturbation with a bat handle in the Visitors' Changing Room that I judged it unkind and possibly unwise to interrupt her. My Commandant and the General, who had carried their partridges away from envious and disapproving glances and into the Scoring Box, remained there together until I joined them half an hour later.

'After luncheon,' said the General glumly, 'we've actually got to get off our bottoms and do it.'

'Do what?'

'Deal with these refugees at double time and a half. And those Trade Union Johnnies will be watching us like hawks. Any sign of anyone's getting pushed around on the one hand, or getting a bit of privilege on the other, and they'll go squealing to the War House. And the War House will have to take action whether it wants to or not.'

'But surely, sir,' I said, 'this is a preliminary and largely theoretical manoeuvre. No one can take it too seriously. Besides, it *is* actually War Office policy that people *should* be pushed around in these circumstances – if they make a nuisance of themselves.'

'Try telling that to the War Office if those bastards complain.'

Even as early as 1957 the Unions' special brand of sanctimonious malice had somehow endowed them with a moral authority which no one dared to resist.

'And another thing,' the General said, 'those clergymen will make trouble if given half a chance. If I put a foot wrong about God – set up one too many tin tabernacles in the Reception Area, or one too few – then the Churches are going to come crashing down on my neck.'

'Tell you what,' said my Commandant, 'pre-emptive bid. You know, three heart call.'

'Meaning?'

'Meaning you've got a long string of hearts and an outside ace.'

'Meaning here and now?'

'Announce an imaginary bomb on Shrewsbury – there's your outside ace. Then say survivors are to be ferried to a new Reception Area in Wales – and there's your long string of hearts. By the time you get them there it will be time to stop the exercise: so the whole controversial bit, who's to sleep where and live off what, and what's to be done if the proles turn Bolshy – you can put all that off till next time and announce a successful exercise in emergency rerouting of survivors. Adaptability and all that balls. Neither the Churches nor the Unions can get at you over that.'

'And when the next time comes? We're going to have this sort of exercise every six months, you know.'

'Six months in the Army is an eternity,' my Commandant said.

The new Reception Area wasn't quite as far away as Wales (that, said the General, would have been overdoing it); it was on Ludlow Racecourse, the drive to which would almost exhaust the time that remained for the exercise and yet not seriously inconvenience anyone of importance.

As for myself, however, the choice of venue made me exceedingly uneasy. Sitting in the bare bar with the Commandant and listening while the CDF quarrelled with the Unions about the allotment of official accommodation (there was just time for *that* before the exercise ceased) I reflected on the last occasion, some two weeks ago, when I had been here for the actual Races. I recalled broad scowls from the credit bookmakers as I falsely assured them their cheques were 'in the post'; and I shuddered as I thought of the humiliating dash to the Tote to make a cash bet with a flyer I had scrounged off one of my subalterns, hoping to save something from the horrible wreck…

For Ludlow was only one of the many attractive Racecourses which clustered round Shrewsbury and on which I had steadily been ruining myself for the last year, ever since I had come to the Regimental Depot to command the Training Company. The ready availability of Courses was compounded by the old-fashioned notions and sheer good nature of the Commandant. As he saw it, one's duty as an Officer at the Depot was to be seen around the County doing 'the right sort of things' and thus boosting the repute of the Regiment: so provided one was prepared to play cricket three times a week, either for the Depot itself or 'the right sort' of local club, then one was welcome to go racing for the other three, for to be seen racing, though not as commendable as to be seen at the wicket, was pretty well what was expected of Regular Officers of a decent County Regiment on Home Service in their own County. (As for the Training, the NCOs and the National Service Officers could look after *that*.) *Mutatis mutandis*, much the same system obtained in the winter: provided one went shooting or hunting three days a week, then one could go racing for the rest with the Commandant's blessing – this being the warmer in winter as National Hunt Racing was somehow more 'the right sort of thing' than the Flat.

The sum of the matter was, then, that since I cheerfully did my stint at cricket and rough shooting, I was allowed, almost encouraged, to attend all the major Race Meetings and many of the minor ones from Aintree south to Chepstow and from Hereford east to Woore…a licence to beggar oneself if ever there was. Mind you, I had my moments; one November day in 1956 I won a massive Yankee (four horses cross-doubled, cross-trebled and accumulated) which got me out of a bad spot of bother and put me two thousand pounds (in those days a huge sum of money) in the clear. But instead of quitting I got greedy (do it again, boy, at higher stakes): away went the two thousand which I had and three thousand which I hadn't; the bookmakers were at first patient, then restive, and by now overtly disagreeable; and there I was on that dreary non-racing afternoon at Ludlow, faced with absolute and irremediable social and military disgrace.

As we left at the end of the exercise the Commandant looked out over the crepuscular Course and remarked,

'Nice place this. I'll join you next time they race here.'

At once a vision came to me of walking with this amiable gentleman between rows of jeering bookies; the sweat began to trickle in my crutch, and there and then I made my confession. The Commandant was uncensorious but mildly taken aback. Although he knew I was a betting man, he hadn't, apparently, conceived of me as a plunger. Such trouble as this he had not at all expected; and of course from his point of view (i.e. the Regiment's) it was the worst sort of trouble in the book. Not the 'sort of thing' which would go down well in the County. However, as I say, he did not recriminate or complain, he merely remarked that in his young days there had been a saying, 'If you can't pay the bill, look for the fire escape,' after which he promised to give me his considered view of the matter on the following morning.

When this came the Commandant was still calm and undismayed.

'It seems from what you've told me,' he said in a light and casual voice, 'that very soon now we're going to have a pack of bookmakers baying for you at the Barrack Gate. In which case we'd have to have you Court-Martialed. Not paying your bookies is conduct unbecoming to the character of an Officer and a Gentleman – in case you didn't know.'

'I knew,' I said.

'Well then. I can't stop the bookmakers pursuing you, but I can help you to keep out of their way until you're a civilian. Until you've *resigned*. You'll still be in bad trouble with the Jockey Club or whatever, but at least there'll be no Court Martial – a very great relief to me and to you too, I should imagine.'

I nodded and quickly wiped away a tear. For this was handsome behaviour by any measure.

'No time to waste,' said the Commandant briskly. 'Lose yourself. As from this second you are on leave: no leave address, because you're touring the Balkans or some bloody place. If no one can find you, no one can Court Martial you. *So lose yourself utterly* until your resignation is safely in the *London Gazette.*'

'But I can't go to the Balkans. I can just about get to London.'

'A very good place to hide. You just lie low, dear boy, and leave me to tell the tale if I have to.'

'How long will it take – to get my resignation through?'

'Two months – with a little luck. It used to be immediate – as soon as you sent your papers in – but that was when you paid your own fees at Sandhurst. Now the Army pays, so the boxwallahs at the War House reckon they're entitled to be awkward – for at least nine months very often.'

'But this will only take two, you say?'

'I've got a friend,' said the Commandant carelessly, 'who's got another. So there it is, dear boy. I'm sorry it's all worked out like this, but at least there won't be a bloodbath – provided you vanish like the proverbial lady. I want you out of this Depot by lunchtime.'

As the train slunk out of Shrewsbury Station bearing me away to my 'tour of the Balkans', I walked through to the Dining Car for lunch. In those days important trains to and from the West Midlands produced a four course meal, which I now enlivened by calling for a whole bottle of Nuits St Georges: for it is to be taken for granted, as Trollope somewhere remarks, that ruined men always have enough ready money about them to eat and drink very handsomely. As I ate and drank, I reflected. There had been great days and jolly days with the King's Shropshire Light Infantry, but really I was not cut out for a soldier and it was not at all a bad thing that my career in the Regular Army (which had only ever begun because of a fit of necessitous pique at the end of my time at Cambridge, when no one else would employ me) had come to a definitive conclusion. It was high time for the next thing, while I was still young enough (twenty-nine) to put myself about a bit. While I was still an undergraduate, I had been introduced to several Literary Editors (Joe Ackerley of *The Listener* paramount among them) who had given me odd jobs of reviewing: now I would go and knock on their doors and request some thing more substantial and permanent.

In short, I decided to commence 'Man of Letters'. But meanwhile, as the train carried me to my new life, a tear or two might be shed, a smile or two indulged, as I briefly recalled the traumas and fiascos of the old.

One day in the Kenya autumn of 1955 the KSLI had fielded an XI against the Nairobi Club for a whole day match on the latter's ground which adjoined the commodious Clubhouse. Our own team consisted almost entirely of Officers who had been brought down into Nairobi from their distant and isolated Companies in the Aberdare Mountains especially for the occasion. The logistic extravagance entailed was entirely justified, it appeared, by the importance of the match, which was in fact a ponderous exercise in public relations between the Regiment and the Colonial Service, the Nairobi Club side being largely made up of District Officers or Commissioners, with a sprinkling of Kenya Policemen. There were, in consequence, many spectators of high rank or sycophantic inclination, among them Major General Frothbury.

As there were no official umpires for the match, competent volunteers from the audience stood shifts of an hour or so, and eventually, late in the afternoon, Frothbury expressed a genial wish to take a turn. It was assumed by all, and asserted by his demeanour, that he had at least an adequate knowledge of the Laws of Cricket, and after five Staff Officers had struggled for the honour of helping him into a white coat he duly took post at the 'Club end' of the wicket.

The state of the game was delicate. The Nairobi Club had declared at 3.30 for 232 runs for 7 wickets, leaving the KSLI until 7 p.m. (three hours, if we allow for the break between the innings and a brief tea interval) to beat this total. Although the fast outfield was in our favour, we had none of us had much practice at playing on matting wickets and the Nairobi Club bowling was reputed to be very tight. By 5.30, when Frothbury strutted on to the ground to umpire, we had made 121 for 5, which put us well up with the clock but otherwise in bad case, as the two batsmen now at the wicket were our last two batsmen of substance, and once they were out the enemy would be right into our tail. One of them was a young National Service Subaltern called Kenyon, a correct and neat player without, however, very much power behind his strokes; the other was the only non-commissioned man on our side, a certain Sergeant Jellico, whose brisk natural talent was marred by an unorthodox grip (left hand right at the top of the handle and right hand rammed down on to the shoulders of the bat).

General Frothbury proceeded to take against both of them. As Kenyon told me afterwards, when they were at the bowling end together Frothbury would make remarks like 'Get on with it, will you, and stop finicking about' – regardless of Kenyon's clear tactical duty as anchor man, which was not 'to get on with it' but to stay put, and also regardless of the regulation which forbids the umpire to advise or rebuke the players save only in respect of the Laws. Sergeant Jellico received more conspicuous treatment: the General took his bat from him and demonstrated the orthodox grip. When the Sergeant, unrepentant, continued to use his own, the General put on an affronted scowl which deepened and darkened when Jellico drove two balls in succession through the covers for four and slammed the last of the over past deep mid-wicket for three.

This meant that Jellico must now face the first ball of the next over, which would be bowled from Frothbury's end. The first ball the Sergeant received, a real sod as Kenyon said later, narrowly missed his off stump.

'Well, I told him about his grip,' said Frothbury to Kenyon, 'if he gets himself out he's no one to blame but himself.'

'I think he's had it too long to change, sir,' said Kenyon.

'Nonsense. Too swollen-headed to take advice. What's his name?'

Kenyon told him.

'Sergeant Jellico,' said the General, storing it away. 'Nothing I hate more than a conceited NCO.'

The second ball of the over was far less savage and was propelled in a huge arc over the bowler's head for six. The third was swept away off the leg stump, dangerously but effectively for four. Frothbury's face worked in discontent. The fourth was slashed hissing towards cover but must, as it seemed, pass wide of his left hand.

'Come on, sir,' Jellico called.

Both batsmen started for the run; but before they had taken two strides cover had miraculously gathered the ball with his left hand.

'BACK,' shouted Jellico. He stopped dead and dived back towards his crease.

But for Kenyon it was much harder to stop. He had been backing up properly as the ball was bowled and was therefore going at much greater momentum than Jellico. However, he juddered to a halt and turned...too late, as cover-point had flipped the ball straight back to the bowler, who crisply broke the wicket.

'How's that?' the bowler said.

'Out,' said the General.

Kenyon began to walk.

'Not you,' said Frothbury. 'The other man. Sergeant Jellico.'

'But sir,' said Kenyon, 'the wicket was broken at my end.'

'The end to which he was running.'

'We hadn't crossed, sir,' said Kenyon, and continued on his way.

'You come back here,' yapped the General, 'and you,' he bawled down the wicket, 'you, Sergeant Jellico, out you go.'

Jellico gaped at the General, while Kenyon, a decent but feeble young man, started to dither.

The Captain of the Nairobi Club XI now walked up to Frothbury and said, very pleasantly, 'Slight misunderstanding, General. Often tricky, this kind of thing. But the non-striker's wicket was broken, and since the batsmen hadn't crossed – '

' – It's me,' said Kenyon, trying to be firm, 'that's out.'

He turned and marched away.

'YOU COME BACK,' squealed the General like an electric saw. And then, to the Nairobi Club Captain, 'Just teaching that Sergeant a lesson. He called the run, then he funked it. He should have kept straight on and let young Kenyon get to his end. Anyway, he needs pulling down a peg.'

The Nairobi Club Captain smiled a ghastly smile and took a deep breath.

'I'm afraid that has nothing to do with it, sir. The Laws of Cricket state – '

' – That the umpire's decision is final,' snapped Frothbury, who was not a General for nothing. 'You come back here, Kenyon. Sergeant Jellico is out.'

The Nairobi Club Captain beckoned wearily to the other umpire…a GSO II in Frothbury's Headquarters, who cravenly deposed that his attention had been distracted by a mosquito and that he had missed the incident altogether.

It was at this stage that somebody at last behaved rather well. Sergeant Jellico, realising that unless the General had his will there would be no more cricket that day, strode from the wicket looking neither to right nor to left but (so the loungers under the fans of the pavilion bar subsequently asserted) blinking very slightly with disappointment, for after all he had been batting with zest and valour and might well have won us the match.

It was funny, I reflected, as the train pelted South and the wine did its work, how often important cricket matches played by the KSLI contrived to be undignified or unedifying, if not in the play itself, then in their social effect or their aftermath. Some time before the Kenyan affair, there had been a notable occasion in Berlin on which a two innings match versus the King's Own Yorkshire Light Infantry had to be converted into a three and then into a four innings match (so incompetent or 'tired' were the batsmen on either side) in order to provide some sort of spectacle for the visitors invited to meals or drinks on the ground during the two days allotted. And some time before *that* there had been a piece of pure Maupassant at Brunswick…

The match against the Lancers at Brunswick lasted exactly two overs, during which nothing much happened except that my friend Andrew Wootton, a non-cricketer who had volunteered, in a lean season, to take the field for the sake of the outing, was observed by all to be wearing black socks and grey gym shoes with his off-white flannels. At the end of the second over it had begun to rain, and after we had hung around for three and a half hours it was agreed that the match should be abandoned. One of our hosts then volunteered to show us round Brunswick. After a quick circuit in the KSLI bus, our guide suggested that the bus should be parked centrally and the KSLI cricketers released to find what amusement they might and then to rendezvous later.

'If you like,' he said to myself and Andrew, 'I can show you the brothel quarter. It's still there, walls and all. There's a very pretty Gothic Gate.'

'Oh yes, please,' squawked a round-faced Ensign called Jack Ogle, who was good at overhearing things; and so off we went in the rain, Andrew Wootton loping along indifferent to wet in the front, while our guide, tubby Jack and myself jostled for places under our only umbrella.

'At the bottom end they display themselves in the windows,' said our guide. 'The top end is more tasteful. It's madly out of bounds, of course. If the MPs catch us we're for it.'

'How can they catch us in civilian clothes? We might be any old tourists.'

'They're trained to sniff out Army personnel. Not hard in our case – we're all wearing Regimental ties or blazers. They'd recognise them a mile off, then ask to see our Identity Cards. Luckily it's pretty early – they generally come out at night. But even so,' said our Mentor, 'we don't want to hang about.'

Nor did we. Everyone was speedily accommodated in a 'more tasteful' house at the smarter end of the street, and very shortly we were reunited outside the front door. All of us, that was, except Jack Ogle.

After ten minutes, 'He must be playing extra time,' said Andrew, who was looking exceedingly glum. 'Failure to score, do you think? Or is he having a second innings?'

'All I know,' I droned dismally, 'is that I'm tired of standing here in this bloody rain shitting myself lest the Red Caps arrive. Let's leave him to find his own way back to the bus.'

'*Not* quite the thing,' said our host, 'to leave one's chum behind in a cat house. Not in our crowd, at any rate.'

'Nor in ours,' I apologised. '*Tristitia post coitum* setting in rather heavily, I'm afraid.'

It set in even heavier during the next fifteen minutes. The rain got harder and our nerves got tauter. Andrew began a long discussion on our chances of having caught the pox. By the time he had finished they seemed about 66 to 1 in favour. Just as he was concluding this lowering exegesis Jack Ogle appeared at last, looking self-conscious. We hustled him straight out through the pretty Gothic Gate and not until we were a quarter of a mile away did anyone speak.

'What on earth were you doing?' I said. 'Having another round?'

'I could only just afford the first.'

'You certainly spun it out,' said Andrew.

Jack giggled.

'Not on purpose.' He giggled again. 'I didn't mean to tell you,' he said, 'but I can't not. Just as I was getting there in fine form, the wireless by her bed started playing 'God Save the Queen'. For some reason, you see, she was tuned into the BAOR network. As soon as she heard it, she started barking orders like a Gauleiter. "Up get," she shouted. She made me get off the bed and stand to attention, then she clamped on her knickers and hung a towel on my John. "Him we do not see while your Anthem die orchestre do play," she said. But of course all this was so off-putting that it went straight down and the towel fell off when there were still two bars to go. "To the wall turn," she shouted, and whisked me round and stood me in the corner. God, I did feel a prick.'

'What was left of it.'

'As soon as the bloody thing stopped, she flew out of her knickers and on to the bed, all ready to go again. But I just couldn't get tuned up. All that shouting. I was worried about you chaps too.'

'So what happened?'

'She showed me some pictures. Goings on in a girls' orphanage. Junior matrons with senior inmates. The gardener's boy with the whole lot. Still no good.'

'How very depressing.'

'You still haven't heard the worst. I've only just realised it myself.' He opened his coat and examined his shirt, closely and despairingly, as if willing it to change colour or something of the kind. 'After we'd given it up as a bad job,' he said, 'I was in such a hurry to get out to all of you that I forgot to put on that sweater I was wearing.'

'Pity. But not the end of the world.'

'*My mother gave it to me.* Oh God,' wailed Jack. 'It took her three months of loving care and labour to knit it – and I've gone and left it in a Kraut knocking shop where I couldn't even come.'

Remembering, after twenty-six years, Jack Ogle's description of the pornographic pictures vainly produced to him at Brunswick, I am reminded of the series which was hung round the room in which the Beef Steak Club at Cambridge drank sherry before dinner. I was never a member of the Beef Steak Club, but my name was put up for it and on one occasion (about three years, I suppose before the little outing in Brunswick) I was invited as a guest for inspection.

As I was in those days unversed in such matters, the Beef Steak collection of Erotica stirred me from the very fundament. The series started with the arrival of a mischievous little maid in the hotel room of a large and soignée lady of mature years. Looks of approval and mock timidity are at once exchanged by the couple, after which the tableaux proceed (if they are still extant) through seven stages of mounting enormity to ecstatic oral consummation.

It is not surprising, then, that I went into dinner in a state of some excitement which did not fully subside for a good hour. My host was sympathetic to my condition but my neighbour on the other side, a dreary Old Etonian called Owen Ives, subsequently denounced me to the President as having 'fingered himself all through dinner and being in an unfit state to drink His Majesty's health'. The President allowed that this was unseemly and was clearly inclined to rule that it constituted good reason for removing my name from the list of candidates, despite my defence, that I had only been checking my fly, and my host's contention that it would have been nothing out of the way even if I *had* been doing what I was accused of; for, said my host (a considerable classical scholar) susceptible members had often been known *ipsas mentulas educere et ad maximam voluptatem titillare* under the table during the soup. Anyway, my host concluded, Owen Ives was a fart.

The debate was interrupted by the collapse into the fire, face forward, of a member who was afterwards asserted to have been pissing into it. I never found out how the matter of my candidature was resolved, as I decided not to press it but to join instead a dining club called the True Blue, the Liberal answer to the diehard Beef Steak, more flexible in its membership, more imaginative in its menus and more various in its conversation. True, it did not have a collection of rude pictures to randify one before dinner, but it had something much more valuable than that: Noël Annan.

Noël Annan was at that time (1951) a young, bald and brilliant don, reputed to have run a spyring during the war, of great influence, both political and intellectual, in his college and mine (King's), a vivacious not to say stagy lecturer, newly married but with a long previous record as gay bachelor, party-giver and social impresario. I was never quite sure of Noël's precise office in the True Blue Club, but he seemed, in some vague way, to be responsible for providing the liberal esprit. To this end he conjured up a series of rather louche guest speakers, perhaps the louchest of whom was Alan Pryce-Jones, in those days still editing *The Times Literary Supplement* – when, that is, he wasn't lunching with dowagers or tinkling among lady novelists' teacups. As far as I know, Alan had only ever published one book, and that under the pen name of Arthur Pumphrey, a mediocre account, called *The Pink Danube*, of what happened to a precocious adolescent when he went on his travels after being sacked, like Alan, from Oxford. On the strength of this undistinguished but agreeably pert performance, pseudonymous for legal reasons but widely attributed to Pryce-Jones by well coached friends, its author enjoyed considerable literary prestige and unquestioned access to ducal drawing rooms. Clearly, a man who had won such flattering accolades with so little exertion of mind and body might have something helpful to say to a lazy but clever boy like myself, eager as I was to grasp the fruits of success without the tedious preface of planting and growing them.

I was therefore all ears when Alan rose to sing for his supper and (I hoped) to ease and accelerate the mechanism of my advancement with his lubricant worldly advice. As I should have known, Alan was much too shrewd a number to share the secret of effortless success with thirty odd greedy and unscrupulous young men; but what he said, though not what I had longed to hear, has nevertheless remained with me till this day as a matchless piece of civilised wisdom.

The True Blue Club, he said, purported to be a society of liberal men; let us therefore hear in what liberality consisted. This was nothing to do with any particular political or intellectual theory, it was simply a matter of practice. For the liberal three things must be paramount: the right to travel without let wherever he wanted; the right to occupy himself as he saw fit, always provided he was prepared to foot the bill, of whatever kind, himself; and the right to speak his mind aloud. These freedoms, said Alan, were practical matters, depending on facility and regulation; so long as we were vigilant they would prevail; but let us once take them too easily for granted or forget their primacy, then there were people who, often with the highest ostensible motives, would gladly steal or wrest them from us (as indeed had become very apparent after five years of Socialist rule). So let us be watchful in our generation; and let us never be deceived by smooth-tongued or loud-mouthed assertions that the 'sensitive nature of the circumstances' or the 'collective will of the people' or 'the sanctity of equality and social justice' required our three freedoms to be modified, qualified or waived.

Much impressed by all this, I voiced my enthusiasm for Alan Pryce-Jones and his message to Christopher Laughton, a fellow member of the Club and of King's, a tow-haired urchin for whom I entertained a kind of sentimental lust which he resolutely refused to assuage. What a splendid speech, I told Christopher; just what we all needed to hear, twenty times over and in full round voice.

'Some of us,' said Christopher primly, 'have got beyond that kind of thing.'

'What on earth can you mean?'

'I mean that some of us are aware that there are more important things than the freedom of the upper class to amuse itself – which is what Pryce-Jones was really on about. He was talking about travel for pleasure and rich living.'

'*And* paying the bills *oneself.*'

15

'Easy enough for the rich.'

'He also spoke about freedom of speech.'

'By which he meant freedom to pervert the truth and hoodwink the masses into continuing to serve their capitalist masters.'

'Oh. Can we stop this dreary discussion and go to bed?'

'Certainly. Goodnight.'

'I meant together.'

'Certainly not. I have Keynes and Engels in the morning.'

'Lucky Keynes and Engels…'

Oddly enough, I had been introduced to Christopher by a totally non-political and non-intellectual acquaintance called Micky Tollman Green. Micky, who was all peaches and cream, I had met at a cricket match the previous summer: we had been on opposing sides and had not spoken, but we had, as the saying goes, 'spotted' one another – and did so again when we found ourselves sitting together in a lecture on Roman History the following October. Micky was much more responsive to sentimental lust than Christopher was, though he suffered hideously from guilt – not exactly moral guilt but shame at letting down his manliness ('What would the other men on the XI think?'). Even my carefully prepared little lecture on the behaviour of the Greek male, and its probable emulation by 'the other men on the XI' if he did but know, failed to reassure him. Each time with Micky was 'absolutely the last' until the next. Eventually he found himself a nice but rather clinging girl, and by way of compensation he had introduced me to Christopher, with whom he had been at School.

'I know you'll like him,' Micky said, 'he's just your type and very intelligent. The only trouble is that I'm not sure that he'll – er – do it.'

Christopher did not – er – do it. Furthermore he wasn't nearly as much fun in other ways as Micky, who took uncomplicated pleasure in days out and sporting assemblies, which Christopher despised. Inevitably, Christopher refused to accompany me to the Varsity Match at Lord's the following summer, but Micky, who had got a few days off from his girlfriend ('Her beastly mother's ill'), agreed to come with me instead.

'But you mustn't try to – you know – because Maureen wouldn't like it.'

'She need never hear of it.'

'I tell Maureen *everything*.'

At Lord's we met, by arrangement, a friend called Dickie Muir, with whom Micky sometimes used to play Lawn Tennis (oh, those white flannel shorts – I can almost *feel* them after thirty years) and with whom I did a lot of drinking and giggling. And still do, I'm happy to say, after all this time, although Micky disappeared totally from our lives as soon as we left Cambridge. But back to Lord's. In those days the Universities had players like Hubert Doggart and

Peter May, whom you could recognise by their style from a mile off. For this reason, as well as the fact that Oxford and Cambridge were still attended largely by proper chaps from proper schools with a proper sense of priorities instead of by lower class swots from Tyneside and Newcastle, the match at Lord's was pretty well subscribed. On this occasion in the early fifties the stands were quite as crowded as they would have been for an important county game, and so we had some trouble in finding Dickie. By the time we ran him to earth at last, in one of the squalid bars on the North side of the ground, it had started to rain. To make matters worse, a message now came out of the tannoy system for Mr Michael Tollman Green, who was to telephone Miss Maureen Fletch at once. Micky went as pink as a hunting coat and started to sweat from under his short blond hair.

'She's found out I'm here.'

'But if you tell *everything*, she surely knew,' I said.

'I only told her I was going to London. I didn't mention Lord's. She thinks games are childish, and anyway they make her jealous.'

'Silly bitch,' said Dickie.

'Oh, please don't say that. *Who* can have told her?'

The end of it was that Micky went to ring up Maureen at her mother's house in Potter's Bar only to find out that Maureen had had no idea at all he was at Lord's and had not, of course, at any stage telephoned the ground. The whole thing was a hoax − and the damage, from Micky's point of view, irreparable, because now that he had rung up Maureen and announced (naturally enough in the circumstances) that he was speaking from Lord's at her request, she (a) knew that he had gone there and (b) held him guilty of deceiving her.

What punishment was in store for him he could not tell. But he agreed, as he was not on Maureen-duty again for another four days and there was no point in making himself miserable in the meanwhile, to accompany us (since the rain continued) to *Kind Hearts and Coronets*, a film with Dennis Price and Alec Guinness which was currently drawing large and hilarious audiences to the Leicester Square Theatre.

'She must never know I've been to the Cinema,' Micky said. 'She thinks they're full of germs. Lord's *and* the Cinema would just about finish her off.'

But hardly had the film started when a message was projected on to the screen by means of a slide (they still did that in those days) to say that Miss Maureen Fletch was waiting in the Foyer for Mr Michael Tollman Green.

'Please come with me,' Micky said. I can't face her without someone to support me. Oh *dear*, what can have happened?'

So we went together to the foyer, where I was staggered to see Christopher.

'Come with me,' he said fiercely; then seized my arm and swept me away and into a taxi before either Micky or I could open our mouths. It swiftly transpired that Christopher, though he had hitherto heard my suit only with contempt, had been made so jealous by the notion of my little 'Memory Lane' outing with Micky that he had followed us to London, engineered the hoaxing and torment of Micky by way of revenge, and was now, as a result of my temporary neglect, perversely possessed of that same lust for me as I had suffered all these months for him. I took him to my Club, smuggled him into my bedroom against all the rules, and did my very best for him; but all I could think of was poor little Micky as we left him in the foyer, bright pink with confusion and very near to tears, with the consequence that my first and last bout of *amour* with the delectable Christopher was a total and humiliating flop.

The next day at Lord's Dickie and I met Giles Peregrine, who had served in the Rifle Brigade with Dickie and had instructed me while I was a Cadet at the OTS at Bangalore in 1946. Christopher and Micky had both gone their ways, which was something of a relief, and the skies had cleared as if in celebration. Giles was getting very worked up by Doug Insole's habit of pulling balls that were on his leg stump, and although Dickie pointed out that Insole did this only when the balls were full tosses or pitched pretty short, Giles still went grinding on with his thesis that Insole was a cross-bat player who would be rendered quite useless by the slightest deterioration in his sight – i.e. in a very few years at the most.

The combination in Giles of ball-aching persistence and sanctimonious utterance (he spoke as if cross-bat strokes were some hideous evil which he had been divinely appointed to search out and damn) reminded me of an occasion at Bangalore, some three years previously, when both he and I were playing for the Garrison against a scratch Mysore XI in a so-called 'Mysore State Trial', the first of its kind to be held since the end of the war. We were playing on the OTS ground, one of the few in India to have a grass wicket and one of the most amiable I have ever played cricket on: the boundaries were shaded by palm and casuarina; a distant view of the big wheel on the Cantonment Fairground lent an incongruous charm; the pavilion was cool and ample, with long, cavernous verandahs of the finest colonial fashion; and in the late afternoon the sound of the silly temple bells came rippling across the outlying paddy marshes.

As I remember the incident, Giles and I were sitting in the pavilion waiting to bat, while James Prior, an old school friend of mine who had luckily been sent out as a Cadet in the same draught as myself, came up and offered us a drink. I should explain that intercourse between white Cadets and white Officers (Giles was then a Captain) was very easy at the OTS at Bangalore, which had been founded in order to turn mature planters and the like into Officers with the minimum of fuss or formality and therefore had a tradition of treating its students as if they were more or less commissioned already. So lackadaisical were the proceedings of the School that it was said that a man could fail the course only if he died, went mad, or had to be treated more than three times for the Pox. What with all of this, then, there was nothing out of the way in James' inviting Giles to have a drink without even bothering to call him 'Sir': they were, after all both gentlemen and both Greenjackets.

'Thank 'ee, no,' said Giles, 'I shall have to bat at any moment.'

'Thank 'ee, yes,' said I, 'Tom Collins.'

'You,' said Giles, 'will be going in to bat next wicket down but one. You cannot bat on Tom Collinses.'

'Walter Hammond,' I said, 'is rumoured to bat on nothing else.'

At this stage someone put 'These Foolish Things' on the pavilion gramophone. For some reason it was the only record in the building and although there must have been another tune on the reverse it was never played. 'These Foolish Things' and the drifting temple bells: they were the music of that season, monotonous but magical, at least in kind memory's ear.

> A cigarette that bears a lipstick's traces,
> An airline ticket to romantic places...

'You,' said Giles, 'are not Walter Hammond.'

> Oh, how the ghost of you clings,
> These foolish things,
> Remind me of you.

James came back from the bar with the drinks – his and mine. Giles scowled.

'This is a serious match,' he said. 'It is the nearest either of us will ever get to playing in First Class Cricket. A Mysore State Trial. It would be frivolous, it would be impertinent, it would be *degrading*, if, halfway through the afternoon and just before you were due to bat, you drank that Tom Collins. It would be letting down the side – no, worse, far worse, it would be letting down the Raj itself.'

> A tinkling piano in the next apartment,
>> That secret look which told me what
>> your heart meant...

James, with the perspicacity of a future politician, realised, as I did not, that Giles was deadly serious. His pompous tone could easily be taken as having been 'put on' for purposes of teasing or irony; but then, as I should have known, Giles did not go in for teasing or irony; now as ever he was sincere, relentless, totally assured of his rectitude and his mission – which was, in the present instance, to prevent me from drinking my Tom Collins. James knew this, scented danger, and removed my drink with the remark that he would have it kept cold for me till after my innings. I myself, on the other hand, refused to believe anyone could be in earnest over anything so trivial, did not care to have my pleasures interfered with, snatched the drink back from James, and drank down half of it at a swallow.

At this moment a wicket fell. Giles rose, checked the straps of his pads and collected up his gloves.

'I'll settle with you later,' he said to me, then clumped down the steps from the verandah.

> Oh, how the nightingale sings,
>> These foolish things
>> Remind me of you.

'You fool,' said James as Giles marched to the wicket. 'Why do you have to make things so difficult for yourself?'

'He surely won't do anything. My drinking habits, off duty, are none of his business.'

'Haven't you got his number yet? My dear Simon, Giles Peregrine is a busybody – a man of moral principle. He applies those principles to every little thing that happens, and whenever he can he will ensure that what they enjoin is strictly practised. It will be interesting to see how he punishes you for defying them.'

The next wicket fell, and I went out to join Giles while 'These Foolish Things' sighed and faded behind me.

In the event I batted very well. Whether it was that I was in luck, or that the Tom Collins had given me just the little lift I needed, or that I was determined to show Giles how fatuous had been his injunction to abstain; whatever the reason, form, fitness or a kindly mood among the gods, I batted smoothly, stylishly and swiftly, and in no time at all I had made 18, which included a beautiful six over extra-cover's head. Eighteen: a handy little score, but in no way remarkable: to be noticed one must achieve 40 at least, preferably 60 or 70. Well, I thought to myself, and why not? I played the ball firmly between cover and extra and called Giles for an easy single. He responded, or appeared to, until I was nearly halfway down the wicket. He then turned abruptly, without a word, and went back to his ground, leaving me stranded. A second later I was run out. For 18; handy but not remarkable: forgotten by all in five minutes…when I might, just might, have shone as the star of the Mysore State Trial.

'You see,' said James, 'what men of moral principle are made of.'

'I see.'

'He probably had no malice against you personally; but he was determined to show you that his principles are not to be flouted, that his God is not to be mocked.'

'Fuck him and his principles and his God. Fuck them all dead.'

'Never mind,' said James in his deep, kind voice. 'I'll take you out to dinner.'

'May his bowels and his balls rot and stink in his nose for ever.'

'If you promise not to refer to this dismal affair any more, I will buy you Champagne at dinner.'

Champagne was not cheaply to be had in Bangalore.

'Dear James,' I said, 'you always did know how to comfort a fellow.'

And more than that, I thought, as I remembered how generously and wisely he had behaved, about a year and a half before, during a volcanic crisis that had suddenly bubbled out of nothing one drowsy summer's afternoon, when we were both still boys at Charterhouse.

II

CHARTERHOUSE PINK I

It had all started at a House Match.

It happened that year (1945) that my House (Saunderites) could field five members of the School XI, two of whom, Peter May and myself, had already got our 1st XI Colours. Then there was a particular friend of mine called Ivan Lynch, who was Captain of the House XI, James Prior himself, and one now dead, alas, called Hedley Le Bas, who was Head of our House and, incidentally, of the whole school as well. As may be supposed, Saunderites, with such supplies of talent, had started clear favourites to win the House Cricket Cup, and Hedley, Ivan and James were exceedingly keen we should do so. Myself, I did not care very much, so long as I had some fun and cut a creditable figure; and what Peter May thought in the matter no one ever knew, as he was not, at the age he was then (something over fifteen), much given to utterance. Judging by his later form, I should say that he was determined to do his level best to help us to win without being inclined to recrimination or resentment if we did not.

All that aside, however, the thing had turned sour on us. Talent notwithstanding, we had performed pathetically in the first two rounds (a heavy loss and a shady draw); and in order to retain any chance of winning the Cup we absolutely had to win the match in which we were presently engaged. We were no longer favourites, though in some quarters, so it was said, a recovery was still expected of us. If so, such expectation was fast fading; for now, on a languid evening in mid-June, our situation was desperate.

Our opponents had made 130 all out, a score we should have passed blindfold. Peter May was already the best schoolboy batsman of the century; James and Ivan both purported to bat at 1st XI level; so did I; and there were some promising younger players in the tail. But Peter had been bowled by a vicious shooter; James had been unluckily run out by Ivan; Ivan had been caught on a short boundary having tried to hook a six; and I myself had been stumped off my first ball, having leapt out like Trumper (or so I conceived) to drive the thing over the bowler's head. Our score was now 47 for 4, and Hedley Le Bas, a bowler and a reserve wicket keeper, was going in to bat at No. 6.

'An irresponsible stroke of yours,' said Ivan to me pompously, 'considering the state of the match.'

'I didn't think much of yours,' I said.

'I had at least made 17 and it wasn't my first ball.'

'Well at any rate,' I said, 'I didn't run anyone out.'

'You weren't there long enough to run anyone out. Though your stroke was so ridiculous that you could almost be said to have run yourself out rather than to have been stumped.'

'Stop squabbling, you two,' said James.

It was about then that the trouble started.

'Sorry, old man,' said Ivan, and nudged my knee with his.

'Sorry, Ivan,' I said, returning the nudge. 'And now I must go and have a pee.'

'I'm afraid you can't, Raven,' said one of the younger boys who was waiting to bat, 'the rears in the pav are out of order. There's a notice.'

'Then I shall have to go behind the pav.'

'You can't, Raven,' said another boy with infuriating smugness; 'the Scouts are practising putting up their tents behind the pav.'

'Then I shall have to go back to House. What a slog.'

'You can't do that,' said Ivan. 'People will think you're sloping off in a sulk because you've made an egg and we're losing.'

Losing we were worse than ever. Hedley Le Bas was out the next second to a drooping full toss which he fatuously tried to scythe away to leg.

'Look,' I said, 'I'm sorry, but I must have a pee. The only place left seems to be at the side of the pavilion.'

'All the players will see you,' said a pert little blond of thirteen who was keeping the score book.

'I'm too desperate to care.'

So I had my piddle on the side of the pavilion. The only person who noticed was Hedley Le Bas, who was walking in from the wicket and was thus pointed straight at me.

'You oughtn't to do that,' he said, as soon as he'd taken off his pads. 'It makes a bad impression on the younger boys.'

23

'It's not my fault that the pavilion rears are fucked up. They all understood.'
'Did they?'

'Well, James didn't mind. If there'd been anything wrong he'd have said so.'

Even in those days we all had enormous faith in the wisdom and equity of James Prior. Hedley grunted in what seemed to be assent.

'Forgiven, Hedley?'

'But not quite forgotten. I do not like my monitors to make a public spectacle of themselves, with or without the approval of James Prior.'

'You're the only one that actually saw.'

And this, of course, was the trouble. *As a result of being out*, Hedley had seen. Hedley was in a bad temper because he had only made 3; Hedley was in an even worse temper because we were going to lose the match and with it our last hope of the House Cup; and all this rankled to such an extent that Hedley, although an easy-going and intelligent man, was making a production out of an episode which he would normally not even have noticed.

'What,' he said, 'do you suppose Peter May thought?'

'I suppose he thought that here was a chap who badly wanted a piss...having a piss.'

'Boys as talented as that are highly strung.'

'Rubbish. He's not Mozart or somebody.'

'He could be Bradman or somebody.'

'Bradman wouldn't care. Australians don't care where you have a pee. They're far too coarse. Anyway, May didn't actually see me.'

'He must have heard. God only knows what he thought.'

On this cantankerous note our last wicket definitively fell for a total of 61. Defeated, disgraced, disgusted we trailed back to Saunderites. Hedley said no more about the peeing incident but started to elaborate a theory that a surplus of talent had led to facile over-confidence.

'Anyway, that's that,' he said. 'Now we must concentrate on the Arthur Webber.'

The Arthur Webster Cup was awarded annually to the best all round House Platoon in the Junior Training Corps. (In those days Public Schoolboys belonged to the JTC, residual legatee of the old OTC, while everyone else was in the Army Cadet Force.) Hedley, as Under Officer and Platoon Commander, had a great deal of personal prestige at stake here, and now sought to hearten the dismal little band of cricketers by persuading them that great things were in store for them on the field of honour. None of this impressed me, as I was immune from military zeal and indeed belonged to the Air Training Corps (a sloppy outfit which wore shoes instead of Ammunition Boots) especially in order to avoid the martial excesses which Hedley was now extolling; but I was delighted to think that the dear fellow had found a new interest so quickly, and fondly imagined that my urinary gaffe (if gaffe indeed it were) would now be dismissed from his consciousness for ever.

And so I think it would have been, had not Fate decreed a most unlikely and unlucky sequence of events which was put in train on the next day but one.

The Charterhouse XI was on its way from Godalming to play Tonbridge School at Tonbridge. A change of train had been made at Guildford. The train in which we were now travelling had no corridor and no convenience attached to the compartment in which we were seated…'we' being Peter May, Ivan Lynch, Hedley Le Bas, James Prior and myself, the whole Saunderite set, plus my friend and fellow-scholar of the Classical Sixth, a merry-witted boy called Robin Reiss.

After we had been travelling for about three-quarters of an hour with many halts, 'You're not going to believe this,' I said, 'but I must have a pee.'

'Oh God,' said Ivan.

Hedley looked up sharply but said nothing.

Peter May looked straight in front of him as if he hadn't heard.

'Why didn't you go at Guildford,' said Ivan.

'No time.'

'Plenty of time if you hadn't insisted on buying that *Lilliput* at the book stall.

Lilliput, *Men Only* and *London Opinion* were the three wicked monthlies of my youth, crammed with coloured pictures of nearly naked ladies, decorous indeed by modern standards but in those days passing fierce and inflammatory.

'*You* liked looking at that *Lilliput*,' I said.

As indeed they all had, except Peter May, who, when offered it, had not lifted a hand to take it or moved a single muscle of his body in any direction.

'Much better,' said Ivan, 'that you should have had a pee.'

Hedley scowled. Peter sat. Ivan pouted. James pondered. Robin Reiss twinkled. I shifted sweatily from ham to ham.

'Does anyone know,' said James, 'how long it is before we reach Tonbridge? Robin, you live round here, don't you?'

'Yes,' said Robin, twinkling more than ever. 'Tonbridge is about forty minutes.'

'Many stops?'

'Lots,' said Robin gaily, 'but none of them long enough for anyone to have a pee.'

'That settles it,' I said.

I stood on my corner seat, crouching to avoid the luggage rack, took out my piece, and made pretty good shift to aim my jet through the gap between the ventilating panels – a narrow target even though they were open as wide as they would go.

'Bravo,' said Robin.

The train slowed and lurched into Tonbridge Station while yet my golden stream showered from the window.

'Mind that Postman,' Robin said.

'Why didn't you tell me we were almost at Tonbridge?'

'Time to get out,' James said.

We gathered our gear and slouched up the hill to the school.

That was the first time I ever saw the Head at Tonbridge, a ground on which I have been many times since and come to know as well as any in the Kingdom. Trees and a long expanse of playing fields to the West; a green bank and then a lawn to the North; more trees, with margins of grass to the East, and beyond these the undistinguished yet satisfying nineteenth buildings, which sit so well in their place; and to the South the roofs of Tonbridge dipping to the Weald, the Weald rising to a ridge, and the white clouds scudding along its spine on the bright and breezy days when the Head is at its best.

But such days were far in the future. *That* day in 1945 was not bright or breezy: it was grey, still and very damp. Tonbridge, having won the toss, elected to bat and were all out for 37; and the rest of the morning and most of the afternoon was spent by me in watching Peter May and our Captain, Tony Rimell, while they piled up superfluous runs which would not even, once the Tonbridge total was passed, count in their own averages. Still, I had my Colours safe, so it didn't matter much that I had no chance to shine. No chance to shine, after all, means no chance to be eclipsed. No doubt I should have passed that grey afternoon pleasantly enough, sitting on the balcony of the Tonbridge pavilion, had not Hedley Le Bas arrived up there in fierce remonstrance.

'Disgusting exhibition on the train,' he said.

'I couldn't help it, Hedley. If it was going to be forty minutes to Tonbridge – '

'I – It wasn't forty seconds.'

'But Robin Reiss said – '

'Robin Reiss is a well-known joker. Couldn't you have used your intelligence? If the train was really going to take forty minutes more to Tonbridge, we should not have reached Tonbridge Station until well after 11.30 – the time at which the Match was due to start. And you know very well that Tony Rimell would never have arranged a scruffy performance like that.'

This was a valid point.

'I'm sorry,' I said.

'What do you suppose Peter May thought?'

I was getting thoroughly sick of this particular question.

'He didn't seem to notice.'

'And what do you suppose he thought when you offered him that *Lilliput*?'

'The same. He just didn't seem to notice.'

'He was probably dazed by shock,' Hedley said. 'It was almost as though you were pimping for the girls in that paper. God knows what damage you may have done to Peter.'

'He's made a pretty sharp recovery,' I said, as Peter drove the ball up the Northern Bank to complete his fifty.

'Mental damage.'

'Because he was offered a *Lilliput*? They're lying about ten inches deep all over the House.'

'The other thing.'

'Because he saw somebody peeing out of a window?'

'Not so much that…though it wasn't a pretty sight…but because he saw someone whom he is supposed to respect behave with complete lack of self-control and discrimination. You nearly hit that Postman. Someone might have sent for the Police. As Head of the School, I shall have to instruct Tony Rimell, as Captain of Cricket, that you are not a fit person to represent Charterhouse in the 1st XI.'

'For Christ's sake, Hedley.'

'I mean it. You've put yourself beyond the pale.'

Hedley departed. James Prior came and sat down next to me.

'You look awful,' he said.

I told him of Hedley's intention.

'Will Tony Rimell listen to him?' I said.

'He'll have to. Hedley's Head of the School. Anyway, everyone listens to Hedley. He has a way with him.'

'I cannot understand,' I said, 'what is this endless drivel about Peter May. My crime seems to be that I have shocked or damaged Peter. What nonsense,' I said, as Peter sent the ball hissing through the trees to slam like a siege missile into the Chapel door.

'Haven't you understood?' said James.

'Understood?'

'Hedley keeps wicket – but we have Oliver Popplewell as our wicket keeper, and a bloody good one. Hedley bowls outswingers which swing the whole way from his arm in a slow curve like a slack banana. Hedley bats like an imbecile gorilla. In short, Hedley is only in this side until somebody in the 2nd XI makes some runs or takes some wickets, and very well Hedley knows it. Now, this is his last quarter and he hankers, he yearns, for his 1st XI Cricket Colours. Since he will do nothing spectacular enough to earn them, his only hope is to survive in the side till the end of the season, when Tony will have to follow the custom and make up the number of Colours to a full eleven.'

'I see. And his only chance of surviving that long is a shortage of players. So he's decided to get me out of the way for a start.'

'Right.'

'Oh, *James*.'

'It serves you right. *You've* given him the chance. You were in an impregnable position as far as cricket went – but you've gone and lost your name with all this stupid pissing.'

'You didn't mind it.'

'I was brought up on a farm. And of course Hedley doesn't give a damn either – he's far too upper class. But your behaviour, if denounced with suitable moral fervour and deplored with sanctimonious reference to the innocence of Peter May, could certainly disqualify you from playing for the XI for the rest of the season – making a better chance of a permanent place for Hedley.'

'All those days out with you and Ivan...I couldn't bear to miss them.'

'Well then. If you promise me to pull yourself together from now on and hold your water like a man, I think I can arrange matters.'

'Oh James. How?'

'The thing to remember, old man, is that Hedley is keen on his Colours rather than on actually playing in the side. He is not a cricketer at heart.'

'How do you know that?'

'Because he is not sentimental. All real cricketers are sentimental men.'

A day or two later Hedley appeared with his wrist in a heavy bandage. It was announced that he would not be able to play cricket again that season, but that in recognition of his services already rendered he would be awarded his Colours as Honorary Twelfth Man and allowed, as such, to accompany us on all our away fixtures.

'Which means,' said James, 'that when Tony Rimell comes to make up his lists at the end of July he'll have to make the 1st XI up to Twelve. Eleven chaps in the side – and Hedley comes extra. Twelve Colours are not really in order. I had a terrible task persuading Tony.'

'But surely…it *is* rather bad luck on Hedley, not being able to play any more.'

'I have already told you. He's not that keen on playing. So he was quite happy to go along with my little scheme and wrap up his wrist in a bandage.'

'Oh.'

'Also, he was relieved that he'd have no further reason for doing *you* down. He hadn't really fancied that. Although he may not be sentimental, he isn't a shit.'

'No. Only a fake.'

'Not even that, perhaps. He desired his Colours so much that he was prepared to give up leading the House Platoon to victory in the Arthur Webster Competition; because obviously if he's not fit for cricket he's not fit for Corps. You know how much the Arthur Webber meant to him in terms of prestige. Yet he was prepared to give it all up to make sure of his cricket Colours – so perhaps,' said James, 'he is a sentimental man after all.'

I am afraid lest I have given rather an unfair impression of Peter May, who has so far figured in these pages as a po-faced booby who batted like an automaton. What I should now like to make very clear is that Peter, as a man, had intelligence and a good deal of charm; and that as a batsman, so far from being a robot programmed always to select and play the most efficient stroke possible in the given circumstances, he had an individual brilliance which often led him to select and play the most satisfying and beautiful, even the most spectacular, stroke possible in the given circumstances – and sometimes in direct defiance of them.

Of the latter gift, more in a moment. First a little tale to demonstrate the fundamental good sense and sensibility of the man.

Although he came to Charterhouse in the Autumn of 1942, Peter May was still under fourteen in the summer of 1943. He was therefore still young enough to sit for a junior Scholarship, and indeed too young, by the Headmaster's decision, to play for the School Cricket XI, though the cricket master, the Captain of Cricket and George Geary, the professional, were all convinced that he was good enough.

Peter accepted the Headmaster's decision with equanimity and played with great content for the Under 16 XI…where he learnt a great deal more about cricket than he would have learnt, at his age, in the 1st: for the master who ran the 1st was a nice but nugatory sort of man, whereas R L (Bob) Arrowsmith, who ran the Under 16, had a rare gift, reinforced by picturesque and memorable utterance; for impressing the necessary disciplines on talent, or even (as in Peter's case) on genius.

However, the substance of this anecdote lies, not in the benefits which accrued to Peter through being kept down for a while, but in the interpretations which were variously made of the matter. It was known that it was the Headmaster's veto which kept Peter out of the XI, but it was not known on what moral or social ground the veto was based. Some said the Head Man had judged Peter to be in danger of injury if he played among boys so much older, some thought that the danger was not of injury but of Peter's own conceit or others' insalubrious attentions; some opined that the Head Man did not want a Lower School Hero round the place nor yet an object of envy, and some that he was afraid the Press would get hold of the story and run annoying articles about a thirteen-year-old prodigy. On the whole, however, the view which prevailed was the most pedestrian: the Head Man, it was generally asserted, did not want Peter's work to be interfered with and his chances of a junior Scholarship impaired by the demands of the many whole-day and away matches which, even during the war, were still played by the 1st XI.

In the event, Peter did not win a Junior Scholarship. I remember hearing at the time that he came very near it but that his performance was somewhat tenuous and lacked flair. The general and immediate view was that Peter had got 'the worst of both worlds'; that having been denied his pink 1st XI cap in order that he might win intellectual laurels, he had in the end been crowned with neither. The obtrusive were not slow to express this sentiment to Peter himself. I was the first.

The list of Junior Scholars Elect had just been posted in the Cloisters. Peter, having examined it, was walking away with a subdued air. I was going the opposite way in order to quiz the list.

'Any luck,' I said, as Peter passed me.

He shook his head.

'Pity,' I said fatuously. 'You've been made to give up your chance of a pink hat and got nothing in return. You've got the Head Man to thank for that.'

Peter was a shy boy, who during the two and a half quarters (terms) he had been in the school had said very little indeed. Now, reluctant to speak but determined that justice should be done, he struggled to present his own notion of the affair.

'I think,' he said very slowly and carefully, 'that the Head Man decided as he did, not to stop my cricket wrecking my hash (work) but to stop my hash spoiling my cricket. I could hardly have made much showing in the XI while I was worrying about a scholarship, but I could manage all right in the Under 16.'

In short, Peter was attributing to the Headmaster the kindest and most sensitive of all motives: the Head Man has seen, Peter was trying to say, that the big thing in my life is cricket, and he has made sure that this has not been spoiled for me by my being too early exposed in high places while I am under other and necessary pressures.

Whether this was or was not the Head Man's true motive, I never found out; but it has always seemed to me that Peter's defence of the Head Man, in the face of my loud-mouthed comment, was grateful, generous, and, for a boy of his years, exceedingly subtle.

Whatever the reason behind the Headmaster's edict, Peter continued to play for the Under 16 instead of the 1st XI even after the Scholarship exams were done; and in consequence I am now able, as a member of the same Under 16 side, to give an eyewitness report of an incident which vividly proclaimed the genius of Peter's batting and also illustrated the combination of anticipation, perversity and panache which informed it.

Not long after the conversation in the Cloisters, I was Peter's partner at the wicket during a crisis in the Under 16 Match against Eton. I was having a bad season, out of luck and out of form, was batting low in the list, and was most unlikely to do much to dig us out of disaster. But I could, I told myself, be of service if I could only *stay there* for a while, giving Peter time to gather runs. In the end, I was too feeble and too futile even to defend my wicket for more than a few minutes, but during those few minutes I saw an unforgettable sight.

I was at the bowler's end, while Peter was facing the very fast deliveries (for our class of cricket) of a tall and fibrous redhead called Bob Spear (later in life a distinguished judge of racing). Peter was having no trouble with Bob, who pitched the ball well up on a wicket that was fast and true; and what followed may even have been an indication of boredom on Peter's part, an attempt to get entertainment out of doing the easy thing the difficult way. In any event, having efficiently driven the first two balls of Bob's over to the long off boundary in the approved manner and off the front foot, Peter took a quick look at the third, which was an obvious half volley just outside the off stump, and then, instead of making another routine front foot drive, elected to hit it for four off the *back* foot, with the same ease and accuracy as he might have despatched a very long long-hop, midway between mid-off and the umpire...greatly to the astonishment of both, who watched the ball pass between them with huge, goggling eyes, as though it had been an emanation of the devil.

Now the great point about Bob's bowling, as I have already suggested, was that it was, for boys of our age, very fast indeed. The speed and coordination required to hit it, when well pitched up, off the back foot yet in front of the wicket, very hard and straight back where it came from, were only less remarkable than the perverse ingenuity which conceived and selected such a stroke. The showmanship with which it was carried off was superb, consisting in a total lack of overt enjoyment or sense of the unusual, merely in a slight shake of the head as though to indicate mild displeasure at not having lifted the ball for six instead. Anticipation, perversity, panache.

And, of course, genuine modesty. The quiet and sometimes embarrassed manner in which Peter behaved in the midst of his triumphs reminded one of the poet Horace when he disclaimed personal merit for having written his poetry and gave credit for all to his Muse:

Totum muneris hoc tui est
    quod monstror digito praetereuntium
Romanae fidicen lyrae:
    quod spiro et placeo, si placeo, tuum est.

This is all thy gift
That I am pointed out by the fingers of those that pass
As the minstrel of the Roman lyre.

That I am filled with the breath of song,
And that I please, if please I do,
Is of thy bestowal.

Reading these lines, one understands why everyone liked Horace. It was probably for much the same reason that we all liked Peter May.

III

THE GREEN YEARS

'Pittifer joe' Potts was also a modest man. Forty years of teaching Classics and Cricket at St Dunstan's Preparatory School at Burnham-on-Sea had made him, one might hazard, more contented and more humble by the year. And yet there was much of which he might have boasted. He was, for a start, a brilliant teacher of Greek, and managed to push enough of it into me, starting from scratch and during the single year I was at St Dunstan's, to win me a Scholarship to Charterhouse during the summer of 1941. What was more, Pittifer Joe was a marvellous instructor in that most difficult of all strokes, the Leg Sweep. Yet he took no undue pride in these attainments, just attended quietly to the needs of his pupils, swift to correct but slow to anger – until one day in that summer of '41 he revealed a streak of violence and brutality which, latent and unsuspected over the full forty years he had served the school, now burst over our astonished heads like Vesuvius over the lotus-eaters of Pompeii.

It happened in this wise. At the end of the Easter Term the maths master had very properly followed the call of the bugle, and the school had been compelled to employ a middle-aged temporary called 'Wally' Wallace. Although Wally knew little mathematics and less science, he was quite a plausible bluffer and had the wit to discover straight away which boys had some reputation at his subjects and then, as it were, to pace himself by them. If he were uncertain how to solve a problem, he would not flounder about trying to do it himself, he would set the whole class on to it and then announce that the school swot had come up with the correct answer. The school swot ('Lotty' Loder he was called) would then be invited to come up to the blackboard and demonstrate his solution to the accompaniment of grateful and approving nods from Wally…who, however, was calamitously found out on the day when Lotty had been introduced by his neighbour to the delights of self-abuse.

Wally by now had such trust in him that he summoned him to the blackboard without even bothering to look at his work; whereupon the wretched child came limping forward with a huge erection clearly visible under his grey shorts and no solution to propose to his audience. After a few feeble efforts at improvisation he asked to be allowed 'to go to the bog, sir, please', stayed there exploring the full possibilities of his newfound hobby, and left Wally to do his own job for once.

And a sad mess Wally made of it. However, no one complained, because we all liked Wally and those of us who were cricketers much admired his graceful batting and the excellence of his instruction in the nets. Whatever his maths might be, his cricket, in a phrase of the time, was the real MaCoy. And this it was which eventually led to his explosive confrontation with Pittifer Joe Potts.

Wally had very properly been appointed assistant cricket master on his arrival, and for some weeks conducted himself as modestly and as prudently as a lieutenant should. The only slight trouble was that Wally was a 'Leg Glance' man who delighted, at the wicket as in the classroom, in letting others do the work and deflecting their power to his glory. Now, Pittifer Joe, as I have already mentioned, was a 'Leg Sweep' man: he believed that one should positively hit the ball and that there was something unmanly, unBritish and even unChristian in merely deflecting it. From this it will be plain that the difference between Wally and Pittifer was not just technical or even stylistic – it was fundamental and it was moral. Nevertheless, such were the efficiency and the deference with which Wally filled his subordinate role that for some weeks, as I say, all went well. Both men sensibly contrived to avoid making Leg Sweep versus Leg Glance into any kind of issue…until the day of the Scholars' Picnic.

This took place early every June in honour of those boys who had won Scholarships to Public Schools in the May examinations. Before the War the school had travelled to Cheddar Gorge or Dunster Castle for the celebration: in 1941 it was held a few hundred yards down the beach by which we lived. The great feature of the day was to be The Dutch Game, as we called it. For this the school was divided into fifteen groups of five boys; each group ranged in age from eight to thirteen, and spent the entire day from eleven in the morning constructing a fort of sand to resist the tide, which would begin to encroach on our labours some time around 4 p.m. The fort which was judged to have held out the longest would win the competition, and the group which had constructed it would receive a florin a head – half a crown for the group leader.

Of all the childhood games which I remember, I think The Dutch Game was the most thrilling. The tension mounting as the tide rose, the desperate reinforcements and adjustments as the first trickle lapped up some tiny channel, the haste and huddle of the final retreat within the walls of the fort (obligatory, by the rules, when the first proper wave reached the ramparts)…it is these I would choose if the gods offered me a few hours back as a boy. But matchless as The Dutch Game was, there was one other game which ran it pretty close and obviously, in the view of Lotty Loder, beat it altogether. Since his induction into masturbation on the day of Wally's unmasking, the ingenious fellow had refined a series of subtle and varied methods which he confided and later actually exhibited to such of his acquaintance as expressed interest. Hitherto, for whatever reason, there had been no question of 'doing it to each other' or even of 'doing it together'; one was simply permitted to watch. But the Scholars' Picnic, in this matter as in others, was to prove a feast of revelations.

Now Lotty Loder (who despite his auto-erotic frenzies had achieved an Exhibition to Blundell's) was a group leader in The Dutch Game. Even quite early it was observed by Wally Wallace and others that Lotty's fort was progressing very slowly. Wally, an oddly innocent man, could not imagine why: the rest of us could have told him that it was because Lotty kept whisking one or other of his group into the sand dunes for a look at 'Lotty tickling his pee', as the exercise was currently dubbed. After the third of these expeditions, this made with an intelligent and sultry ten year old, Lotty returned in a state of some bewilderment and came lolloping along the beach to talk to me.

'It's even more fun,' Lotty said, 'if you tickle one another. Young Hayward suggested it. I can't think why I never thought of that before.'

'*I* thought of it before,' I said.

'Why didn't you tell me?'

'It makes *them* cross. It happened at my last school and there was a dreadful row. We were told it might ruin our whole lives.'

'Oh. Does it ruin your whole life if you just do it to yourself?'

'No. But they're not too keen on that either.'

Lotty went thoughtfully away. But clearly my warning had not gone very deep, as soon after lunch I saw him disappear again with 'young Hayward'.

Pittifer Joe came on the scene.

'Where's Loder?' he said. 'His fort's jolly feeble.'

'He's gone to the bog in the dunes, sir.'

This, as I had supposed, for the time being satisfied Pittifer Joe, who now hung around giving me unwanted advice about the design of my own fort. But at last, 'Loder's taking a long time,' he said. 'Wallace,' he called to Wally, who was ambling along under the dunes, 'just have a look for Loder, please. He's somewhere in there and he's neglecting his fort.'

Wally turned without enthusiasm to climb the steep dunes. Pittifer, noticing Wally's reluctance and not entirely satisfied with delegation of duty, started walking up the beach after him. Something must be done very fast. Always a slow thinker, I was paralysed, my mind a blank. Fortunately there were quicker wits than mine in the group.

'Sir,' said Broxton I (a tall, morose, precocious boy, with legs like toothpicks), 'Sir,' he called to the departing Pittifer, 'can you please explain something?'

Pittifer turned.

'If the Leg Sweep is better than the Leg Glance, why did Prince Ranjitsinjhii always do Leg Glances?'

'Who told you that?'

'Mr Wallace, sir. In science yesterday.'

'*Did* Mr Wallace say that, Raven?'

'Yes, sir,' I lied, by now having some notion of Broxton I's tactic.

'Wallace – please come here.'

Wallace, halfway up the dune and not at all sorry to be recalled, plodded down through the fine sand and back on to the beach: Pittifer Joe went to meet him.

'Did you tell the Sixth Form in the Science Period yesterday,' said Pittifer levelly as they met, 'that Ranjitsinjhii always played the Leg Glance and not the Leg Sweep?'

'I might have done,' said Wally amiably. (Having no science, he usually allowed the period to turn into a conversational miscellany and in his own casual way imparted a lot of valuable general knowledge.) 'Yes, I might have done,' he said. 'It's true, you know.'

'It is not true,' said Joe sternly.

Although I could not see his face, I could tell from his tone that he had thinned and primmed his mouth into what we called his 'confiscating' expression. ('Nasty little boy, eating sweets in form. Watch me now. I'm going to put them all on the fire. One by one. One...two...three...')

'Oh, come along,' said Wally. 'You know that photo in the *Jubilee Book of Cricket*. "Ranjitsinjhii glancing the ball off the Leg Stump".'

'There is also a photograph, in the Lonsdale Library book on Cricket, of Ranjitsinjhii sweeping to leg. He did not *always* glance.'

'That photo,' said Wally earnestly, 'has no definite caption. It only says "Ranji playing to Leg".'

'He was playing off the front foot. He must have been sweeping.'

'It is quite possible to *glance* off the front foot.'

'His bat is at an angle for sweeping.'

Lotty came out of the dune with Hayward. Hayward looked jubilant. Lotty looked even more bewildered than he had the last time, and rather haggard with it. What was that story, I thought with some alarm, about the brain turning to water?

'He could perfectly well be glancing,' said Wally, mild but persistent, 'even with his bat at that angle.'

'He was not glancing,' rasped Joe, 'he was sweeping.'

'All right, have your own way,' said good-humoured Wally. 'All I really meant was that Ranji glanced much more often than he swept.'

'Not true. Lies. Beastly lies.'

For some reason, Wally's concession had infuriated Joe more than anything yet. His face, I reckoned, must now be at its 'Filthy little pig' stage, which it normally reached only in cases of cheating or theft.

'Lies,' said Joe, low but intensely malignant. 'Where have you been, boy?' he yelled at Lotty as he slunk past towards his fort.

'Going to the bog, sir.'

'Lies,' shouted Joe, transferring his rage, apparently without even noticing, from Wally to Lotty. 'Horrible lies. Look at your face, the rings round your eyes, you've been polluting yourself, you'll go blind, you'll go to hell – '

' – Steady on,' said Wally. 'You can't go accusing people of that sort of thing.'

Luckily Hayward had got out of Joe's arc of vision before Joe spotted Lotty. Otherwise, I thought, his accusations would have been far worse.

'I hate LIARS,' howled Joe. (Yes; howled.)

He seized Lotty by the hair and jerked his head backward and forward, faster and faster.

'Stop that,' said Wally.

He hit the inside of Joe's elbow very hard with the wedge of his hand. Joe released Lotty's hair, nursed his arm, and bowed his head. Wally nudged Joe off along the beach. No reference was made to the incident, nor did Pittifer Joe lose his temper, ever again.

During later discussion of the day, while all mention of the quarrel was carefully avoided, questions were nevertheless asked about why Lotty Loder had loitered so long in the sand dunes. A normal 'Lotty session' took three minutes flat: this time he and Hayward had been gone fifteen.

'What on earth was going on?' we insisted.

Lotty sweated and blushed, refused to gratify the curiosity of the general, but later confided in myself. What had taken so long, it transpired, was that Lotty had had his first adult orgasm ('White stuff coming out') and had nearly fainted from pleasure.

'I had to hang about and pull myself together,' Lotty said.

Hayward had been delighted, relishing the unusual nature of the performance and attributing Lotty's ecstasy to his own skill. But Lotty was bothered. What was this remarkable phenomenon? Always before he had had 'the feeling', along with a lot of 'throbbing and juddering', and then it had 'sort of exploded' and gone away, leaving a slight discomfort 'in my pee', as he explained, which, however, vanished in ten minutes or so, whereupon he was immediately able to start up again. But this time he had felt – well – as if he had been 'drained', and hadn't 'got keen again' for nearly an hour, by which time he was sitting in his fort with his team surrounded by the sea. He had been about to suggest that they all did it together, only the Headmaster's wife had been paddling in that area and it had seemed unwise. But the real point was, Lotty said, that he must know exactly what had happened to him in the dunes. Hayward had been vaguely reassuring and had quoted a rhyme which his elder brother, now at King's School, Bruton, had taught him:

> First it tickles and it prickles,
> Then it trickles:
> Then it squirts and it spirts
> For hours and hours
> When you see Harcourt Minor in the showers.

But there was an element of hyperbole here which Lotty mistrusted, and in any case the thing was too frivolous to carry the authority for which he craved. Now, I seemed to know a lot about all this, with all the talk of the row there had been at my last place: could I please enlighten Lotty? Was this afternoon's occurrence in the natural order, or had he been overdoing it?

So then I told him. It would seem, I said, that he *had* been doing it rather a lot by other people's standards, but otherwise everything was as it should be. It hadn't yet happened to me, I went on, because I hadn't yet got 'hairs down there' ('Ah,' said Lotty); but sooner or later I would and it would, and it was the same for everybody. 'For girls?' said Lotty. *Mulatis mutandis,* I replied. I then went on to explain the mechanics of sexual intercourse and the conception of children, which was, I said, what the whole apparatus was meant for.

'It seems to me you can have a lot of fun without any nuisance of that sort,' said Lotty, who was not an Exhibitioner Elect of Blundell's for nothing.

In fact, it now appeared, Lotty found the whole arrangement so ridiculous ('I mean, imagine trying to stick it in your mother.' 'You're not *supposed* to stick it in your mother.' 'Well, in Matron or Mrs Mack the cook. You'd look absolutely *daft*.') that he suspected me of having him on. What was the *provenance* of the information, he wanted to know? In what circumstances had I come by it? How could I authenticate it? Since he would not be satisfied save by the most accurate, detailed and logical account of how I came by my knowledge, I was compelled to give him the full story...

...Which can conveniently begin at the Oval in August, 1938. A boy called Crawford, a friend of mine at my first prep school, had a father who had tickets for the timeless test against the Australians. I was invited to accompany Crawford *père et fils* to several days of the match, and there we now were, watching Hutton as he plodded towards his world record. Whatever you may hear to the contrary, take it from me that it was a pretty dreary performance; I was far more interested in the man on my left, who kept peeling great strips off his fingernails with other fingernails. How long, I wondered, before he had none left? This question was not to be answered, as the man left shortly afterwards, as soon as Hutton broke Hammond's record. But by that time there was a much more absorbing drama in the offing, something which we had been working towards ever since we arrived in the Stand at eleven o'clock that morning.

Imagine us there. Crawford and myself, in grey shorts and turned down knee socks topped by our school colours (red and green), Aertex shirts and horizontally striped school ties, grey jackets and big grey floppy sunhats which sported the school riband...imagine us there, Crawford and me, one on either side of Mr Crawford, who was in a dark blue chalk-striped suit, and had iron-grey hair cut very short and an iron-grey Hitler moustache. There we had been sitting, as I say, since eleven o'clock, and now at last Mr Crawford was about to put the boot into his son's belly in the manner which he must have been planning ever since we sat down.

Mr Crawford had set the thing up by asking for an account of the 1st XI Cricket season at our school. Both Crawford and I, though only ten, were in the XI, and we started on an artless history of the matches played, interrupting and supporting each other, strophe and antistrophe, sticking mostly to fact but occasionally issuing half-baked tactical or general judgments.

The first match had been against Fan Court, where all the boys were Christian Scientists and constantly dying, we assured Mr Crawford, of ruptured appendices because they were never allowed a doctor. Fan Court had made 57, which was a pretty feeble score. One of their batsmen had wet himself with fear of our fast bowler and had then fainted. We afterwards heard (said Crawford) that he died of sunstroke because he wasn't given any medicine, only prayed for. No, I said; it couldn't have been sunstroke because it was a very chilly day in early May; it was infantile paralysis. What happened in the match? prompted Crawford Senior.

'We won with 4 wickets down,' said Crawford. 'I made 62.'

'How can you have made 62 if the other side only made 57?'

'We played on after we'd won.'

'How many had *you* made when you passed their score?'

'Nineteen, Daddy.'

'Then that's all,' said Mr Crawford with evident satisfaction, 'that counts. Nineteen not out. *That* is what goes into the averages. How many did you make, Raven?'

'Didn't bat, sir. I'm a bowler.' (As, in those days, I was.)

'Did you get any wickets?'

'Three, sir.'

'Jolly useful. They say one wicket equals 20 runs. Say 15 in prep school cricket. So you got the equivalent of 45 runs – much better than 19 not out.'

And so the morning had gone on.

By the time we reached the Bigshott match, two patterns had become abundantly plain: the pattern, dismally familiar to all cricketers, of poor Crawford's form as a batsman, which had started brilliant but turned steadily sour; and the pattern of Mr Crawford's inquisition, which consisted of probing into every one of his son's performances, eliciting the maximum disgrace from the bad and somehow contriving to discount or even discredit the good.

'At Bigshott,' said Crawford, setting his teeth, 'they don't have proper lavs. They go in pails. They make the boys empty them themselves.'

'Only as a punishment,' I put in.

'What about the match?' insisted the remorseless Crawford *père*.

Well, we had made 136. Crawford had made 2 and I, batting at No. 10, had fluked 17. Then they went in to bat. I had taken 2 wickets; Crawford, who was given a trial bowl, had taken none – *but*, I pointed out loyally, had had two sitters missed off his second over.

'I hate bowlers,' announced Mr Crawford, 'who whine about missed catches.'

'I didn't whine,' said Crawford. 'I didn't even mention it. Raven did.'

Mr Crawford appeared not even to have heard. I then went on to describe how their best bat had been in with their last, how their best bat had got the bowling and had a whole over left in which to make the 7 runs needed to beat us, how he had hit a brisk four off the second ball, and had then driven the fourth ball so hard that you could hear it hissing and everyone thought it must be another four – only Crawford at extra-cover had thrown himself down to his left, to take a miraculous catch six inches from the ground and win the game for our school.

'Sheer fluke,' said Mr Crawford.

'Mr Edwardes said that it was very lucky –'

' – Sheer fluke –'

' – But,' continued Crawford patiently, 'that I deserved the luck for being quick enough to get my hands there.'

'Mr Edwardes should know better than to encourage small boys to get conceited.'

By this time I was beginning to dislike Mr Crawford very much indeed. The odd thing was that he hadn't behaved at all like this during the earlier days of the match; he had been a bit sombre but perfectly agreeable, remembering to hand out ice cream money and quite prepared to smile (if not without patronage) at our brash little jokes. Why had he suddenly turned so nasty?

That is a question I couldn't answer then and still cannot. Perhaps he had received one bill too many in the post that morning; perhaps he had failed to satisfy his wife the night before. However that may be, the fact remains that he became more and more unpleasant to his son as the day went on and by the time that the applause for Hutton's record had subsided he was ready to stick in the knife and twist it.

We had now arrived at the Lambrook match, the penultimate of the season. Lambrook had made 97. At the start of our innings wickets fell swiftly but Crawford, who was beginning (too late) to run into form again, had batted steadily and after 45 minutes was apparently in a position to win the match for us, his own score being 23 and that of the team 59 for 5. But at this stage he had stepped back to pull a short ball, slipped and skidded into his wicket...after which disaster we were all out for 72.

'Jolly bad luck,' I said.

'Sheer carelessness,' said Crawford Major. 'Anyway, people who play cow shots deserve everything they get.'

'I was trying to hook,' said Crawford miserably.

'Hooking is for people who can play the game. You didn't even get your Colours. Did Raven get his?'

Raven had got his. So would Crawford have, had he not made a blob in the last match (a shooter), given away 24 runs off his first over, and missed two skiers (out of the sun).

'I wonder you weren't sick on the pitch,' said his father, 'to top it all off. It would have made an apt comment on your entire season's play.'

Now, I hope I have made it clear that Crawford was a jolly nice boy. Although all in all he'd had a wretched season which had ended in cruel humiliation, he had made no complaint and had clapped as cheerfully as anyone, in the circumstances, could possibly expect of him when the rest of us went up the Assembly Room to receive our Colours. But now he had had more than he could bear. Even his one great achievement, the match-winning catch against Bigshott, had been treated by his father with contempt. He needed to get his own back; he needed someone to blame for his misery; he needed a plausible excuse, other than mere 'bad luck', for his failure. And so, like many before and after him in similar predicament, he drew a great big stinking red herring right across the trail, diverting the hounds that tormented him to the pursuit of others.

'It wasn't my fault,' he said, 'I was worried about Colonel Killock.'

There was a long silence.

'Colonel Killock? What about Colonel Killock?'

'Oh, nothing. Nothing, Daddy, nothing.' But it was already too late.

Lieutenant-Colonel Killock, a married man with two sons, had retired from the Indian Army three or four years previously and had come to our school to teach football, rugger, PT, mathematics and English. He was extremely good at teaching all of them; he was one of the finest natural schoolmasters I ever met, a man whom one would wish above all things to please and would obey as if one's life depended on it; a firm man yet flexible and tolerant, of apparently inexhaustible good humour and good will.

He liked playing with little boys' penises, and he did it so deftly that we positively queued up for him. He also liked letting us play with his own, an object of gratifying size, agreeable texture and startling capacity. One of his particular favourites had a tent which he put up in a remote part of the pine woods which surrounded the cricket ground; and as soon as cricket for the day was over, Crawford and I would hurry through the warm pines to 'The Tent' (as it was known), inside which several boys, ranging in age from nine to thirteen, would already be lolling about with their shorts round their ankles, exploring one another's anatomy and waiting for the arrival of 'Colonel K'. It was a scene of great erotic fascination, vividly memorable to this day, of Petronian power and indecency.

It may be imagined, therefore, that the information which Crawford's father now had from him really set the fuse sizzling. To be fair to Crawford, I think the uneasiness of mind of which he had spoken was genuine: there was obviously something not quite right, to say the least of it, about five boys and a grown man practising circular *fellatio*: however much one enjoyed it at the time, one felt a bit dubious when it was over. Whether or not this uneasiness had affected Crawford's cricket is another matter again, and in any case irrelevant. For what was happening, as I have already tried to convey, is that Crawford was instinctively using 'Colonel K' to create a diversion as a result of which he would be exonerated, at someone else's expense, from any blame for his failure. In fact, of course, he found that he was not only exonerated but was actually deferred to — as long as he kept the revelations coming. Crawford, then, did not stint: any guilt he might feel at his treachery to his companions of 'The Tent' was swiftly allayed by assurance that it was his moral duty to tell all; and so, gleaming with self-righteousness and self-importance, tell all he did.

'They' made a very good job of hushing it all up. The evident approach of war was cleverly exploited in order to arrange that Killock should rejoin his old regiment, which was only too pleased to have a good man back before others grabbed him. It could therefore be egregiously announced, when Colonel K did not appear among the Surrey pines next September, that he had been requested to return to military duty in India. It is a matter of record that he had a 'good war', after which he and his wife started up a 'pre-preparatory' school for boys aged between six and ten. He must have died (which he did suddenly some fifteen years later) an exceedingly happy man.

As for the rest of us, we were dealt with by a combination of enlightenment and threat. In the first place, we were told the full 'facts of life' from Alpha to Omega, in order to straighten us out about the precise (and perverse) nature of our recent experience. We were then told that if ever it all got out none of us would be allowed to go on to his public school. Because we were all so young, 'they' said, 'they' were prepared to forgive us: others would not be so accommodating, so from now on just keep your dear little hands to yourselves and hold your busy little tongues, *or else...*

Mr Crawford and Master Crawford were full of nuisance, Master C because his pleasure in the role of principal delator had made a strutting little monster of him, and Mr C because he was the only parent in the know and was constantly threatening to tell others if the affair was not handled exactly as he thought it should be. Since this would involve calling in the police and the public burning of Colonel K, 'they', who abhorred the idea of publicity and incidentally liked Colonel K as much as the rest of us did, had a problem on their hands…which 'they' managed to solve by agreeing to educate young Crawford free till the end of his time. Thus Crawford *père* was silenced and the boy perforce tolerated. Since he was, *au fond*, a thoroughly decent boy, he returned before long to his natural and agreeable self, from which indeed he would never have departed, had it not been for his father's malice at the Oval. Although Crawford and I often discussed the possibility of 'doing it together again', we decided that 'their' warning was too savage to be neglected. From now on, pleasure under the pines was strictly solitary.

Thus and thus it came about that I was competent to inform Lotty Loder of the full facts of life and to reassure him that his experience in the dunes on that afternoon of the Scholars' Picnic had been, physically at least, entirely *en règle*. 'They' would certainly pass a wet orgasm: what 'they' would not care for, I said, was the idea that young Hayward's ministrations had brought it on. For the rest – well, now he knew.

I had, on the whole, a satisfied client. Lotty's initial incredulity about the facts I offered him had been overcome by the evident sincerity of my tale of how I came by them.

'It must have been fun at your first school,' Lotty said wistfully, 'before it all came out.'

'It was. Tremendous fun.'

'I can't see it happening here. With Wally or Pittifer Joe.'

'Pittifer Joe would have had a fit if he'd caught you and Hayward.'

'Gosh, it was lovely. When that stuff started coming out…'

'I haven't seen that – not since Colonel K. Come on, Lotty; show me.'

And good-natured Lotty obliged.

IV

CHARTERHOUSE PINK II

I did not achieve such emission myself until the following October, by which time I was at Charterhouse. Though agreeing with Lotty that it was very delectable, I could not agree that it was anything to faint about. However, I repeated the process with huge enjoyment and almost daily until the following March, when a rumour was put about that 'shagging' (the elegant Carthusian vernacular for masturbation) gave you a terrible disease called syphilis. The story had been started by a boy whom I had scarcely met at the time but was later to know well: William Rees Mogg.

Our first encounter of any consequence occurred entirely by accident a few days after the 'shagging' rumour had started. During those days I had been continent for very fear, and I was now canvassing the opinion of my friend, Conrad Dehn, in the matter, while we walked on the boundary of a pretty little cricket ground where 'Maniacs' (the 4th XI) would play in the summer.

'It's all a great lot of nonsense,' Conrad said. 'Syphilis, or the Great Pox, is contracted from sexual congress with an infected person – usually, though not necessarily, a woman. How many women have you had lately?'

I shook my head and tittered.

'If you should get it,' Conrad continued, 'you'd certainly know all about it. Bloody great spos (*sic*: another piece of Carthusian vernacular) all over your apparatus – and then all over the rest of you. Have you had any of *those* lately?'

'No, thank God. But everyone says that Rees Mogg says –'

' – I know. There he is, sitting on that bench. Let's settle this.'

William was sitting alone, surveying the empty cricket ground with a poetic look. We sat down on either side of him.

45

'There'th thomething tho forlorn,' said William, 'about an empty cricket ground.'

'What else would you expect it to be in March?' said Conrad the realist. 'What we want to know is this: what is all this balls you've been putting round about shagging giving people syphilis?'

'My motive is twofold,' said William, 'first, to see how many people are stupid enough to believe it; and secondly to discourage shagging, since my Church holds solitary vice to be a mortal sin.'

William was a Roman Catholic.

'Come to that,' he went on, warming to the theme, 'my Church holds that any sexual act, unless conducted within lawful wedlock *and intended for the procreation of children*, is a mortal sin.'

'So even husband and wife can't do it just for the fun of it?'

'No.'

'Are they allowed to enjoy it if they are genuinely trying to have children at the same time?'

Conrad, later a formidable QC, enjoyed going into subtleties of this nature.

'They are allowed to rejoice in it,' said William, 'as an act of union under God and in the furtherance of His will.'

'And are they allowed to do…amusing little *other* things before they do it properly?'

William thought not.

'Thank God I'm a Jew,' Conrad said.

'Jewith law ith pletty thtrict ath well.'

'Thank God I'm not a *proper* Jew,' Conrad emended.

'Let's get back to the point,' I said. 'You admit, Rees Mogg, that this story about shagging giving you syphilis is only a spoof which you've got up to annoy people?'

'To *test* people. And to deter them.'

'Well, it won't deter me any more,' I said.

'But you did believe it — just for a time?'

'I thought it as well to be cautious.'

'If there is one kind of sinner,' said William, 'who will be thrust into the Seventh Circle of the Inferno, it is the kind who is deterred only by motives of wordly caution. You are both destined for Hell. Dehn because he is a Jew who scoffs at Jewry; and you, Raven, because you are an Onanist.'

'What's that?'

'Someone who spills his seed upon the ground.'

'Then I'm not the only one round here.'

46

'Do you know what Hell is?' enquired William. 'It is like an abscess in the gum, getting worse every minute forever. Once in a hundred years it stops, to remind you how lovely it is not to have it, and then, after five minutes or so, it begins again.'

'If there is a God in Heaven,' remarked Conrad, 'He will certainly send *you* to Hell, Rees Mogg, for spreading false rumours and frightening your fellow human beings.'

And with this we rose and went on our way.

But there was something about Mogg's discourse, frightening or not, that I found pleasing. To begin with, it was succinct; and whatever else it was, it was not trivial. It turned on serious issues which were seriously, if sometimes rather grotesquely, presented and illustrated. It was also polymath. William, under the pretext of being delicate, spent much of his time, while others were doing disagreeable things called 'War Work', reading volumes of history, philosophy and literature, particularly those of the English 18th Century. Not only, then, did he know a lot, not only could he 'tell you things' if he chose, but he also had the fascination of someone who had used his wits to better his lot and in general to lead a more interesting and comfortable life than the rest of us.

Just how delicate William really was is anybody's guess. He certainly looked pretty awful, but that may have been due to an aversion from washing and an economical habit of cleaning his teeth with school soap. What was not in doubt was that, delicate or not, he had somehow convinced all the key personnel (House matron, House tutor, even the Headmaster) that he was. He had given it to be understood, and it *was* understood, that if he was made to do anything in the physical line which he didn't want to do then the consequences might be dangerous and even fatal. And so, while the rest of us, inexorably coerced, stamped up and down drill squares, cleaned out lavatories, cut down trees and stooped for long hours to gather potatoes from the earth, William sat in front of the fire in the Library (even as a very junior boy he had his own chair which no one dared sequester) becoming more and more knowledgeable not only about books but through them about the world.

I think, now, that one of the reasons why no one ever challenged or investigated Mogg's status as a permanent invalid was that he gave such thoroughly good value in return for being indulged. When all the nasty business of the day had been despatched, when parades had been dismissed, gardens weeded and dishes washed, Mogg would appear, fresh from the Library or his bed, to enjoy with the rest of us whatever pleasure was going forward, an evening cricket match, perhaps, a concert, a debate, or just an *al fresco* gossip, and would so much enhance that pleasure by stringent and witty comment, fantasy and anecdote, or by hilarious personal denunciation, that no one could bear to accuse him of having spent the day shirking while others perspired or froze. He entertained us too well for us to offer him offence or to imperil the leisure from which he derived his power to enchant.

Consider, for example, Mogg's acquaintance with Bob Arrowsmith. R L Arrowsmith, who has already appeared in these pages as master in charge of the Under Sixteen Cricket XI, was a brisk and accurate teacher of the Classics, a man of duty who left no chore undone and no stone unturned, a devout Christian who practised what he unofficiously but clearly preached, a hater of idleness or hypochondria. If any man could see through Mogg and detest what he saw the other side, you would have said it was RLA. And yet he took more pleasure in Mogg's company than anyone. They were constantly to be seen walking the touchline together or criticising some match in the Fives Courts (for Mogg, though he played no game, was an educated aficionado of all). It was even said that Mogg had once had tea in RLA's lodgings in Pepperharrow Road, an unprecedented privilege. What spell had William cast on this man of iron? There could only be one answer: like everyone else 'the Arrow' quite simply accepted, without asking any awkward questions, that William was a weakly boy who must not be pressed into hardship or exertion. Bob was not exactly conned or deceived or imposed upon, he was lulled. For it was, after all, *unthinkable* that William, spindly, spotty, chesty, learned, lisping William, should go for a Cross-Country run or execute about turns in the rain. It would be deeply and offensively wrong: it would be a crime against seemliness, against harmony, almost against God Himself, to put William into football shorts or ammunition boots. He was to be enjoyed, nay cherished as he was – a literate, civilised and thoroughly amusing boy, matchless company…as indeed was Bob himself. They deserved each other, Bob Arrowsmith and William Rees Mogg, in the best possible sense.

Or again, take William's friendship with VSH ('Sniffy') Russell. Russell was a fine scholar in a rather different *mode* from RLA; much concerned with intricacies of meaning, he had a tendency to seek out doubts rather than to proclaim certainties (which was what the Arrow went in for), and he often indulged his passion for semantic theorising or metaphysical speculation, both of them exercises well outside the taste and scope of RLA. Like RLA, however, he was a convinced Christian who acted on his beliefs: though perhaps more tolerant of minor deviance than RLA, he would never have condoned major evasion of daily duties or wartime tasks; and he was quite as shrewd as RLA when it came to spotting techniques of fraudulence. Yet

48

'Sniffy' too accepted Mogg's role without question. Mogg was there to cultivate his mind, to entertain, to comment, to discriminate, but on no account to take an active part in anything physically arduous or distasteful. In VSHR's case, however, a certain irony was discernible: this took the form of pretending to believe that Rees Mogg would fain be cured if he could be, would be only too happy to shed debility, were this but possible, to rise up from his bed and walk – and indeed to leap about and caper joyously, like all other healthy boys of his age.

'Poor William tells me,' said VSHR to me one day in Mogg's own presence, 'that he will not be well enough to attend early morning school tomorrow. He has a cold coming on.'

'Oh dear,' I said.

'But of course he would like to come if he could because I am setting a test on the accidence of the Greek New Testament, and he would love to beat you all at it and demonstrate his superiority on the subject.'

'But when I have a cold,' said William, 'I have palpitationth until ten thirty in the morning. I really think I muth stay in bed.'

'Ah,' said Sniffy, and twinkled in my direction. 'I too suffer from palpitations, and my doctor has made up a marvellous new prescription for me. You must try it, William. Two teaspoonfuls with water just before bed. And then tomorrow morning you'll wake up as fit as a greyhound, which will make a nice change for you, and you'll come scampering along to do my accidence test at seven thirty.'

Sniffy Russell produced a medical-looking packet. William examined it.

'I have an allergy,' he said gravely, 'to at least three out of the five ingredients listed here.'

'Oh, what a shame,' said VSHR, twinkling more than ever, 'would you like me to send the test up to your House so that you could do it in bed? I'm quite sure you wouldn't cheat.'

'I really think I would sooner be conserving my strength,' said William. 'I find the doggerel Greek of the New Testament so repellent that it undermines my religious faith – not a happy matter for a Catholic.'

They then discussed the 'Common' Greek of the original Gospels, Sniffy praising its moving simplicities, William condemning its clumsy pronouns. The matter of the Test itself was apparently forgotten…until the marks were announced the following week.

'Rees Mogg: nought,' Sniffy read out.

'Why nought, sir? You usually give me an 'aegrotat' when you can't test me.'

'In this case, dear boy, I *was* able to *test* you. You remember that conversation we had the afternoon before the Test was to take place? I was convinced, by your repeated vilification of the "Common" Greek use of the pronoun *Autos*, that you were entirely ignorant of the subject and utterly insensitive to this particular kind of usage – which is every bit as legitimate, in its own way, as the Classical. Let me repeat,' proclaimed Sniffy with relish, 'Rees Mogg: nought.'

Mogg took this with a bow and a smile; but Sniffy Russell was not allowed to get away with it for long.

A week or so later there was a cricket match between the 'Yearlings' (first year boys) of Sniffy's House (Hodgsonites) and those of my own House (Saunderites). Sniffy, who supported his House with desperate loyalty even in activities to which he was personally indifferent or averse, had been got to understand that if the Hodgsonite Yearling team could win this game they stood a very good chance of finishing the season at the top of the Yearling League. He was, in consequence, frantic for Hodgsonites to win and, although he himself had never been able to distinguish between a long hop and a yorker, was on the ground ready to watch a good thirty minutes before even the most punctual players.

While VSHR was eagerly and ignorantly canvassing the opinions of those who now began to join him about the chances of the forthcoming affair, William Rees Mogg was lurking like a spy with a bomb, precisely knowing and patiently awaiting the circumstances which would prove most favourable to its felicitous combustion. At this point I should explain that William, being a nonplayer but exceedingly knowledgeable and accurate about the game, was very much in demand to act as Umpire in the inter-House contests at all levels that went on almost daily (despite the War), and that he was now so well regarded by a grateful Captain of Cricket that he could virtually 'choose his match'. Today, he now declared, he had chosen this one. There was no complaint by either side; indeed both felt themselves honoured that so veritable a Daniel had come to judgement; and no man was more delighted by the compliment thus paid to his Yearlings than VSH ('Sniffy') Russell.

William was very soon joined by some nonentity allotted from the Umpires' Pool, and together they swayed out to the wicket. (Since William always swayed when he walked, anyone who tried to keep step with him was compelled, by some rhythmical peculiarity, to sway too.)

'I'll take the pavilion end,' William said.

'Right you be, Mogg,' said the nonentity, 'stumps at six?'

'If they're still at it.'

Although Yearling Matches were normally of two innings, for some administrative reason (a temporary shortage of pitches, I think) this game was to be of one innings only. Saunderites, having won the toss, elected to bat; and

Hodgsonites, pursued by VSHR's almost hysterical clapping, now took the field.

There is no need to dwell on the Saunderite Innings. A bad team in a bad year on a bad day, they finicked and fiddled and fluked some 43 runs, leaving Hodgsonites two clear hours to pass this wretched total on a gentle wicket. Pundits of either House were forecasting a victory to Hodgsonites by at least six wickets, while VSHR pranced back and forth in front of the pavilion like Minnie Mouse doing a tap dance in an early Disney.

'We've never had the Yearling Trophy in Hodgsonites,' he was saying to anyone who would listen, 'at least not in my time as Housemaster.'

' "The man that once did sell the lion's skin," ' said Mogg as he passed Sniffy on his way out to the wicket, ' "Was killed with hunting him." '

'*What* did you say, William?'

'κοὐκ ἔστ᾽ ἀέλπτον οὐθέν, sir,' said William. 'Sophocles. In the vernacular: you never know your luck till the wheel stops turning.'

'Very true,' said VSHR: 'one must walk humbly under the gods. But you won't deny – now will you, William? – that we're off to an excellent start.'

'It is not my business to analyse or comment on the play,' said William: 'merely to regulate it.'

And with this he flicked his fingers for the nonentity, led him swaying on to the pitch, and took post with his back to the pavilion, a lean and faceless spectre when regarded from where Sniffy was sitting among his darling Hodgsonites.

'Mogg was being rather tiresome,' Sniffy said to the Hodgsonite Captain, 'I fancy he's one of those people who don't like it when their friends are doing well.'

'I know what you mean, sir,' said the fourteen-year-old Captain of Hodgsonite Yearlings. 'I'm afraid he's not the only one on the ground. All cricketers are like that, you see. None of us likes anyone except himself to make more than two.'

'Gracious, such cynicism,' said VSHR 'It reminds me of what they say about Maurice Bowra. If you get knighted, he'll never speak to you again. But if you're sent to prison, he will come and feed you enormous cheques through the bars to help you when you are let out.'

VSHR always assumed in conversation that you knew as much as he did (e.g. who Maurice Bowra was) and was on the whole well liked for the assumption.

'Good luck, good luck,' he now cried, rising and clapping his hands above his head as the Hodgsonite opening pair left the pavilion. 'Smite the uncircumcised Philistine.'

There was a cascade of giggles, during which the Captain and Vice-Captain managed to settle Sniffy down on his seat in a more or less orderly manner.

'Please keep still, sir,' said the Captain. 'It makes the batsman nervous if there's movement in the pav.'

'Oh dear, oh dear, what have I done?' moaned Sniffy, rolling his eyes in a ghastly fit of contrition.

'Nothing, sir, nothing at all. But please to be still from now on.'

The first ball was a full toss which hit the Hodgsonite No. 1 on the shoulder.

'How's that?' said the bowler facetiously.

William gently raised his finger.

The Hodgsonite Captain and Vice-Captain looked puzzled; but such was William's prestige as an Umpire that the event was allowed to pass.

'Must have been dropping fast,' said the Vice-Captain. 'One can't get the trajectory right from here.'

'*Me miserum*,' keened Sniffy. '*Eheu, eheu, eheu*.'

'Never mind, sir. Lots of good men left.'

The next good man sent his first two balls ballooning over the pavilion for six. VSHR wriggled like a four year old.

'Over a quarter of the runs already,' he said.

The batsman now called a shortish run to extra-cover. As he was lowering his bat to run it in over the crease, Mogg stepped sideways and forwards, causing him to swerve and crash into the bowler, who was waiting behind the stumps. As a result of being barged by the batsman, the bowler fumbled extra-cover's return.

'Interference with the field,' said Mogg. 'Possible run out there. Kindly leave the wicket.'

'But I was *forced* – '

' – Pray leave the wicket, sir,' said seigneurial William; and once again, such was his prestige that the decision was, albeit bleakly, accepted.

Twelve runs for two wickets. The last two balls of the over passed without incident.

The second ball of the second over, though struck over square leg's head quite firmly, failed to reach the boundary. The batsmen ran a comfortable three. William, now umpiring at square leg, performed a signal which no one had ever seen before, like an old fashioned piece of physical jerks but with one arm only.

'Two short,' he called to the scorers, 'only one run to be tallied.'

The next ball was snicked into the gloves of the wicketkeeper, who dropped it. But since the bowler had begun to appeal before the ball had reached the wicketkeeper, the appeal had to be answered – and was.

'Not out,' said the nonentity at the bowler's end.

'I beg your pardon,' said William, swaying over to his colleague, 'but I think I had a better view than you did. The catch was perfectly valid.'

'But he dropped it,' said the furious batsman.

'He had the ball under control,' William said, 'and then got rid of it. You don't have to hang on to it for ever, you know.'

There was a long pause. The nonentity looked at William and William looked back at the nonentity.

'Very well,' said the latter at last, and raised his finger.

Back in the pavilion VSHR was looking thoughtful.

'Surely that catch was dropped,' he said to the Captain, who had risen to go in, 'even I know that.'

'You *could* just say that the keeper had it just long enough,' said the Captain, who was a very conservative little boy and did not believe in the perfidy of his seniors…but certainly began to a minute later, when he was given out lbw off his first ball which pitched outside his leg stump and turned sharply from the off.

The last Hodgsonite wicket (fairly and squarely bowled – the only one often) fell for 17 runs some fifteen minutes later. As the triumphant Saunderites came in from the field, their Housemaster (and Headmaster), Mr Robert Birley, stalked majestically on to the ground, confident that he was in time to enjoy at least ninety minutes' play. Since he loved a cricket match above all things, he was very desolate when told that play was over, even though his own House had won. He was now saluted by William, to whom, as I have said, he was well disposed, and together they walked over to console Sniffy Russell.

'An extraordinary run of misfortune, sir,' said William easily, 'I've never seen anything like it.'

'It was my fault,' wailed Sniffy. 'I was arrogant, hybristic. I presumed. I crowed too soon.'

'Funny game, cricket,' said Robert Birley. 'Eleanor [Mrs Birley] says her school was once out for three and their opponents made only one.'

'Strange things happen,' said William blandly. And to VSHR, 'I thought your boys were very sporting, sir, all things considered. One or two started to protest my decisions, but I soon set them straight.'

Sniffy's underlip began to tremble. Tears glistened in his eyes.

'Such an opportunity,' he breathed, 'lost, for ever lost.'

'Of course,' pursued William, 'they had some excuse for being a bit fwactiouth. After all, the odds against so many unlucky dismissals were enormous…about the same as the odds against – what shall we say, sir? – finding a page of the Greek Testament without that dreary little word *autos* on it.'

The Headmaster looked puzzled. VSHR blinked, pursed his mouth, fingered a little tuft of hair beneath his underlip (which was still trembling), and marched quickly away, pausing occasionally to slap his ribs and hooting all the time with dry, savage laughter.

After the match, Mogg and Robert Birley started pacing the boundary together, deep in discussion. James Prior and I walked away to 'Crown' (the school tuck shop).

'You know what they're talking about,' said James, 'Mogg and the Head Man.'

'No. But they look pretty thick.'

'The Head Man wants to make Moggie Head of the School next Oration Quarter [Michaelmas Term].'

'A-haaaaa.'

'But the trouble is that Jasper Holmes refuses to have Mogg as Head of Verites.'

William's Housemaster, Jasper Holmes, a chunky, health-foodish, do-it-yourself number, much given to wearing shorts and sandals while doing it, was one of the few people who had never succumbed to William's attractions. William, who reciprocated his dislike, once compared him to 'one of those Shakespearean clowns: a capering buffoon, hugely pleased with himself, forever interrupting more interesting people, and quite incapable of even being funny.' On another occasion William had remarked, 'Jasper is the sort of man who used to join those communes in the thirties, you know the kind of thing, where they went in for raffia work or making lampshades, and all lived self-consciously and prudishly in sin. But of course Jasper would have been too boring and sanctimonious even for them.'

'So,' James Prior now continued, 'what is the Head Man to do? His mind is made up, his word is given, Moggie has accepted the post with well-feigned modesty: but Jasper won't budge.'

'Can he be first in the School and second in Verites?'

'At this very moment, I suspect, some compromise is being fudged up.'

We looked back at the distant strolling pair. Even the Headmaster swayed when he walked with William.

'Sweet William,' I said, 'so that's what he's been after all the time.'

'Didn't you know? You must have been the only person in the world who didn't.'

'I did notice...that he's taken to coming to School Chapel sometimes instead of going off to his Papist menagerie.'

'That's part of it all. If he becomes Head of the School, he'll have certain ceremonial duties in Chapel which the Head Man wouldn't want him to miss – and which he himself most certainly wouldn't want to miss, for all the grace in the Catholic Heaven. So he's coming twice a week, for a bit of net practice so to speak. I gather that one of the ways he's been sucking up to the Head Man is by hinting that he *might* just apostasise and come over to the dear old C of E. The Head Man would love that – it would make that filthy little Irish priest so sick.'

I should say here and now, as it makes no part of my future narrative, that William did in fact become Head of the School and made a very good one. He swayed down the aisle of Chapel, hands clasped in front of his navel, with enormous dignity, conducted several labyrinthine intrigues with refinement and panache, and had his revenge on Jasper Holmes (who still refused to appoint him Head of Verites) by inventing a new nickname for him: Clara Cluck. Whether he left the Church of Rome, I do not know to this day; for although I still see him from time to time, there is something about his demeanour (the Editor of *The Times*, like God, is not mocked) that has deterred me from enquiring.

'Anyway,' James was saying, 'the trumpets are going to sound and William is going to be proclaimed King in Judaea. If I were you, I should abstain from witticisms on the subject. William's celebrated sense of humour does not embrace jokes about William.'

We now arrived at Crown, where I bought us both ice cream and 'red drink' in Bloods' Window on credit. Mr Veale, the faithful elder who ran the place, reminded me respectfully that all accounts were due for settlement monthly, and swept his cap off his head and down to his knees when I promised to pay him at the end of the Quarter.

We then went next door to the 1st XI pavilion and upstairs to see George Geary, the cricket pro, and his assistant, Rainsford. They were both sitting over the ever-bubbling glue pot in George's 'shop', George whitening a cricket pad and Rainsford trying to dry one of his calico shirts from the scant sideways heat of the paraffin ring which ministered to the glue pot.

It may come as some surprise, to boys now at school and accustomed to cricket pros who frequent the Masters' Common Room, that George Geary, of Leicestershire and England, was cleaning *my* cricket pads on *my* command, and was very glad to do so as he would be able to charge a shilling for it on my school bill. (Mercifully George, unlike Veale, had his accounts paid to him by the Bursar.) It will come as a further surprise to the democratic young that I called George 'George', or sometimes, if piqued with him, 'Geary', and that in theory at least he called me 'Sir'. In fact George eschewed vocatives; but Rainsford made up for him by inserting at least two oily 'Sirs' in every sentence.

While George had been famous in his day, Rainsford's past was so totally obscure that it defied all investigation. It was rumoured that he had been, variously, a convict at Dartmoor; a prison warder in Hong Kong; a professional conjurer; a lancer; a steeple jack; and, the most probable speculation, the professional of some London Cricket Club, at that time (or at any rate up to the War) quite a common type of appointment. Whatever the truth of the matter, he was a wretched bad cricketer. For a start, he taught us to play back in the outmoded and inept Victorian fashion, with the bat alongside the rear leg and the front foot pointed like a ballet dancer's. If I further remark that he taught us to roll the ball instead of spinning it and to stand in the field with our hands open in front of our waists (like a picture in the *Lonsdale Book of Cricket*); that he smelt, that he creaked, that he croaked, that he leered, that he was at once sycophantic and familiar, and that he had atrocious teeth; if I add that he looked, in his chalk-white calico kit, like a down-at-heel and drunken mortuary attendant: then you may well wonder why he was employed as a pro for all the four summers during which I was at Charterhouse and for very many more. The answer is both simple and astounding: we all *liked* Rainsford: God alone knows why: perhaps just because he *was* so ghastly. There was something almost innocent in the repulsiveness of his appearance and demeanour: no one could have looked so horrible and not done anything about it unless he were simpleton or saint.

But if the rest of us liked Rainsford, George Geary positively loved him. Perhaps that was why he was employed, to keep the invaluable George contented; perhaps George had even had Rainsford put in his contract, so to speak. Of this at least there is no doubt: during the Cricket Quarter the two men were inseparable, together in the 'shop', in the nets, watching junior games for talent, sleeping in the same lodgings, fishing all day long in the River Wye on Sundays. Perhaps this last is an important clue to the mystery of Rainsford's inexplicable appeal: for no fisherman, as John Buchan once remarked of Tiberius, can be wholly vile.

'I wonder,' Ivan Lynch once said to me, 'where George and Rainsford go in the winter.'

As well ask what song the Sirens sang, or what name Achilles assumed among women. They were there in May and in September they weren't: like all the best things in this world, they were seasonal.

'Catch anything last Sunday?' said James as we arrived.

'A dace, sir,' said Rainsford.

'A gudgeon,' said George, 'mine.'

'That pad of mine,' I said, pointing to the one which George was whitening, 'it bends at the knee. So does the other.'

'Of course it do. Your knee bends so the pad bends.'

'I mean it *flops*. The top flops right over and hangs down.'

'Where did you buy it?'

'From you.'

'Yes, sir,' said Rainsford. 'I mind the occasion, sir. It was the day the ring went out, sir, and the glue got cold, sir. Last year.'

'Last year?' said George. 'And *here* you are complaining *now*.'

'I didn't want to hurt your feelings. I thought they might get better.'

As a matter of fact the pads which George sold were famous for flopping at the knee. Everyone's did, and it just wasn't done to mention it, as James now reminded me.

'There's no guarantee with pads,' James said. 'You know that perfectly well. *Caveat emptor.*'

'What's that?' said George.

'Let the buyer watch out.'

'You get a square deal in my shop.'

George put down my pad and started gluing someone's bat together.

'Perhaps you could put some pads in to stiffen them?' I said.

'Put some pads in what?'

'Put some pads...in my pads. In the knees,' I said desperately.

'All right. But whatever I do, you won't get any more runs because of it.'

'Mr Raven gets enough as it is,' said Rainsford, sucking up.

'Mr Raven wants more,' said James maliciously. 'Mr Raven's highest score for the School this year is 43. Not enough to get him a place for the Southern Schools at Lord's.'

George put down the bat he was gluing.

'So that's what you're after?' he said.

'It would be nice, certainly.'

'Let me tell you a thing. If you stay at this school for another 200 years, and never get a day older, and play cricket morning, noon and night, you'll still have no more chance of playing for the Southern Schools at Lord's than of farting all seven verses of "God Save the King".'

'So now you know,' said James.

The various diversions of the afternoon had prevented my writing the Greek Prose which I was due to show up to the Master of the Classical Sixth the next morning. A L ('Uncle') Irvine was not pleased.

'Because you fluked a Scholarship at King's last April,' he said, 'you seem to think that you can ignore your work now.'

I expressed rather casual contrition.

'What you need,' said the Uncle affably, 'is to be punished. I have a mind to ask the Headmaster to forbid your going away with the XI tomorrow. But such punishments are for little boys.' He paused and gave a short, sharp laugh. 'Something…more Promethean is in order for you,' he said. 'Now go. And good luck for tomorrow's match.'

'Thank you, sir. But what exactly is my punishment?'

'You'll find out,' the Uncle said.

The Uncle was a rotund and beautiful old gentleman with a deep, succulent laugh, like Falstaff's. While he openly proclaimed his supreme and unswerving faith to be placed in the 'Three Cs' (Classics, Cricket and Christianity), he also had a passion for English Literature (especially poetry) and the plastic arts. He sung a pretty bass, played a fair game of Fives, knew trees and flowers. He was always ready (like Sir Pitt Crawley in *Vanity Fair*) 'to crack a jest' with you even as you stood in the dock awaiting his sentence; but normally his jokes were in better taste than Sir Pitt's and were accompanied by a long and generous belly-rumble of laughter, of the kind with which he had warmed our hearts and bodies through the sad and undernourished winters of the War. It was this – or rather the absence of this – which worried me now. The laugh which he had given just before dismissing me had been untypical: it had not been leisurely and amiable; it had been brusque, and it had been at my expense…not indeed spiteful, for the Uncle was wholly without spite, but – well – retributive. The Uncle had smelt something coming, something which he didn't altogether care for but was going *to serve me right*…and so amply was it going to do so that he could even afford a little pity, to express a genuine wish that I would enjoy myself ('Good luck in tomorrow's match') before the Furies arrived with the reckoning.

When the Furies appeared, a few weeks later, they were not immediately recognisable by me, first because there were only two of them, and secondly because both were much preoccupied with making jokes. (I should have known better, even then, than to be deceived by *that*.)

They were called C M (or Maurice) Bowra, Warden of Wadham College, Oxford, and A B Ramsay ('the Ram'), Master of Magdalene College, Cambridge; and they had arrived to conduct the Annual Examination of the

Classical Sixth. If there *was* a Fury about the place, I should have said, it must surely be Hugh Trevor Roper, a conceited, angular and predatory young man, still in uniform, who had come to examine the historians. But History and Trevor Roper were nothing to me: *I* was to answer to witty Bowra and the gently prattling Ram…both of whom would surely take kindly to a clever, amusing, successful, handsome boy like me.

At first all seemed to be going well. In so far as the two examiners were out for anybody's blood they seemed to be out for each other's: Bowra, who considered the Ram to be soggy and sanctimonious, excoriated him with oral scalpels; while the Ram, bleeding cruelly on the sacrificial table, yet contrived, with his piteous bleats, to raise interesting doubts as to the purity of Bowra's scholarship, the soundness of his College administration, and the orthodoxy of his moral character. Lulled by the strophe and antistrophe (reported to me with relish by Sniffy Russell) of these recriminations, I deluded myself into thinking that my papers had been rather well done (despite total lack of preparation) and were in any case quite good enough to satisfy two old mountebanks, to whom I had made myself particularly charming and in front of whom I had made 50-odd in dashing style for the Scholars versus the Rest of the School – surely so signal a service to Scholarship as to render mere examinations irrelevant and to procure me, of itself, a brilliant place in the List.

Disillusion was swift and ugly. The Headmaster sent for me the day before the results were due to be announced. The two examiners had apparently enjoyed my company and my batting, deplored my early election to King's, pitied and despised my presumptious efforts to pull the wool over their eyes, and brought me out precious near the bottom of the List – below several scholars of the year junior to my own.

'Mr Irvine has suggested,' the Headmaster said, 'that it might save you embarrassment if I permitted you to absent yourself from Hall when the results are read out before the School tomorrow.'

Good old Uncle: extending what charitable unguent he could to mitigate my long foreseen (by him) and most just chastisement. But one had one's pride.

'No, sir,' I said. 'Thank you very much, but I'll come and face it out.'

And so I did, sitting in the front row, while the Ram looked down at me from the platform with unctuous disdain and Maurice Bowra glinted at me with a combination of malice and amusement, as if to say, 'Oh yes, you're a cute little cookie all right, and don't think *I* haven't got your number.'

Later on the Uncle greeted me with one of his friendliest smiles.

'Of course you'll do much better again next Quarter,' he said; 'but it's always a worthwhile experience to be tried and found wanting by dons of such distinction.'

Dons of such distinction... Well, Amen. But I often wondered, as time went on, what the Uncle or the Headmaster, or even the rather more sophisticated Sniffy Russell, would have said if they'd been told the tale which Malcolm Bullock (of whom more hereafter) told me some years later: how Maurice Bowra, bent on pleasure one dark night, discovered at daybreak that he had mistaken a tin of black boot polish for the more appropriate sanitary colloid.

V

Red Beret

After I was sacked from Charterhouse in the autumn of 1945, I volunteered for the Army. King's had made it plain to Robert Birley, to his pleasure as my friend and to his deep discontent as a Christian moralist, that they considered my offence ('the usual thing') to be entirely trivial and that they would certainly not withdraw my Scholarship; but they also made it plain that what with the end of the War and the sudden rush of ex-servicemen they had no time or space just yet for me. So the Army it had to be (a very good job, too, as discipline and discomfort were exactly what I most needed), and I duly applied for and was accepted by the Parachute Regiment, which I joined, after Primary Training, in the early Spring of 1946.

Now the War was over, the Parachute Regiment was changing its style. No longer was it a shower of hard-bitten and scruffy ex-convicts descending from the sky armed with flick knives and primed with every dirty device known from Bow to Dartmoor; it was becoming a Corps of clean-limbed aspirants to honour, who were drilled and turned out to the standards of the Royal Marines, were disciplined with a formality which at times surpassed that of the Household Brigade, were imbued with the traditional concepts of loyalty and valour, and (almost incidentally) had the phlegm to step out of an aeroplane into nothing relying only on their by no means infallible parachutes. Gone now were the slouching razor boys, the bandy Sergeants who had been booth-boxers, the evil smelling, rum-swilling Lance-Corporals who had turned the Company Stores into a fence or a brothel, and the ex-ranker Officers selected for their foul mouths and biceps. Now we were to be a *corps d'élite*, nothing less. NCOs and Warrant Officers were transferred to us from the Brigade of Guards, brilliant young Officers were poached from every

Regiment of the Line, while those of Field Rank were lean men, hungry and alert. Hail to the new King Hal: and away forever with Bardolph and Pistol.

But of course Bardolph and Pistol (to say nothing of Falstaff) are hardy perennials who do not go away easily. For one thing, they are adept at camouflaging themselves, or appearing to have turned over a new leaf, or at making sycophantic or such other noises as changing times may require. So despite the New Chivalry which appeared to dominate No. 1 ITC (Infantry Training Centre) of the Parachute Regiment, despite the colossal presence of Regimental Sergeant-Major Lord of the Coldstream Guards, despite a Colonel who had been a county cricketer and Captains with glittering rosettes on honourably faded ribands, despite the panoply of England (one might say), Corporal Nym still lurked by the stove in the Stores and Pistol toyed with Mistress Quickly and Doll, forgetting or disdaining to use the 'Early Treatment (Prophylactic) Packet' which authority, being these days, even in the new model Parachute Regiment, more concerned with hygiene than with morals, benevolently provided for such excursions.

Corruption, in short, was still moving pretty near the surface, and with a nose as adept as that of a truffling pig I sniffed it out in the most unlikely quarter.

Captain Isaacs the Cricket Officer, a moderate but knowledgeable player, had managed, by mid-June of 1946, to assemble a very passable XI. This placed him high in favour with the cricketing Colonel; there was even talk of an acting Majority. But to retain esteem Isaacs must retain his XI – which was about to be seriously depleted by the 'Passing Out' of my own intake. Three Recruits in this intake were important to Isaacs' XI: his star spin-bowler, his left-handed opening batsman, and a useful all-rounder (Recruit Lance-Corporal Raven). Our departure for Parachute (Jumping) School was now imminent and with it the debilitation of Isaacs' XI and the forfeiture of Isaacs' putative Majority (of his Captaincy too, perhaps, as even this was only temporary).

In this emergency, Isaacs summoned the three of us to his office and proposed a deal. Or rather, he proposed the possibility of proposing a deal. The hint was that if we would consent to stay behind at the ITC and play cricket, Isaacs would make it well worth our while. He could not be more specific until he was assured of our good will.

My two companions, like the honest, fresh-faced Englishmen they were, said that much as they loved cricket they had joined the Parachute Regiment to parachute, and nothing would persuade them to forfeit or defer their posting to Parachute School. *I* said that keen as I was to do my parachute jumps (untrue), I nevertheless felt a certain loyalty to Isaacs and his XI after nearly two months of playing with them (untrue), and therefore found myself in a quandary (true, though not in the sense I implied, as my real difficulty lay in calculating whether the loss of face caused by evading my jumps would be adequately compensated by the quality of the cricket which Isaacs could offer (poorish) and the magnitude of the bribe which he might conjure – not, I suspected, of the first order).

I, at any rate, was prepared to listen. My two fellow-recruits saluted smartly and marched strongly forth, pure of mind and straight of limb, untainted and unbought. Captain Isaacs sighed with self-loathing as he watched them go. He knew they were right; he admired them for going and despised me for remaining; and he hated himself for treating with me. But I was now the last, the forlorn hope for Isaacs' XI and his coveted brevet. I was a precious, even a rare, commodity, and must be handled with reverence.

'Well, Raven?' he began with affected cordiality.

'Well, sir?' said I.

He sighed again, bitter yet resigned, and began to outline his scheme for my retention.

After 'Passing Out', I was to be held on the strength of No. 1 Parachute Regiment ITC on the pretext that, as a recognised aspirant to a Commission, I would shortly be called before one of the preliminary and local boards in this connection; it was therefore desirable, the inquisitive or censorious could be told, that I should be ready to answer such a summons *instanter* and not have to be dragged back the length of England from a Jumping Course which would, furthermore, be invalidated (so tight was the schedule) if interrupted.

All this was plausible enough. But what, I now enquired, what – er – status would I enjoy? A polite hint that I must know without more ado what price was being offered. Isaacs narrowed his eyes, flared his nostrils, smiled and shuddered at the same time like the recipient of a traitor-kiss, sighed his twentieth sigh, and then laid it all on the line for me with admirable precision. My nominal employment, he said, would be as a Mail-Clerk in Headquarter Company Headquarters. I should now become a pukkah Lance-Corporal instead of a mere Recruit Lance-Corporal; I should have the barest minimum of work to do, being excused all duties after noon each day on the official supposition that I was playing cricket (even if I wasn't); and I should enjoy the absolute and guaranteed good will of the HQ Company CSM, one Serjeant-Major Lewis, who would ensure that I was not subjected to intrusive chores such as Clerks' Drill Parades or Evening PT. Finally, said Captain Isaacs with some self-satisfaction, he had arranged for me to enjoy a remarkable privilege, hitherto bestowed only on the Company Clerk, a certain Corporal Mond. Mond, Isaacs explained, was allowed to sleep and keep his gear in a private alcove of the Company Office, thus avoiding such annoyances as Reveille, Lights Out, Barrack Room Fatigues, Making Up Beds and Laying Out Kit for Inspection, and, in general, all the superveillance and interference which went with military life at low level. Captain Isaacs could now assure me that he had persuaded Mond to take me into his alcove, there being room, if only just, for another mattress: what a piece of work was this, crowed Isaacs, if he did say it himself. For Captain Isaacs, though displeased with what he was doing, was proud and pardonably proud of the package which he had contrived to get together. Those who ever served in the Army of the day and still remember its Tiberian discipline will appreciate his achievement. The last item alone, a bed in private quarters, was a luxury beyond the worth of rubies. No doubt about it: Isaacs was giving superb value. I clinched the deal on the spot, I 'passed out' with my companions two days later, and then, as they packed for Parachute School, I humped my kit down to Corporal Mond's oasis of independence in HQ Company Office.

Although Captain Isaacs had already introduced me both to Mond and to CSM Lewis, I had barely taken either of them in, beyond noting that Mond was a pretty, dimpled redhead and that the Serjeant-Major was wasp-waisted and willowy. These brief impressions had led me to premise an affair between them and to infer that Mond's privileged quarters had been allotted to him by the CSM in grateful exchange for his favours. I had hardly been in my new home for ten minutes when I began to realise how wrong I had been.

'We're here,' said Corporal Mond gravely, 'for Security. Guarding the Company Documents.'

'Do they need guarding? I mean…who on earth would want them?'

'That is just the sort of remark,' said Mond, 'which could get us turfed out tomorrow. You are, of course, quite right; nothing in this Office is of the slightest interest to anyone. But in order to get me installed in here, Serjeant-Major Lou has propagated the theory that a guard is needed for the confidential files, and somehow or other he has got people to believe it. The position, however, is delicate in the extreme. Any scepticism, however privately expressed, could start to radiate ethereal waves of doubt which might sooner or later reach the Company Commander. You must therefore make it an Absolute Article of Faith that we are the Guardians of Mighty Mysteries, and express that view on every possible occasion.'

'Kind of the Serjeant-Major to take such trouble for you,' I said, hinting.

'Nothing to the trouble I take for him.'

Here it comes, I thought.

'He has a termagent wife. He can't fuck her. I do it for him every Thursday night…which keeps her more or less sweet for the rest of the week.'

'Oh.' I had a quick vision of this dainty boy in bed with a kind of Widow Twanky.

'But six nights in seven I have to myself,' said Mond, looking happily round the alcove, 'a very fair proceeding, on the whole. I can get on with my work, you see.'

Mond was writing a book: a history of the Blitz on London. He had consented to my joining him because Captain Isaacs had represented to him that as a Scholar Elect of King's College, Cambridge, I had literary tastes and skills that might assist his labour and edify his leisure. I did not demur, though I could have wished he was writing on a more sympathetic subject.

'But all work and no joy,' enunciated my new friend, 'makes Mond a dull boy. One must have pleasure. Going to bed with Mrs Lou is like doing it with a sack of herringbones. Two nights of the remaining six are therefore dedicated to Aphrodite Polypous.'

'Aphrodite what?'

'Polypous. An epithet of my own invention. It means many-footed, hence many-legged. Many-legged Love, i.e. having it off with several girls at once.'

'Very agreeable, I do see. But where do you get them all from?'

'The NAAFI. They toss their knickers off like confetti. There'll be plenty of legs for you too, if you want me to bring a few pairs along.'

'Here?'

'Here. Don't worry. It's all part of the deal with CSM Lou.'

The weeks that followed were heady and exhausting. It turned out that Mond's arrangements for the delivery of NAAFI delicacies to the Company Office were not quite as comprehensive as he had advertised them to be, but a delivery there positively was, of passably fresh and varied goods, and this quite regular. The average turnout for one of Mond's soirées was one girl for each of us, and just as well perhaps, as there wasn't really room for more in the alcove. Sometimes Mond would organise us into a rather ragged quadrilateral: sometimes he would decree performance by pairs and swap at half-time. On one notable occasion three girls turned up; but the third only wanted to watch, or so she said – and then caused considerable annoyance by masturbating glutinously with Mond's best fountain pen, the one he kept for writing *The London Blitz*. On another occasion only one girl arrived, and I was quite interested and pleased by the attentions which Mond paid to myself on pretext of balancing the threesome.

The girls themselves were hot and good-humoured. True, some of them were unshapely and one or two of them unhygienic, but at that age (eighteen) I had appetite for all that came and more – 'more' in fact taking the form of

Mond, generally at the end of the evenings spent working on his book. As I had begun to suspect during the threesome, Mond was in truth bisexual with a strong bias towards men; and indeed one of the purposes for which he so assiduously recruited the NAAFI girls was to try to assure himself that things were the other way about, that he was principally a womaniser and could take or leave 'the other' where he found it.

So what with the NAAFI sprees and the 'working' evenings (on which the boring Blitz was put aside earlier each time in order to allow more and more leisure for 'the other') the days went on happily enough. The only trouble was, of course, that both Mond and I had special duties, his to 'Mrs Lou' and mine to Isaacs and his XI, in the performance of which we were beginning to buckle. In Mond's case, it was just possible to fob off Mrs Lou with the dexterous use of a device; in mine no such deceit or surrogation was possible. My game was going fast downhill: Isaacs' face expressed surprise, then reproach, then irritation as failure succeeded failure; and my reputation was only (and very temporarily) restored by a fluky 47 against a scratch side of elderly Sappers.

'That young man needs a good kick up the arse,' I heard the cricketing Colonel announce to Isaacs after I had flopped yet again two or three days later.

'He made 47 against the Sappers on Saturday, sir,' said Isaacs with such loyalty as he could still muster.

'Dropped four times,' replied the Colonel, 'hitting across the line like a ploughboy…without a good honest ploughboy's excuse. He knows what to do as well as anyone but he's too idle or too feeble to do it. If I were you, I'd get rid of him.'

In this crisis of my affairs, I was summoned to a WOSB (War Office Selection Board) which would finally determine whether I was fit to be trained for a Commission. Although Westbury, where the thing was to happen, was only a few miles away across the Salisbury Plain, I should be absent a good seven days, for all practical purposes, and for this time at least I was safe from further disgrace. I was also able to recruit my energies a little, there being neither 'work' nor hospitable obligations in the alcove to draw on them. I was grateful to WOSB for providing an interlude of most welcome chastity; for it is possible, even at the age of eighteen, to become utterly sick of sex.

Back with the ITC and much restored in health and morale, determined to repay Isaacs' trust and give of my best for the rest of the season, I dedicated myself with renewed fervour to the special soirée which had been got up by Mond in honour of my return. (For while it is indeed possible to become utterly sick of sex even at the age of eighteen, in youth as in politics a week is a very long time.) On this occasion, unprecedentedly, alcoholic drinks were served. Unknown to us at the time, one of the girls was stupendously sick just after leaving us at 2 a.m. Once again the Furies were on my traces.

For early the next morning, while we were still in bed, there came a huge knock on the office door. Since Reveille had sounded some ten minutes before, whoever wanted admission was in order while we were not. I went to the door in my underpants (pyjamas were not the fashion with Other Ranks in 1946), opened it, and saw Regimental Serjeant-Major Lord on the other side.

Lord, some say, was in his time the most magnificent soldier in the world: standing there on this occasion, as straight as a Doric column and nearly as high, he wore Service Dress (fastened right up to the throat), Sam Browne, breeches and long puttees, and he carried a dark brown pace-stick the bronze fittings of which flashed like Jubilee beacons. Enough to make anyone under Field Rank tremble in his socks. I trembled away on my bare feet, ludicrously brought my knobbly ankles together, and grabbed at my pants, which were about to sag below the hair line.

'Ah,' said this colossal creature mildly, 'a bit of luck to find somebody in. They did say a picquet slept here, but I wasn't certain. I'm sorry to have interrupted you at your ablutions.'

The immediate response to this courteous speech was a gurgling snore from Mond in the alcove. The first essential was to get him on his feet. The RSM apparently condoned a considerable degree of undress at ten minutes past Reveille but he would not tolerate a lay-a-bed.

'Douse that tap please, Corporal,' I called, 'the RSM's here.'

'The Regimental Serjeant-Major,' corrected Lord, gently but very firmly.

'What tap?' groaned Mond.

'The one that just made the row. I can't hear what the RS – the Regimental Serjeant-Major is saying.'

Mond got the message. There were sounds of rational activity from the alcove.

'What can I do for you, sir?' I said.

'These returns… May I come in?'

'If you please, sir. Would you like this chair?'

'Thank you very much… I am sorry, as I say, to disturb you while you're at your ablutions,' said this gentle giant, under whose eye twelve-year men sweated with terror on the parade ground and who had even been known to make a public arrest of another (albeit junior) Regimental Serjeant-Major, 'but these returns are cast in the most vexatious fashion. Whoever is responsible for them has used abbreviations which I have expressly forbidden (such as CSM for Company Serjeant-Major) and has in every case spelt "Serjeant" with a "g" instead of a "j".'

These were Lord's two major abominations. He could not bear abbreviations, whether in speech or in writing; and he was determined that a man with three stripes on his sleeve was a 'SERJEANT', presumably because he thought the 'J' raised the rank from a Music Hall joke to a dignity comparable with that of a Mounted Serjeant of the Middle Ages, who was tactically rated if not socially esteemed as almost the equal of a knight.

'These returns will have to be retyped before they can be shown to the Commanding Officer,' Lord said now. 'I realise, of course, that you are only the picquet here and are not responsible: but will you kindly find the Clerk or the Non-Commissioned Officer who is responsible, and tell him to present himself, in my office, with these returns correctly typed, no later than 0830 hours.'

'Of course, sir.'

I hitched up my knickers again. Lord rose to go. He passed an eye over the alcove, in which Mond was making hysterical domestic motions as of one preparing for the new day.

'I do not see a tap.'

'Tap...sir?'

'You referred, just now, to a tap.'

'The nearest is a hundred yards away, sir. I was requesting my friend here to douse his "yap", i.e. – I mean, *id est* – his conversation, so that I could attend to you.'

'Then if the tap is a hundred yards away, you were not yet engaged in your ablutions?'

'We have to go one at a time, sir. Security. I was just going when you arrived.'

He accepted this. He was a kind man who realised that if you call on people at 6.10 a.m., however legitimately, you must expect to find them somewhat disordered.

'Then please do not let me detain you further.'

I went to the alcove, put on my gym shoes, grabbed my washing kit, and ran. As I ran, I noticed that Lord, who had already left the Office by about the length of a cricket pitch, was thoughtfully inspecting an enormous heap of what (I realised a few minutes later) could only be NAAFI girls' sick.

'Well, who did make out those returns?' I asked as soon as I was back from my 'ablutions'.

'I did.'

'What in the devil's name were you thinking of? Abbreviations. Serjeants with "g"s. You've gone potty.'

'I'd had too much beer at lunch, and I thought the return was for the Quartermaster. Married Quarters, that's what it's all about, bloody fucking thing – Quartermaster's business. *He* doesn't mind abbreviations, and he thinks Serjeant with a "j" is affected. I once heard him say so.'

'Anyhow, it seems that his Lordship shoved his nose in.'

'Can you help me retype it? You could do half of it on the second typewriter.'

'Sorry, sweetheart,' I said. 'I've got to parade in the MT – sorry, Motor Transport – Lines at 0715. We've got an all day match at Aldershot.'

And a very long day it was. By the time I had been slammed for 37 runs in two overs, got myself out hit-wicket for 3, missed their last man off a dolly catch which, if held, would have taken us through into the Semi-Final of the South West District Trophy – by the time I had endured all this and the drive back from Aldershot (during which no one at all would even look at me) I was ready to slit my windpipe.

'Well at least,' said Mond grimly after I had recited these horrors, 'at least you weren't sick on the pitch.'

'Why should I have been?'

'For the same reason you were sick just out there last night.'

'That wasn't me. It must have been one of the bints.'

'It makes no odds. We're blown. When I formed up with that retyped return, "Leave to fall in, sir?" says I. "It's you, is it?" says he. "I thought you was only the picquet in there, not the Corporal Clerk." "Corporal Clerk and permanent picquet, if you please, sir." "I see. Permanent picquet, and too idle to know when someone has thrown his entrails up right outside your door." No answer to this, so, "Leave to dismiss, sir, please?" "Yes please, Corporal. I'm going to make a few enquiries about you and your permanent picquet. Pray ask Company Serjeant-Major Lewis to step this way." '

'Couldn't Lou have squared it?'

'He might have. Only last Thursday was a crashing fiasco with his Missus. She spotted that rubber contrivance and saw me hanging as limp as a daffodil. She's given me the bum's rush and she's given Lou sheer perishing Hades, and the long and the short is, the deal's off. We're out of here tomorrow, Sonny Jim.'

'And I'm out of Isaacs' XI. God knows what will become of us.'

'Poor little orphans. The last night in the old home – so let's make the best of it.'

But on the morrow the Furies found other more interesting business and my Good Daimon flew in to clear up the mess...*my* mess, that is, as he seemed indisposed to do anything much for Mond, who was last seen by me with a kit bag over his shoulder trudging up the hill to Hut 3 (ADM) in HQ Company Lines. I turned away with a sigh (after all, it had been a memorable summer) and carefully cleaned and labelled my rifle before delivering it into the Armourer's keeping.

For I had passed my WOSB and was to be posted out *instanter*. I was to hand in my weapon (oh God, the relief of getting rid of that horrible, *hurting* rifle), report myself to the Transit Centre at the Great Northern Hotel in London, dump my kit there while I went on embarkation leave, and then sail away in HM Troopship *Georgic* to India (still British if only just) where I should train as an Officer Cadet at the Officers' Training School in Bangalore (Mysore State).

But there was one big black blowfly buzzing in this delicious ointment. If anyone ever found out what had gone on in the alcove, if Lord or another should ever learn that though a comatose picquet we had been lively hosts, then the matter would be grave enough to bring about my recall to the ITC for appropriate disciplinary action, or, had I already reached India, my almost certain dismissal from the OTS and degradation as a Private to some British Unit in the Far East. No Good Daimon could exorcise this threat, which was to cast a shadow over even the bluest and blithest days for many weeks to come.

However, nothing happened. There was no summons to the Office of the Commandant at Bangalore. After the requisite number of days and parades had passed, I was duly commissioned, early in May 1947, as a Second Lieutenant in the Oxfordshire and Buckinghamshire Light Infantry, and by that time there could really be nothing to fear. What happened to Mond in the meantime, or thereafter, I never heard. But this much I do know: if there was any subsequent trouble about the orgies in the alcove, he must have covered up for me and taken full blame on himself. I can see Mond doing that...pretty, dimpled, loving, loyal Mond, with his ghastly book about the Blitz and his desperate need to prove himself heterosexual.

VI

MUMMY'S BOY

But back to the autumn of 1946. My embarkation leave was rather distressful.
Here was I, a grown man and now an Officer Cadet, deserving and desirous
of a fortnight of independent and sophisticated pleasure; and here was my
leave pay, all £14 of it – and not even as much as that because in theory I was
to give some of it to my mother for my 'maintenance'. As for *her*, she was no
help at all in sustaining me in my chosen role of aspirant Officer about town:
she still regarded me as a schoolboy, who should and must come straight home
now the term was ended and stay there with no nonsense until it began again.

Neither of my parents was impressed by my posting to India. My mother
regarded it as all rather 'silly' and as liable to give me 'silly, independent ideas'.
My father thought it was 'bad and silly and bad' that the nation should be
paying good money to send 'someone like you' all that way to be trained for
a Commission. It wasn't, he said, as if I were going into the Indian Army – not
that there would have been much point in that either. When I remarked that
Subalterns were still badly needed in the Far East, and that most of us would
probably be posted to British Battalions in India itself or in South-East Asia,
my father expressed peevish scepticism about the function of such Battalions
and the function of anyone as 'floppy' as myself within them, while my mother
became exceedingly resentful at the further opportunities I should have, at
points East of Mandalay, to incubate 'silly independent ideas' – to say nothing
of the fact that when I got leave I could neither be expected nor compelled
to come home for it.

That was the sort of parents I had. My sister was too young to understand
or comment. Only my brother Myles took interest or pleasure in my
situation, partly because he realised it was just the sort of trip I should enjoy,

and partly because he could now tell the boys at Charterhouse that I had smashed to pieces the supposedly unbreachable sanctions imposed by my expulsion: for beyond any question I had now become an Officer Cadet and would shortly become an Officer, appointments of honour which tradition declared to be for ever beyond the reach of a man who had been 'sacked', especially if it had been 'for the usual thing'.

Having touched this topic, I should add that people's attitudes in this regard were very revealing. The Army itself simply did not want to know whether one had been sacked or what for, but it did issue every candidate for a Commission with a formal certificate of moral character which must be signed by a priest, schoolmaster or JP of his acquaintance before he presented himself at WOSB. Since, in the circumstances, I could hardly apply to the Headmaster for a signature, and did not want to embarrass Bob Arrowsmith or the Uncle (both of whom would have taken such a formality rather seriously), I simply forged Sniffy Russell's autograph on my certificate, knowing that while he too would have been reluctant to sign it in the cold light of day, so to speak, he was yet far too good-natured and loyal to denounce one should reference ever be made to him by the authorities. He would probably, I thought, laugh the same high, dry laugh as he had when Hodgsonite Yearlings were cheated by William, and disappear fast in another direction. In the event, of course, my speculations were never put to the test; the certificate was simply filed and forgotten as the irrelevance which it was – though it still gives me pleasure to reflect that my Emergency Commission, and much later on my Regular Commission, were both made possible, in the original instance, by my own crudely forged moral testimony in my favour.

The Headmaster, when he eventually heard of my Indian prospect, was, I think, rather puzzled. He knew that a moral certificate had to be signed in such circumstances, as he had signed hundreds himself. He had not, he knew, signed mine, so presumably somebody else had. Who and why? These questions, though never uttered, were somewhere at the back of his voice when I rang him up to say goodbye, in itself an entirely natural proceeding, as we had remained friends and corresponded as such despite the dismal sentence he had been bound to pass upon me. His sentiments were probably very much those which he entertained towards King's College after the College Council had pronounced my offence trivial and my admission certain: he was glad, as my friend, that things were going as I would wish, but also rather indignant that my wickedness, though punished by him with the gravest penalty in his power, was made so light of elsewhere.

The simple fact was that the immense popularity, over many years before the war, of the ludicrous Billy Bunter and his friends at Greyfriars had made the whole punitive apparatus of the Public Schools, flogging and expulsion, the lot, a universal joke. Even Public School men themselves, though grateful and dedicated *alumni* in other areas, could not be got to regard corporal punishment or condign dismissal as anything other than an hilarious 'jape' – which would in any case be forgotten by the next issue of *The Magnet* (as it were), in which Coker the school rotter, publicly whipped and cast forth at the end of the last number, would be back again after some shadowy process of reinstatement lurking among the studies as slimy and villainous as ever. And of course if expulsion was such a light matter, so was what you were expelled for. Never, after my expulsion from Charterhouse, did anybody so much as raise an eyebrow when the thing was mentioned. Most people merely giggled.

But enough of this digression.

When my leave still had four days to run, I received two letters in the same post: the first, accompanied by a cheque for £10, was from my grandfather (maternal) who himself had been a soldier and took vicarious pleasure from my exotic posting; the second was from Hedley Le Bas, suggesting that I should join him for a day or two at Lord's, or even for all three days, during some Festival Match which was to be played early that September. Since these were the last three days of my leave, I wired Hedley that I would meet him by the Tavern the following afternoon and announced to my family my intention of leaving for London early the following morning.

My father, who had seen about enough of me, took this in good part. My brother, although a little sad, quite understood, he said, that I needed a change of scene. We then spent the whole of my last afternoon at home playing a game of small cricket, which we had first devised as children, on an enclosed terrace in the garden, and after Myles had made 402 while impersonating J D Robertson he was resigned to the indefinite suspension of play (which was, in fact, never resumed, for when I came home again as an Officer I found small cricket beneath my dignity). Thus all was well – except with my mother. At first she had heard of my intention with apparent good grace: 'It'll be so nice for you to meet your old friend at Lord's,' she had conceded. But as the afternoon went on she had been busily distilling discontent inside herself, and when Myles and I came in from small cricket she fizzed and steamed like a witches' cauldron.

'This boy, Le Bas,' she said, 'I know the name.'

'You do. Head of the School my last summer.'

'Yes. One of the boys who got up to filthy tricks, like you.'

'Can't we forget all that.'

'If only we could. But now you're going off to get up to those filthy tricks again at Lord's.'

'We're simply going to watch the cricket.'

'Cricket. Nothing but filthy boys like this Le Bas, playing filthy tricks in the changing rooms...etc, etc...and anyway,' said my mother half an hour later, after poor Hedley was finally disposed of, 'what are you going to use for *money*?'

'I've got ten pounds.'

'Where did you get it?'

'Grandpa sent it.'

'GRANDPA...*sent you ten pounds*? Without asking me? We'll see about that.'

She flew to the telephone and excoriated her unfortunate parent for fifteen minutes flat.

'I've made him agree to cancel the cheque,' she said when she came back, 'he quite sees, now, that he shouldn't give you money to encourage *silly ideas of independence*.'

'Too late. I cashed it at the bank this morning. Special clearance.'

'You...deceitful...little...pig,' mouthed my mother, with all the venom (rather a lot) which she had in her.

But the show was over. Game, set and match to me. My mother, although one of the most infuriating and possessive women I have ever known, knew when she was beaten (which in those days wasn't often) and was skilful at assuming a kind of hurt and sorrowful quietude which, with cleverly interposed acts of kindness, was intended to make one feel guilty – and did. By ten o'clock that evening, so tender had been her concern about what I would like to eat and to do 'on your last night at home', so wistful had been her asides about how 'Myles and I will miss you', that I was on the verge of renunciation. However, Myles saw this coming and took me on one side, 'Don't give in,' he said. 'You know how you'll enjoy yourself at Lord's. You mustn't let yourself be blackmailed any more than you let yourself be bullied.'

Good words and true; but justify myself as I might, I had not a moment's mental peace during the whole journey to London.

'Happy days are here again,' said Hedley Le Bas outside the Tavern. 'A pity about that infernal row down at Charterhouse, but I think we're over the worst of it.'

Hedley, skilful operator that he was, had managed to make his part in the Great Scandal appear marginal, whereas in truth it had been central. He was helped by his already having left the school when the scandal broke, which meant that he could not be summoned and grilled like the rest of us but at the same time could always protest, from a safe distance, that he was being misrepresented. The end of it was that Hedley had been forbidden to appear on Carthusian territory for one calendar year but was not otherwise penalised. Since the year would very soon be done (mid-October) he was indeed 'over the worst of it'. I, on the other hand, was not. It might be many years before I was admitted to the Old Carthusian Club, about which I did not particularly care, or allowed to play cricket for The Friars (the old boys' touring side) about which I cared very much. But I saw no point in going into that now: Hedley would only think I was being envious and dreary, and he would be right.

'Take my word for it,' he was saying, 'old Bags [Birley] knows the ways of the world as well as anyone living. Although he may be playing it rather stiff and stuffy just now, he'll come round just as soon as he sees that we're not letting it get us down. In my case, I was accepted for a Commission in the Life Guards, then they found my heart was a bit dicky, so I was given an immediate place, in mid-term, at Jesus – returning heroes or no returning heroes, they found room for me fast enough. All done by money, of course, and Bags knows that as well as I do, but it *looks pretty good in the score book*: so I'm more or less forgiven already, and by October it'll all be as if it had never been. More beer?'

'Yes please, Hedley.'

'As for you, they'll take you back into the fold just as soon as you get a Commission – and never mind how you got it. The India thing will impress them too. To be an Officer in India is in fact about as unsmart as you can get, but it sounds all right to the middle classes, and Bags is nothing if not middle class. Have a whisky with that beer. You drink half the beer in one go, then all the whisky in one go, then pour the whisky drops into the rest of the beer and then drink *that* in one go.'

'Where did you learn that trick? In the Life Guards or at Jesus?'

'In a pub by the Mill Road. Some of us from Jesus go there to pick up women.'

'I hope you don't pick up anything else.'

'Been lucky so far. Anyhow, all that's got to stop because I'm thinking of getting married.'

'Why on earth?'

'Must have a son, old boy. Le Bas must have a son.'

'But already? Surely, if there's one thing more unsmart than another, it's an early marriage?'

I had him there; but Hedley was saved, as the likes of Hedley are always saved, by sheer chance, which this time took the shape of Gerald Carter, a plodding but good-humoured member of the XI the year previous to our own.

75

'What cheer, old chums? Let's have another of what you were both having. Dismal match, this. I thought it was meant to be a Festival.'

'They're all trying to look good in the score book,' I said, 'to fatten up their chances for next year. Although they may call this a Festival, the new era we live in has no time for all that sort of amateur rot. It's graft and grind from now on.'

'I rather think you're right,' said Hedley, taking a beer and a whisky from Gerald. 'Have you noticed that none of the amateurs are wearing club caps or sweaters, Free Foresters or Harlequins or anything like that? They always did before the war, but now they've been told to wear county colours or nothing. Democracy, you see. It upsets the pros to look at them in their pretty striped blazers.'

'It never upset George or Rainsford,' I said, and drank the second half of the beer Gerald had given me (complete with whisky drops).

'George was too good a player to worry about that kind of thing, and Rainsford was too bad. The sort that are complaining are the mediocre lot – they're always the ones that carry the chips. Blight, P, of Notts – that kind of crap.'

'Exactly,' said Gerald, accepting a fresh beer and whisky from my hands. 'Look what happened the other day down in Kent. Ladies' Day at Canterbury, sun shining, band playing 'Blue Danube' on the boundary, everyone as happy as larks in the sky, and then what happens? Some grimy little pro complains that the music is putting him off. "Fuck that," says the Umpire, "it never put Frank Wolley off. You just play on." (Thank you, Hedley: same again). Then blow me, ten minutes later the same beastly squirt says that the sun shining on the instruments is upsetting him. "You mingy bugger," says the Umpire, "why don't you send for yer cap? That's what it's for, to keep the sun out of yer eyes." "I haven't yet got my cap," says Ferret-face, "and what's more I never shall if I have to play in these conditions." "Conditions?" says the Umpire. "Look you here, laddie: if Les Ames and Arthur Fagg could put up with a band now and then, so can a manky sod like you." So of course the little brute didn't get his way, but you see what a pass things have come to? Some puking junior pro, who hasn't even got his county cap, daring to complain about the Band at Canterbury. They'll start a Union next. Don't they know they're simply there to entertain us?'

'I fear,' I said, 'that we have been born into the wrong age. Just a hundred years too late. (Thank you, Gerald, I don't mind if I do.) We should have been happier with top hats and round arm.'

'And proper grovelling from the Lower Classes,' said Hedley.

Later on, after some of the base mechanicals also drinking at the Tavern had become hostile to our little group, Hedley drove me to the Norfolk Hotel near South Kensington Tube Station, at that time a creaking and crumbling private hostelry which my family always used when in London. As we rounded Hyde Park Corner, I said, 'I'm terribly thorry, Hedley old bean, but I musht have a pith.'

'A pith?'

'A weedle-weedle.'

'A weedle-weedle?'

'For Chrisht's shake, man: a PEE.'

'God,' said Hedley, '*that* again.'

'It'th quite all right, old faggot. The Law shays I can go on either of your off-shide wheelsh.'

'In Knightsbridge?'

'It's either in Knightshbridge, or it'sh in your car.'

Hedley stopped (in those days you could, wherever and whenever you wanted).

'Make it the rear wheel,' he said, 'it's rather muddy.'

'The byelaw,' said James Prior, 'under which you thought you were permitted to urinate on the off-side wheel of a stationary vehicle, has long since been rescinded.'

'Why?'

'Notions of public decency. Increase of public provision for relief. Sheer bloody hypocrisy and prudishness. But the fact remains that it *has* been rescinded, and that you could have been arrested and charged with perpetrating an obscene nuisance – and then goodbye to your Commission. For Jesus Christ's sake, stay out of trouble until you've passed out of Bangalore.'

James and I were on the deck of the Troopship *Georgic*, watching the flying fish as they played among the waves of the Indian Ocean. James had done his Primary and Infantry training with the Greenjackets: by a marvellous stroke of luck (for me at least) the potential officers of his intake had been posted to Bangalore with the same draft and in the same Cadet Platoon as myself.

'I've been finding out about Bangalore,' James said now. 'It's not like an English OCTU, where they'll toss you out for showing a fly button. By the time they've transported you to Bangalore, they've invested so much money in you that they've got to pass you through with a Commission. All you have to do, Simon, is to sit there politely and let the thing go on; and after the prescribed number of weeks you will march off the parade ground as Second

Lieutenant Raven. For Christ's sake, and all our sakes, do it. Do it, and everyone will forgive you everything, because a Commission means success and success means exculpation. Do it, and Bags Birley, Bob Arrowsmith and the Uncle will stand in line to welcome you down to Charterhouse again with open arms and beaming faces.

'But if you make a mess of this,' James rumbled on, 'if you are so wilful or perverse or plain stupid as to make a fuck-up where it is, by common consent, almost impossible to make a fuck-up, then you'll have ditched yourself for good and all, and bloody well serve you right.'

'Hedley said much the same at Lord's.'

'Of course he did. He knows the way the world goes round.'

'But we must…well…have *some* fun at Bangalore.'

'Of course we must. We'll have all the fun that's going, we will have food and drink and expeditions and parties of pleasure, but what we will not have is sex. Repeat after me, Simon: NO SEX'

'NO SEX.'

'No sex with the other Cadets, because even at Bangalore they'll draw the line at that. No sex with white women, even if readily available, because British women in India are, by and large, idle, conceited, pampered and promoted far above their proper class. They are therefore even more prone than most of their sex to interference and malice, and are to be avoided at any cost. And no sex with native women, if only because they stink.'

'What about half-castes? I'm told they're very appetising.'

'So they may be. But they probably have the pox and they certainly have native mothers who chew betel nut.'

VII

RAVEN SAHIB

When we arrived in India we were sent to a Transit Camp called Khalyan (near Bombay) to await transport that would take us South to Bangalore. The only features of the place which I can still remember are a weird conical mountain which spiralled up over it and a seedy fairground with a Death Wall Rider.

'Transit Camps mean idleness and trouble,' said James, 'we must organise occupations for ourselves.'

'I'm told we can get twelve hour passes to go to Bombay,' I said.

'And what would you do when you got *there*, I'd like to know? We shall stay here, Simon, and I shall go to the Officer who is in nominal charge of us, and we shall have football matches and cricket matches and swimming matches and cross-country running matches and–'

'– Isn't that enough to be going on with?'

Some of these things we certainly had, and in this way James continued to keep most of us out of trouble during the very long three weeks during which we lingered in Khalyan. The cricket match in particular was a huge success because of the spectacular comeuppance with which it served Spotty Duvell.

Spotty Duvell (MM) was an ex–Sergeant-Major (very much with a 'g') and Glider Pilot. Now, as a general rule, Warrant Officers who were found fit to hold combatant Commissions at that time were commissioned straight away in the rank of Lieutenant and did not have to undergo training as Officer Cadets. But the authorities had clearly decided that Spotty needed a bit of polishing first, and to India he duly sailed in the good ship *Georgic* with the other 300-odd of us. There was a good deal of controversy as to his exact status. Spotty maintained that until we arrived at Bangalore he would still hold the King's Warrant and enjoy the rank of Company Sergeant-Major (after all, he was still being paid as such) and that he was therefore entitled to the absolute obedience of the rest of us who were still only Private Soldiers. Nonsense, we said: we had now been instructed to assume the insignia of Officer Cadets; *all* of us had been so instructed, including Spotty Duvell, so he could jolly well take down his crown and laurel wreath (in 1946 CSMs still wore both) and put up white shoulder tabs along with the fellow-Cadets who were now his peers.

Spotty did indeed put up white tabs, and also fixed the complementary white celluloid disk behind his regimental cap badge, but he did not take the crown and laurel wreath off his sleeve. All right, so he was an Officer Cadet: he was also a Sergeant-Major. As it happened, this concept very much suited the Officer who had been given the charge of us while we remained in Khalyan: he was short of Warrant Officers, Cadets in transit were notorious for putting on airs with noncommissioned ranks, so let them have their own Cadet Warrant Officer to keep the little buggers in order. Thus authority upheld Spotty's claim, which was thereafter reluctantly conceded.

It followed, of course, that it should have been Spotty who formed up to suggest the programme of games and matches, whereas it had in fact been James. For Spotty was not an initiator, he was a natural other rank loiterer, who would have been only too glad to hang about, vacant and atrophied, for our entire stay in Khalyan. He therefore resented James' action on several levels, and set about trying to discredit the activities which James had put in train by giving loud-mouthed imitations of the Public School accent ('Bah Jove, what a supah toe-ah, Aubrah old sport, whaaaat') and, more harmfully, by ordering people to leave the field in mid-match or mid-race and report for some nugatory fatigue which he had got up out of sheer malice.

Of all the fixtures which had been set up, the one Spotty Duvell most loathed was the cricket match. ('Bah Jove, the mater and the pater are coming to watch us play crickah at Lord's, whaaat. Don't forget your topper, Claude, etc, etc.') No sooner was the first over bowled than Spotty came strutting down to the ground (a murram square with matting wicket) accompanied by his henchman, Syd Tasker, an ex-Sergeant of Military Police.

'Now let's see, Sergeant,' said Spotty. 'We need five men to clean out the latrines.'

'Sir.'

'I think we might detail these men who are sitting here doing nothing. Men, did I say? More like a row of little girls at their first dance, legs together in case they piss their knickers... You,' yapped Spotty, 'you you you and you, report to the latrines at the double.'

80

'Excuse me, Sergeant-Major,' said James, who was Captain of the side that was batting, 'these Cadets are members of my team and are waiting to go in to bat.'

'You speak when you're spoken to, Cadet Prior,' said Sergeant Tasker. 'You you you you and you.'

'If you take them,' said James civilly, 'you will spoil our match.'

'Oh, jolly poor show, whaat, fraightful shame, Monty old chap, and what will his lordship the Marquis say,' snarled Spotty. 'Got ears, have you, lads? You you you you and you.'

I myself was the third 'you', and I did not like the way things were going. For a moment the match continued, but uneasily. By now the fieldsmen were fully aware what was up, and when 'Over' was next called they crossed with furtive, scurrying movements, as if about to be detected in criminal conspiracy.

'There are plenty of people available to clean the latrines,' said James equably, 'who are not playing in this match...which, incidentally, has been organised with the permission of the Officer i/c Draught.'

'Who you went crawling to when I wasn't looking,' said Spotty with naked malignance.

'Only because you arranged nothing for us...sir.'

'Watch yourself, Prior. You're not too important to be put in close arrest...and have those pretty white tabs taken off your shoulder. Now then, you lot: for the last time: you you you you and you.'

'I suppose it's no good my appealing to your kindness?'

'Christ almighty, it brings tears to my eyes, it really does. Poor little toffs, and did the horrid, wicked mans spoil their nice cricket game. You, *you*, YOU, YOU and –'

'– I have a note here from the Officer i/c Draught,' said James, producing it, 'which specifically exempts from today's fatigues all those selected to play in this cricket match, including the two twelfth men, and also two umpires, two scorers, and two men to operate the tally-wag. Here is the list, sir: these five Cadets are all on it.' And then to us, 'Please do not disturb yourselves, gentlemen.'

I think it was this last sentence that really did it – possibly just the last word of all, so quiet and so clear, so evident and total a repudiation of Spotty Duvell...who now completely lost his self-control.

'Why didn't you tell me at once,' he yowled, and snatched at the list. 'You fucking, stinking, slimy little cunt, you – you and your shit-eating nancy friends.'

There was a very long silence. Play ceased as all the players turned to gaze in our direction. Syd Tasker shifted from heel to toe and licked his upper lip. Spotty's face wobbled and then fell apart.

'I...I...' he mouthed.

'As a man of your experience must be aware,' said James, 'you are forbidden to address any soldier in this fashion. If sworn at with good will and good humour, the rank and file will tolerate and welcome a little rough language. If insulted, indeed slandered, in obscene and malevolent terms, they will not. I have only to report this disgraceful exhibition to the Commandant, supported as I shall be by these witnesses, for you to be deprived of your Cadetship and almost certainly degraded to private rank. However, gentlemen,' said James to the rest of us, 'I think we know how to make allowances. You, Sandy, and you, Barry: you're batting well down in the tail. Just accompany the Sergeant-Major to the latrines, would you, please, and be sure he makes a good job of them.'

'Well,' I said later, 'why didn't you tell him at once? About that note? You were leading him on.'

'Oh no. I just wanted to give him a chance to show us his better side.'

'Would they really have degraded him if we'd reported the incident?'

'I doubt it. *He* believed it, because at bottom he is the sort of underdog who believes anything which he is firmly told by his betters. My own view is that he might well have got off with a severe reprimand. Still, it certainly wouldn't have done his career any good. I think he was wise to accept the proferred bargain.'

The next day, Sergeant-Major Spotty Duvell dismissed his jackel and arranged with the Officer i/c Draught for James to be made up as a Local, Acting, Unpaid (O/Cadet) Colour-Sergeant. From now on James was to be Spotty's constant aide. Clearly Spotty, though not an initiator, was an opportunist and a philosopher; he would make (James reported as the days went on) a far better Officer than we had thought.

Certainly, he never forgot himself again.

'You taught me a thing, you did,' he said to James one night when mildly in drink, 'you taught me there's nothing like Class, and if a man hasn't got it he better borrow a bit. That's what you are, Jimmy boy – my bit o' borrowed Class.'

Although the OTS at Bangalore had been founded to train mature and experienced civilian volunteers, and was therefore adult in its attitudes and sparing of regulation, the authorities were aware by now that the Cadets coming into their care were far younger and more vulnerable than they had been in the early forties. The Commandant had therefore decreed that, while the traditional tolerance of the institution should not be renounced, the Cadets must nevertheless have as many amusements as possible 'laid on' for them during their leisure, in order to distract them from the perils of the town. One such entertainment was an educational visit, scheduled to extend over a whole long weekend, to the Gold Fields at Kola. James and I and Sandy and Barry (two Greenjacket chums of James who were wary of me but not unfriendly) were all going, not for the technical enlightenments on offer, but to take part in a Gala Two Day Cricket Match.

'I want no snobbiness from any of you,' James said as we set off in an OTS bus. 'Some of the chaps there will be absolute oiks, of course, the sort of people you'd expect to be mixed up in gold digging, but we must remember that we are the ambassadors of the OTS and the Army, and we must do our best to strike up cordial relations.'

'Yes, James,' we all said.

It was early in the evening when we arrived at Kola, where a crowd of white employees was waiting by the central offices to greet us all and escort us to the various houses in which we should be entertained. As luck would have it, I was separated from James, Sandy and Barry, who were swept away by a stubby and overbearing manager of senior aspect. Meanwhile, I was taken on by a modest and brittle young man, who led me off to his bachelor bungalow and filled me up with gin, curry and whisky, in that order, as a preface to telling me about his life.

This had been somewhat less than satisfactory: his father and mother had drunk the money left by his grandfather specifically to provide him with a decent education, and had then resented and bullied him when he succeeded in winning for himself scholarships just sufficient to put him through a grammar school and Sheffield University. His father accused him of being a parasite on the household and his mother called him a traitor to his country (his call-up had been deferred as he was studying Metallurgy), and the only girlfriend he ever had used to arrive in his lodgings at Sheffield shortly after breakfast every morning and stay with him there or follow him wherever he went until eleven o'clock at night, talking incessantly of the 'home' they would have as soon as he had the sense to leave the University and get a 'proper, paying job'. In order to be rid of her he had to feign three epileptic fits, during the last of which he had banged his head so hard on the fender that he went to his final examination in a state of shock. What with that, and what with having had his work constantly disrupted for the last three months by the alternate quacking and whingeing of the girlfriend, it was, he told me, hardly surprising that he managed to obtain only a Pass Degree.

However, Metallurgists were in short supply, and when the Army had absolutely turned him down for service (advanced and ubiquitous nervous eczema, first aroused by the attentions of his girlfriend and later long nourished by her memory) he was accepted for overseas employment here at Kola. So in the end things hadn't turned out too badly, you might say. He was quite liberally paid (in order that he might keep up his end as a white man), he had two native servants (to the great envy of his mother and the fury of his father), and a cosy little place of his own (and cosy it was) to drink his whisky in peace and quiet. What, I enquired, did he actually do in exchange for these privileges? Well – er – well, he was in the Security Department. A trained Metallurgist...in the Security Department? Yes: you see, they needed an expert to recognise the presence of gold dust in the clothes or on the persons of native workers who tried to smuggle it out of the compound. He looked at me heavily, took a long swig of whisky, laughed out loud, and, 'After all that solemn grind at Sheffield,' he said, 'I now spend my entire professional life looking up black arseholes and under black foreskins – some people's idea of heaven, I suppose.'

He was, in fact, a pretty good sort of man who had no illusions about his own dinginess and absurdity. I often wonder what happened to him when Independence came to the Kola Gold concern, and I rather fear for the worst.

As soon as I arrived with him next morning at the cricket ground, I was taken on one side by Sandy.

'Something awful has come over James,' Sandy giggled, passing his fingers rapidly in and out of his short blond hair and exhibiting a positive sheen of pleasurable excitement on his fourth form face, 'he's taken against the Mem.'

'Taken against the what?'

'The wife of that man who's putting us up. He calls her 'The Mem', or 'Mem' in the vocative. Apparently she's the 'doyenne' – that's the word he uses – of all the Kola wives. She snooted us up last night because we're Greenjackets. *She* pretends to think that the Fusiliers are much smarter – her father was one. James is very put out.'

'Surely he won't rise to that bait? After all his talk about our being ambassadors. She's just the sort of person we've got to be nice to.'

'I know. But when you get a look at her you'll see why we're finding it difficult. There,' said Sandy, and pointed.

A sort of giant upright pug dog, on two legs like barrels, was dismounting from a tonga. It carried a parasol and was supported by two native bearers. An enormous strawhat, smothered in botanical decoration, crowned and sheltered it; the massive, white-stockinged legs, jammed into white brogues, somehow, incredibly, propelled it; a kind of shrill drawl announced its arrival, in a series of prolonged hoots.

'Can't…you seaah…I'm heaaah,' it said, 'jildah, jildah, cheah…bairaah.' (Can't you see I'm here. *Jilde, jilde* (quick, quick), chair, bearer.)

'I do see,' I said. 'Has there been a row yet?'

'No. Though there nearly was when she called the Rifle Brigade a "Parvenu Regiment".'

'So it is.'

'I know. But James says a woman like that can't be allowed to say so and get away with it. He's planning what he calls a "Heffalump Trap".'

I remembered the technique from nursery readings of *Winnie the Pooh*. In order to trap a Heffalump, one arranged a piece of ground to look particularly pretty and well kept, and so particularly tempting to an ill-conditioned Heffalump to trample on. And when it did, it went crashing through into the trap beneath, where it was left bellowing furiously until at last it quietened down and promised to mend its manners.

'From the look of her,' I said, 'he'll have to get up quite early in the morning to construct it.'

'It seems that her husband is Captain of their cricket team. James is working on that.'

'But he's about a hundred years old.'

'That's what James said. "No fool like an old fool",' he said, ' "we should be able to fix something." '

'But what's got into James? He knows he mustn't tamper with elderly managers – however disagreeable their wives may be.'

'I thought I'd tell you,' said Sandy, jittering with expectation, 'because you've known him longer than any of us, and you might be able to do something to stop him. Though I don't think you will be,' he added happily.

As I walked across the ground towards the Pavilion my host (Ted) rejoined me.

'You'll find our lot's a sporting team,' Ted said, 'but tough. They remind me of some of the Sheffield League sides I used to watch. The only trouble is our Captain. He is fascinated by the personality and practice of W G Grace. He thinks that he's W G reborn.'

'A fairly harmless delusion?'

'But don't you remember? W G was a marvellous cricketer, but he was also omniscient, arrogant, and over-fond of refreshment at lunchtime…all of which turned him into a bully and even a cheat.'

'Ah.'

'Kola Bert – that's what we call our skipper – Kola Bert reincarnates the very worst of W G. But no one can do anything because he's so senior. And as for his Mem…'

Ted shuddered.

As I passed this lady on the way into the Pavilion (with some difficulty as she was parked slap in the doorway) four bearers appeared with cold drinks, pots of tea, plates of cakes etc, and set them up on a series of tables which substantially increased the obstacle to entrance. Her husband now came up (wearing an Old Carthusian blazer) and diffidently recommended a slight shift of her apparatus, but was told 'not to be a bloodah fool, Bertah, Ah've onlah just got comfah.' He departed with a muffled snort, clearly about to take this defeat out on someone else, while I hurried on to the Visitors' Dressing Room.

'He's wearing an OC blazer,' I said to James, who was putting on the specially thick white socks that were knitted for him by his mother.

'Who is?'

'Bertah – the chap you're staying with. He's wearing an OC blazer with thick stripes – like a wop ice cream.'

'Is he?' said James dangerously.

'James…what *has* he done to you?'

'It's his wife. Great rorting carnivore. But he's as bad. OC blazer indeed. There's no such thing. Bob Arrowsmith once told me.'

'But I tell you he's wearing it.'

'Then he's had it made up. As bad as wearing a made-up evening tie. Worse.'

'Ted, my host, says he thinks he's W G Grace. And cheats to prove it.'

'Come over here, please, Barry,' said James to sinuous, sinewy Barry Tooman, our first spin bowler.

Barry came.

'Now listen carefully,' James began.

The first day's play in the Kola Match was pretty dull, but left the possibility of an interesting finish. Giles Peregrine, our Captain, had won the toss, put us in to bat, and declared at teatime at 372 for 6, an average opening score for the ground, which was very small and very fast (whence the dullness of the play, which was apt to be a monotonous succession of easy boundaries). The Kola XI had reached 180 for 3 in reply when stumps were drawn for the day. On the form they were showing, they would probably bat on to equal our score by about lunchtime the next day, thus leaving the afternoon to settle the issue.

At close of play on the second day, there would be a quick buffet, after which we Cadets must leave at once for Bangalore. On the evening of the first day, just concluded, there was to be a Gala Dinner for both teams, we had been told, in the Boardroom of the Company. Men only. Thus it seemed unlikely that James would again encounter the Mem in any substantial fashion, and I was hoping that absence, making his heart grow fonder or at least less loathing, might lead to his abandoning his scheme for the humiliation of her husband the next day.

This consisted in getting Barry Tooman, with Giles Peregrine's connivance, to bowl very high donkey drops, which would descend almost vertically on the old man and show up his incapacity in shame-making slow motion. It was, on the face of it, a harmless enough idea, but it seemed to me that it could lead to just the sort of ill feeling which James himself had told us must in no case be conjured, and it also seemed that this whole business was somehow unworthy. Why did James have to bother himself about this dismal couple in the first place? True, the Mem was about the most appalling example of her species ever put on view, but Kola Bert was just ageing and pompous, nothing worse, and in any event at all they would both vanish from our lives for good and all at dusk tomorrow. It did not seem to me that her mild (and accurate) jibe at the Rifle Brigade and his donning of a vulgar and unauthorised blazer need give rise to vengeful stratagems. So at least Sandy and I were telling James as we walked up the steps of the building (Graeco-Buddhist) which contained the Boardroom, and so, I was happy to observe, he now seemed to be thinking for himself.

'Right you be,' he said, 'I was just being childish.'

Then we entered the Anteroom. The first thing we saw was the Mem. Enthroned amid a crowd of Kola cricketing sycophants and wielding a Tom Collins like a sceptre, she gazed down with sumptuous disdain on all which and whom she beheld, ourselves among them.

'What is that fucking woman doing here?' muttered James. 'A men's dinner, they said.'

'She,' I hazarded, 'is bound to be the exception...the one who may not be excluded, the one to whom the Laws do not apply, just as the Queen of England, alone among women, may enter the Pavilion at Lord's.'

'That could be it,' said James. 'The Head Bitch.'

Clearly he was outraged and even rather frightened by the Mem's appearance at this masculine function. So was I. Who knew what vile processes of bullying, nagging or blackmail she had deployed to get herself there? We were also outraged by the behaviour of the husband. He surely was in a position to stop her. If he had not done so, it meant either that he was downright feeble (in this area at least) or that he enjoyed according such lone privilege to his wife and so by extension to himself. Either way he must be punished: the plan for tomorrow would now, after all, go forward as it had been conceived; and it was greatly hoped among us that before the sun next set the Mem would have been brought as low as her lord, by the humbling of Kola Bert.

In the event, Kola Bert came in to bat at No. 7, when the score was 280 and the time half past twelve. Thus the Kola team had 92 more to make in order to equal our first innings' score, and until a few minutes previously none of us had doubted they would get them by luncheon (1.30 p.m.). But the arrival of Kola Bert at the wicket was definitely encouraging; for it would appear to indicate that we were now into the tail. To judge from Bert's flaccid fielding, he had long been too far gone for cricket, and if his position as No. 7 was in true accordance with his relative merit as a batsman, there could only be even worse rubbish to follow him. If, on the other hand, Bert had put himself in at No. 7 out of vanity or selfishness, then here at any rate was a quick and easy wicket. We grinned self-indulgently as Bert asked for guard and took up his 'W G' stance with left foot cocked. Barry Tooman took a three pace run and launched the first of his hyperbolic donkey drops.

Even a good player finds it hard to deal with Dollies. They take for ever to arrive, they are very trying to watch in the air, they madden otherwise cool men into desperate, ill-tempered swishes, and even if perfectly struck they do not fly sweetly off the bat but either stop dead after twenty yards or, if lofted, sag dismally into the hands of long off. We all waited for Kola Bert to wind himself up like an arbalest for some clownish stroke which would end with his falling on his wicket (or something of the kind) – and were a good bit mortified when he leaned easily back and hooked the ball full toss, as it descended, clean out of the ground. He then did the same thing twice more, at which stage Giles whispered to Barry, who reverted to his normal style of leg break bowling. Not that this troubled Kola Bert. To the fourth ball of the Over, which was on a good length and turning just outside the off stump, he played quietly and precisely back, getting a sight of the new Barry, and both the fifth and sixth balls, which also turned outside the off stump, he cut very late and most exquisitely for four.

Barry's Over had cost 26 runs. Bert remained unhumbled, quite conspicuously so. How could we, I thought, how could we have made such a stupid mistake? We had surely been playing the game long enough to know that an elderly man who does not put himself out in the field may yet be a most accomplished batsman. Ted had not said that Bert was no good, just that he had a fantasy, which could sometimes prove tiresome, about being W G Grace. Fantasies of this order could inspire as well as derange: I remembered Myles' 402 on the terrace in the role of J D Robertson ('Another spanking boundary for "J D").

'Jollah gad shah, Bertah,' honked the Mem from the midst of her manifold refreshments in front of the Pavilion door, 'you shah the little baggahs.'

It was impossible to distinguish whether the last word intended beggars or buggers. Whichever it was, it conveyed an almost physical disgust.

Not to go into the details of our discomfiture, I shall say *tout court* that Kola Bert made an immaculate 49, which included every stroke in the book; and that when he was given out l.b.w., one run short of his fifty and on a highly questionable decision (he almost certainly snicked the ball before it hit his pads), he went with a good grace and without hesitation, as a gentleman should. No ugly flush of the face, no shaking of the head, no reproachful look at the umpire, no slamming and slapping of baton pad as he departed: he simply went, followed, I'm happy to recall, by a huge volley of clapping, and received by the Cadets on the boundary (who had now concluded their educational tour of the mines) with a cheer to warm his heart till the day it turned to dust.

As he entered the Pavilion, he stooped to give his wife a quick and sweaty kiss on the cheek. 'Bravah, bravah,' she bleated, 'oh bravah, dear old chap.' Watching from the boundary for the next batsman to emerge, I saw that a single tear (of pride? love? gratitude? pity?) was running down her ogreish jowl, and I forgave her all.

'What I never understood,' said James, when we were discussing the incident a long while later, 'was why that man Ted told you that Bert was an ill-tempered cheat.'

'He explained, after the game, that it would have been a very different matter if Bert had done badly. He might even have refused to go out. It had happened – according to Ted.'

'Seems odd to me,' James said. 'If he was that sort of chap, he'd have shown *some* sign of annoyance or recalcitrance at being given out even when he had done well. He might have pulled himself together pretty quick and gone with a smile in the end, but for a few seconds at least the bad sportsmanship would have shown. It always does. But not in this case – not for a single flick of the eyelid.'

'It's my view,' James went on, 'that Kola Bert was absolutely pukkah right through. That was what I got wrong at the time. I thought that if Barry got him all knotted up with those high lobs, he'd lose his rag and make a fool of himself. Then, later on, I thought, at luncheon perhaps, the Mem would push herself in on the act, reckoning aggression to be the best form of defence as such a woman would, and that with a little luck she too would lose her wool and give me the chance to pick her off.

'But the origin and basis of the entire scheme was the notion, promoted by Ted and confirmed by that horrible OC blazer, that Bert was hairy at the heel – which simply wasn't true.'

'I dare say Ted got it all wrong,' I said, 'he had chips along both shoulders, to say nothing of nervous eczema.'

'But what about that made-up blazer?' said Sandy. 'That was real enough.'

'I've written to check the record,' said James. 'There's no doubt Bert was at Charterhouse. He was a Saunderite – contemporary of Ronald Storrs.'

'But as you pointed out,' Barry persisted, 'there is no such thing as an Old Carthusian blazer, or at any rate it is not officially recognised. Bert was out of order there.'

'But was it really so very dreadful?' said James. 'I was furious at the time because I was narked by that bloody Mem woman. Another day I'd just have laughed. It was probably she that had it made for him – stupid kind of cock-up these women make when they will interfere. Particularly a stuck up blowsy old bitch like that.'

'She wasn't so bad,' I said. For the first time I told them about the tear.

'Crocodiles put on the same performance,' said James, 'it only meant she was going to eat another piece of him when they got home.'

'I don't know. Tough she may have been, but then you've got to be if you're going to live out here.'

'Fat lot you know about living out here,' said Barry.

'I wish,' I said, 'that I was going to have the chance to learn a lot more. Seems such a damned shame – to go home after only six months.'

For the appointed day had duly come and gone, and now we were all four Second Lieutenants, four brand new Second Lieutenants just about to go home. Independence was to be bestowed on India earlier than anyone had thought; Attlee's Labour Government was 'bringing the boys home', not only from India but from other parts of the Far East, as fast as possible; and so far from being urgently despatched to points East of Mandalay (as I had boasted to my parents we should be) we were sitting in the most run down and visibly rotting Officers' Mess (Napier Mess) of all the four such in the Transit Camp at Deolali, waiting for a passage back to England with the lowest possible priority.

'What makes you think we shall ever get home?' Sandy now said.

Deolali was so famous for frustration and delay that it had given its name to a form of madness – Deolali (sometimes pronounced Doolali) Tap. Men were abandoned there for ever, the legend said: your papers disappeared through a crack in the floor, after which you lost your official identity and with it your pay, your rations and any possibility of a passage, so that there was nothing to do but turn your face to the wall and die. But generally there was an intermediate period: before you took to your bed for ever, you made a last effort, uttered a final protest, which took the form of hideous fits of gibbering and foaming – Deolali Tap.

We had been there three weeks. At first the Field Cashier had looked kindly upon us and advanced us plenty of money against arrears of pay: now, when we skulked into his office, we were peremptorily waved away by a Lance-Corporal. Clearly we had no further claim; we were losing our substance, our identity... Any minute now we should be attacked, as inexorably and mortally as if by Rabies, by Deolali Tap. Something must be done to revive us, to make us aware again, or we were surely lost. It was in this predicament, as the result of an idle boast by Spotty Duvell that he could out-drink any man in Deolali, that James issued his Challenge and A GRAND DRINKING MATCH was proclaimed along the Lines. At last life had meaning and interest enough to make us bustle again.

James and Spotty were both to deposit Fifty Guineas, making a Purse of One Hundred Guineas for the winner. (Although everyone else was counting his Annas, James and Spotty, each being the man he was, had ample resources.) The Match would take place at Nine p.m. on the night of June 10, 1947, in Napier Mess. Two Judges were appointed by common agreement; and the Laws which they had to enforce were these:

> I. At Nine of the Clock on the Afternoon of the Day Appointed, the Two Principals should present themselves on the Ground (Napier Mess); and at Ten Minutes after Nine they should come to the Scratch (the Mess Bar), where they would exchange Compliments in a gentlemanly fashion.
>
> II. At Fifteen Minutes after Nine the Judges would supervise the pouring of the first potation, a Double Whisky for each Contestant. Each Contestant must then drink his Whisky, neat from the glass, by 9.20, at which time the Judges must be satisfied that both potations had been absolutely consumed, and would then cause to be poured two more of the same amount of the same Liquor. These in turn must be consumed by 9.25, when two more potations would be poured, etc, etc, etc.

III. The First of the Principals to puke on the Ground (i.e. anywhere in Napier Mess), to faint, have a fit, fall and be unable to rise, die, or declare himself unable to consume, in whole or in part, a properly presented potation, would be disqualified and The Match and The Purse would thereupon be awarded to his Opponent. But if both Principals puked on the Ground (i.e. anywhere in Napier Mess), fainted, had a fit, etc, etc, etc, *after consuming an equal amount of Liquor* (in which matter the Judges' Computation would be absolute and final), the Match would be pronounced a Tie. It was to assist the Judges in this respect (e.g. in the assessment of partly consumed potations) that the Contestants were required to drink their Whisky neat from the glass. However, there would be no objection raised against the Contestants' drinking chasers of water, or any other liquid they might favour, from separate glasses.

IV. Spectators would be admitted, but they must keep a distance of not less than Five Yards from the Principals and the Judges; and the Stewards would ensure that a passage of Four Foot wide was clearly marked and respected by all, to enable the Contestants to reach the Jakes without let or hindrance. *Nota bene*: Voiding of Bladders or Bowells by the Principals would be perfectly in order, always provided:

a) Such functions were performed in the proper Offices of the Jakes;

b) Contestants were back on Scratch (i.e. at the Bar), having fairly finished their current potation and being ready to receive the next, by the time allotted;

and c) Contestants admitted one Judge to accompany them into the Water Closet to determine whether or not they threw up (*vide* Law III).

V. Bets might be struck with the Principals up to the time appointed for the Match to commence. Once the Principals had arrived on the Ground they might no longer take or lay the odds on or against themselves or each other. Spectators, however, might wager among themselves *ad lib* both during 'orders' and 'in running'.

As the days passed and excitement mounted among gentlemen of the fancy, Spotty emerged a clear favourite at 6 to 4 on, though respectable sums were invested on James (by those who could still find them) at 7 to 4 against. As much as 100 to 1 was offered in some quarters against a tie, and 500 to 1 (generally thought to be rather mean odds) against the death of one Contestant. I myself staked two Rupees (about three shillings), at 2,000 to 1, on both Principals dropping dead and ten Rupees (all I could raise for the purpose) on a victory for Spotty at even money – a price briefly on offer when a rumour that Spotty had the clap (started by me) caused fluctuations in the market.

'Damned disloyal I call that,' said James when he heard.

'One has to take the practical view. I know you're a reliable drinker but you haven't quite had Spotty's experience.'

'I don't get drunk, if that's what you mean.'

'It's exactly what I mean. There's nothing in the Laws saying the winner has to be sober, only that he mustn't be sick or pass out. Spotty has had practice – almost every night he has practice – at getting drunk, i.e. drinking the stuff by the bucket, *without being sick or passing out*. You have had no such practice. You're not even having it now.'

'I don't have to make a hog of myself just because of the Match.'

'But you will have to make a hog of yourself in order to win it. You might at least find out what it feels like...have the odd net, so to speak.'

'But *you* don't want James to win,' said Sandy spitefully; '*you've* backed Spotty Duvell. So why are you giving him all this advice?'

'Because I don't want to see Spotty Duvell walk all over him. The honour of Charterhouse is at stake here. James must put up a good show. What on earth will Hedley Le Bas say,' I said to James, 'if he hears you've collapsed after the first few rounds of a public Drinking Match? Whatever would Bags Birley feel about it?'

'I fear lest Bags would deprecate the whole proceeding,' said James, 'whatever the result.'

'Not if you win. To win is to succeed, and as you yourself once told me, success brings its own exculpation.'

'So in the last resort...you really want me to win – although you've had a bet against me?'

'That's about it.'

'It makes no sort of sense.'

'It makes admirable sense,' I said, 'it means financial emolument in case of personal disappointment. By the same token, I've also had a bet that you and Spotty will both fall down dead. Should this sorrowful calamity occur, 2,000 Rupees would at least be some kind of compensation.'

The day before the match it became clear that if everyone who wanted to attend were to be allowed in, Napier Mess would totter to the ground. The entire Transit Camp was buzzing with almost hysterical excitement, and literally hundreds of pounds' worth of bets had been struck by men of all ranks from the Commandant himself (or so it was rumoured) down to the very punkah wallahs. Since Napier was one of the Officers' Messes all non-commissioned spectators were automatically excluded, but even then the crowd would be enormous. In the end, it was decided that the Principals and the Judges should have the right to make a certain number of nominations, and that for the rest a further 100 cards of admission would be distributed by ballot. Ticket holders, when their names were made known, were offered anything up to £20 by crooked Quartermasters who were making important books on the event or by senior Officers either in transit or on the Staff. I myself was one of James' nominees.

'You don't deserve it,' he said as he handed me my pass, 'and if you sell it I'll kill you.'

'I wouldn't miss this for a dukedom,' I said, and almost meant it.

'In that case,' said James, 'I invite you to be one of my seconds.'

Next to hearing the news of my Scholarship at King's and of my 1st XI cap, it was the proudest moment of my life.

At exactly 9 p.m. on the appointed evening, James entered Napier Mess attended by Sandy and myself. All of us were wearing Tropical Service Dress, in those bleak days the nearest one could come to Full Dress or Ceremonial. James' lapels carried the insignia of The Norfolk Regiment (the Greenjackets were not accepting anyone back from Bangalore as Officer of *theirs*, and thank you for your kind application); while Sandy sported the Petard of The Royal Fusiliers and I displayed the Bugle Horn of The Oxfordshire and Buckinghamshire Light Infantry (Wellington's beloved 43rd). Though I say it myself we made a brave group – and so, I am glad to report, did Spotty Duvell and his seconds, who were already on the Ground. Lieutenant Duvell (for he had been granted two pips straight away in recognition of his former seniority) flaunted the Rose of Yorkshire, while the two Ensigns who flanked him both bore the Sphinx. (Take heed, take heed, for we shall see such heraldry no more amid the drab artisans who man the Army of our age.)

The two groups bowed to each other, then stood easy and talked low and nervously among themselves. The crowd buzzed and seethed; the Stewards marshalled it well back, and marked the route to the Jakes with white ropes; the Head Barman, in high turban, stood strictly to attention behind two rows of twenty glasses; punkah wallahs plied their fans with a frenzy as if the penalty for sloth were death. No doubt about it: Napier Mess, like Todger's, could do it when it tried.

At 9.10 there was a long roll of kettle drums, followed by total silence. The two Judges (one of whom wore the crepuscular Kilt of The Black Watch, while the other carried the Harp of Ulster on his breast) beckoned to James and Spotty. The seconds of either party backed off, to a special row of seats by the double door which led to the verandah. James and Spotty advanced to the Bar, bowed again to each other and shook hands; then each retired to his own place, some three yards respectively to left and right of the Head Barman, whither he was attended by one Judge. There was another roll of kettle drums; the Head Barman measured two exact doubles into the left hand glass of either rank; the Judges stepped up to him, agreed the measures, and carried them to the Principals; and at a sign from the Senior Steward a rocket went up from the verandah to notify the masses outside the Mess that The Grand Drinking Match was now in train.

Spotty took his double in one go. (I thought of Hedley and Gerald at the Tavern.) He did not chase it with water, as his theory was that the bulk of the water increased the likelihood of his throwing up. James, on the other hand, drunk his whisky in sips, taking a gulp of water from a separate glass between each sip; for *his* theory was that the water rendered the Usquebaugh less toxic and therefore more readily assimilable. Thus Spotty had nearly five minutes to wait, after taking his bumper, until James had sipped his way through his first glass, which the Judge at his elbow announced had been fairly drained with twenty seconds to spare. A green flare was then fired from the verandah to inform the crowd that both Contestants were safely through the first round; the kettle drums sounded once more; and the Head Barman measured double whiskies into the second glass of each rank of twenty.

And so the thing went solemnly on for the first six glasses. Spotty continued to drink in single sconces; James continued to sip whisky and gulp water. Both had unquestionably put up empty glasses within the time and the conditions ordained: neither showed the slightest sign of having been affected by what he had drunk: neck and neck, nothing to choose.

But after draining his seventh glass Spotty belched very fiercely; and towards the end of his eighth James had to reswallow a sip which had obviously come back. During the ninth round both parties were in trouble with their bladders; both retired with a Judge apiece, Spotty after his customary bumper, James when he was about a third the way through his glass; and both returned, certified by the Judges to have pumped only, James just in time to sip and chase his way (with some bulging of cheeks) through the remaining two-thirds of his portion.

And so the ninth green flare rose toward the eastern stars, proclaiming that after nine rounds neither Champion was yet unhorsed.

Meanwhile the 'layers' inside the Mess were doing brisk business 'in running'. The quiet dignity of James' demeanour had caused the odds against him to ease a shade, and at one time they were as low as 5 to 4; but his slight disorder in the eighth round brought them swiftly back to 6 to 4. As for

Spotty, his crudity of method at first put the backers against him, and at one stage you might have had even money about him, for the first time since the discredited rumour of his clap. His mighty belch, however, somewhat reassured the punters, on the ground that it was better out than in. 6 to 4 on was now standard about Spotty, while James was slipping away, because of a slight sweatiness in his appearance on his return from the loo, to 7 to 4 against and even 2 to 1.

'Your man's fraying at the edges,' said one of Spotty's seconds to Sandy.

'Our man will stick it till he busts,' Sandy staunchly replied.

The tenth drink was a very dicey one for both competitors. Spotty retched in agony after his self-imposed sconce, and once again, for a couple of minutes or so, you might have had even money. But not for long, because Spotty shook his head and grinned, having evidently recovered for the time being, while James' sweating sickness was getting worse every second. Great glistering pools gathered beneath his eyes, then cascaded down either side of his nose, along the clefts between his nostrils and the corners of his mouth, then over his chin and on to his tunic, which was already darkened, round armpits and shoulders, by the creeping stain of the perspiration which had worked through his shirt. Then at last, despite all social and sartorial habit, he decided to loosen his tie – a concession which improved his looks a little and enabled him, though not without much heavy breathing, to finish his tenth glass.

At this stage both men seemed, for whatever reason, to get another wind. Grimly but not desperately they despatched their eleventh and twelfth glasses (having by now consumed about a bottle apiece), each sticking to the method he had used from the beginning. James was keeping up a good rhythm of sip and gulp, I noticed, while Spotty got through his two periods of waiting in a relaxed yet alert posture which promised ample capacity still in reserve. But at this very moment of apparent steadiness and calm there was a sudden and ugly transformation.

For just as the bookmaking Officers were offering 33 to 1 against either Contestant's consuming more than 20 glasses, James' face turned to something like Captain Hook's 'rich, green cake', and Spotty, having given two or three deep and uneasy swallows, came groggily to his feet. By now their thirteenth glasses were before them. Spotty seized his, downed it in one, then sat again, swivelling his eyes and contorting his mouth, looking all in all as though he were watching his wife in flagrant adultery while himself under heavy constraint. No question about it, though: his thirteenth glass was down. How would James respond? Most nobly. Realising that he would never get his glass down by slow stages, he rose to his feet, flung back his head, then tossed the dose off and clamped his mouth shut like a vice.

Thus James, standing, and Spotty, sitting, faced each other at the crisis of the drama. At first it seemed to me that the Match now turned on who could keep his stomach down the longer. But then did it? The Laws said that if both Contestants 'puked on the Ground (i.e. anywhere in Napier Mess), fainted, had a fit, etc, etc, after *consuming an equal amount of liquor,* the Match would be pronounced a tie.' Obviously, in order to win, James not only had to hold down his load longer than Spotty, he also had to get it out of the Mess before he chucked it up; equally obviously, he could not move until released by Spotty's prior incontinence, except to the loo whither a Judge would attend him; finally, one had to remember that in three and a half minutes' time both of them would be served with a fresh drink, the arrival of which would raise problems on several most interesting levels.

In the end, both buckled at the same time. Spotty simply opened his mouth, like a drunk don in a Rowlandson print, and sat there while vomit cascaded vertically between his thighs. As for James, his cheeks and lips bulged and bulged and bulged until his lips must surely part or his face explode into fragments…had not Sandy, inspired, called out, 'OVER HERE,' and pointed to the double door which led on to the verandah. Quick to take a hint even *in extremis,* James hurtled through the door, opened his lips, and squirted thirteen double whiskies and twelve tumblers of water in a proud and graceful arc, high over the balustrade of the verandah and on to the massed soldiery below.

There was now grave controversy between the two sets of seconds. True, both Principals had been sick at the same time and after consuming equal amounts of whisky; but (said we) James had deposited his burden *outside* the Mess, whereas Spotty had incontestably fouled the Ground itself. Granted (said they); but since James' person was on the Mess verandah, i.e. still in the Mess or on Mess territory, when he 'laid his kit', he must be counted to have 'puked on the Ground' even though the 'kit' itself had landed outside.

The Judges, when the matter was referred to them, inclined against James. This business of the vomit's landing outside the Mess, they opined, was a pure technicality: morally and judicially James' performance was on a par with Spotty's. And indeed a tie would assuredly have been proclaimed, bets paid out accordingly, and their respective contributions to the Purse handed back to the Contestants, had it not been for the magnanimity of Lieutenant Spotty Duvell, who lifted his head from the Bar on which it was uneasily reposing and said, like the Englishman and the sportsman that he was: 'Give him the Match. I catted on the carpet. He did it dainty, off the verandah. That's manners, that is: that's self-control. Like I always said, our boy Jimmy's got Class.'

Whether the crowd immediately below the verandah would have agreed with this opinion, I do not know; but so the matter was adjudged. A red flare was fired to indicate that the contest was decided, and then a single white flare (it would have been a pair for Spotty, matching his pips) to signify that the victor was James.

In this fashion was concluded The Grand Drinking Match between Jim Prior and Spotty Duvell, contested at Deolali in the June of 1947, when good King George the Sixth was Emperor of India, a whole generation ago. They asked me to tell the story on television some weeks back, for a programme they were getting up about the Right Honourable J M L Prior, Privy Councillor. I duly told my tale to the camera, but was not altogether surprised when it was omitted from the finished film. It has an Hogarthian air which offends the prim nostrils of our time. But I for one think it a good tale which does honour (of a kind) to two good men; and if any should perchance accuse me of having embellished or improved it in the telling, well, I still preserve, at the bottom of my old Indian tin trunk, the slips for the two losing wagers which I struck – to witness if I lie.

VIII

PIECES OF ORDNANCE

When our troopship reached Southampton in July, 1947, a trim and mannerly Major came on board to address us.

'Gentlemen,' said he, 'the one thing we do not need in England, or in Europe, saving your worships, is Second Lieutenants of Infantry. You are, of course, all Probationary Officers only, and in theory we could withdraw your Commissions. But since this would not be a charitable exercise, it has been decreed that those of you for whom no postings to Infantry Regiments are available (some ninety per cent of you) shall be seconded variously to The Royal Artillery, The Royal Engineers, the Royal Corps of Signals, or the RASC,' for even this smooth and plausible number could not bear to enunciate *that* in full. 'You will be notified, during the course of your disembarkation leave, of your new appointments. Any Officer who fails to give an effective leave address will be Courtmartialed and cashiered *instanter*. Thank you, gentlemen, for your courteous attention.'

'All that way and back,' said James as we filed down the gangway, 'just to become some kind of mechanic.'

James himself did not become a 'mechanic'. He was one of the 10 per cent of us who were posted to Infantry Regiments and one of the 2 per cent who were actually posted to their own – now the Norfolks. As for me, you may be chagrined to learn, my destiny was less distinguished, and by mid-August I was serving as theoretical Commander of a Troop of Heavy Anti-Aircraft guns at Rolleston Balloon Camp in the middle of the Salisbury Plain.

The Royal Artillery at that time comprised some of the smartest Regiments (in every sense) along with some of the most dismal in the British

Army. The Royal Horse Artillery was to be classed with the better Regiments of Cavalry and the Field Artillery with the more bearable Regiments of Infantry; but Anti-Aircraft Regiments whether Light or Heavy (both, I imagine, now extinct), were pretty near unspeakable, and the Coastal Artillery was quite untouchable. From all of which it followed that, although I had not touched the absolute bottom, both my social and my military pretensions had taken a sharp slap in the face when I was compulsorily exchanged from the 43rd Light Infantry into the 77th Heavy Ack-Ack.

Matters were not improved by my sour relations with my Commanding Officer, Lieutenant-Colonel Lewis Pugh. Pugh, as I have since come to understand, was an outstanding Officer, of wide experience, sympathetic intelligence and endearing modesty (he was fond of telling us the story of how he failed to get into Winchester, despite intense and prodigious cramming, and had to go to Wellington instead, for he was what would now be called a 'late developer'). He had been seconded to the Political Service in India before the war (a rare distinction); he was, in principle, a 'Horse Gunner', who was now slumming with Ack-Ack only because of the vagaries of the Artillery Rota of Command; and he was clearly due for early promotion (he in fact ended his career as a Major-General). Why should one have been on bad terms with such a man as this? The answer is very simple: Pugh was a 'lean' Colonel, a dedicated professional soldier and a very determined careerist: I, on the other hand, was simply an 'Emergency' Officer waiting to be demobbed and off to Cambridge. Pugh wanted to run an efficient Regiment (even if it was only Anti-Aircraft), to achieve a high standard of Gunnery, and to be rewarded with Command of a Brigade: I didn't give a damn for this alien unit and its beastly, noisy guns, and was not prepared to discommode myself in order to make a Brigadier of Lewis Pugh.

What made the situation a great deal worse was that Pugh, who soldiered 'by the book', strictly enforced a number of very irritating regulations which were intended to limit or abolish the traditional privileges of Officers in matters of discipline and dress. Thus we were forbidden to wear brown leather fur-lined gloves and made to wear the kind issued to the rank and file, nasty and austere garments of low-grade khaki wool. We were not allowed to carry riding whips but compelled to equip ourselves with mean little sticks of bamboo. We were never permitted to wear Service Dress or Forage Caps; we must appear on parade in the horrible rough Battle Dress of the period, with plebeian berets, dumping Ammunition Boots, and 'blancoed' belts and gaiters of a loathsome substance called 'webbing'.

In short, Pugh went a long way towards taking the fun out of being an Officer. I like to think that had he allowed me to cut just a bit of a figure, if

100

only in the item of the riding crop, I should have accorded him rather more loyalty, but on reflection I am inclined to doubt this: in many ways I was a very unpleasant piece of work at that age (nineteen and a half), idle, conceited, sluttish, self-opinionated, mean-spirited, and deliberately and maliciously obtuse in my refusal to see anyone else's point of view. As far as I was concerned, Pugh's Regiment of Ack-Ack was a dowdy washout, Pugh's efforts to improve it were both laughable and beside any possible point, and Pugh's professional prospects and ambitions were beneath contempt. I was even too perverse to admit that the tedious sumptuary ordinances on which he insisted, so far from being of his invention, were in fact the spiteful and typical emanations of the Left Wing Administration of the day.

I can only say, in defence of my bloodiness, that there were certain aspects of Pugh himself which invited disaffection. Excellent Officer and splendid man as he was, and as I now fully acknowledge that he was, at the same time he himself would have to admit that he did exercise his Officers and men both long and exigently, less for their good or the Army's than for the greater glory here on earth of Lewis Pugh. Despite the minimum of assistance from me, he achieved this: as a result of the exertions which he coaxed, nagged or bullied out the 77th Heavy Anti-Aircraft Regiment (RA) he went on and up to command a Brigade of Gurkhas, a coveted and honorific appointment. How very peculiar, then, of Major-General Pugh to omit, when he came to draw up his entry for *Who's Who*, any mention of the 77th, which was his immediate springboard to higher command. Every other appointment he ever held is listed; his extra-regimental tours of duty in India, his numerous postings within the Royal Horse Artillery or on to the Staff – all is precisely recorded save only for his stewardship of the dreary but for his purpose essential 77th Regiment of Heavy Anti-Aircraft Guns. Can it be that Lewis Pugh was a snob? I wrote to him a few years back to point out his omission and received a rather shifty reply, the purport of which was that he did not wish to hog too much space in the columns of *Who's Who*. Well…he was always, as I remarked a page or two ago, a modest man.

The person who first noticed that the General had omitted the 77th from his entry in *WW* was Conrad Dehn, just the sort of chap who always sniffs out such things, setting aside, as I believe, an hour or two every month to follow up the careers of his old acquaintance. He followed up Pugh's because he too served with the 77th as a Second Lieutenant, had indeed been there some months when I arrived in the later summer of 1947.

'Well, it's a bonus finding you here,' I said.

'I reciprocate the sentiment. And I have to tell you that I have checked up with Charterhouse, and find that you are now absolutely *bien vu* once more.'

'Good of you to take such an interest.'

'I was simply anxious to be able to give exact answers to the questions asked of me when they realised that a fellow Carthusian of mine was coming. I was able to report that you had been lost but were found again.'

'By which you meant precisely what?'

'That for one thing a movement is already in train to make you a member of the Old Carthusian Club; and that for another you will be invited to play cricket for the Friars next summer. They would probably have asked you this year if you had arrived back in England a little sooner.'

'Very gratifying. When am *I* to be notified of all this?'

'At any moment now.'

Conrad's intelligence service was always notably reliable. Within a few days I received a letter from the Secretary of the OC Club, another from the President of the Friars, and a third from the Secretary of the Butterflies Cricket Club, to all of which (thanks to the generous offices of Bob Arrowsmith) I had either been elected or recommended. The Butterflies required an entrance fee, which reminded me that funds were scant and it was time to think out a financial strategy that would procure me adequate exhibition for a dashing young Officer on Home Service. As Lewis Pugh was to decide many years later, there was no obligation, once away from Rolleston, to say much or indeed anything about one's appointment to Ack-Ack: simply to call myself a 'Gunner' would be both truthful and becoming. I might even let it drop that as a Gunner Officer I was deemed to be 'mounted' and was therefore entitled to spurs (even if these were not commonly worn with Battle Dress).

But in any event at all, I must put money in my purse. After some thought I caused the tenuous balance of pay at my disposal to be placed with the main branch of Lloyd's Bank in Cambridge, and then wrote to my maternal grandfather, who lived there and banked with this branch, asking him to have a word with the Manager and give me a favourable chitty. The kind old gentleman did exactly that, and what was more, as I had hoped, he paid a small sum into my Account as a 'Commissioning Present'. Best of all, he also told the Manager that he would be responsible for any amount by which I might overdraw the account, up to £100. This he did, as he told me in his letter, because he realised that junior subalterns were often subject to fortuitous calls on their resources (a very civil euphemism, I considered, for sudden bouts of vanity or lust): I was to understand, he wrote, that since I was under twenty-one the arrangement was unofficial and could be revoked by the Bank at a moment's notice; but he ventured to think that they would be reluctant to inconvenience his grandson. Would I please be certain not to tell my mother either about the overdraft or his present, as I would almost certainly remember how disagreeable she had made herself the last time he had given me money.

My resources, if I included the full amount of the overdraft, were now in the order of £130, in those days, when one could dine *en prince* for a pound, a very substantial sum. I was therefore able, despite the uncertain terms on which I stood with Colonel Pugh, to enjoy the dying summer on Salisbury Plain in easy and ample fashion. This did not go unremarked by the Colonel, who enquired of my Battery Commander what he knew of my finances. The Battery Commander, a good-natured drinking man, said that he understood I had 'family money' (as indeed I had put it about), on hearing which the Colonel rather reluctantly let the matter go at that...until, that is to say, the annoying affair of The Corps Headquarters Match.

What the 'Corps' was in this instance, whether a Corps of Artillery or an Infantry Corps to which we were somehow ancillary, I have long forgotten if ever I knew. All I can tell you now is that this Corps in some way comprehended 77 HAA Regiment, that it had a Headquarters which hung out at Uxbridge, and that this Headquarters had got up a cricket XI which came down to play us towards the end of that September (1947).

Now, Rolleston Balloon Camp, though a dreary place enough, had two pleasing features: a copse of elm trees at its centre, which was handy for country copulatives on the nights of Battery dances, and, about a stone's throw from the copse, a pretty little oval cricket ground. Matches were infrequent, as Lewis Pugh disliked ball games and bestowed such encouragement as he could muster on Association Football, because Soccer was the game which the men preferred and in those early days of Socialism this pernicious criterion was officially paramount and binding; but since it was Corps HQ that asked for a cricket fixture, Pugh was only too keen to set the thing up and even attended the game in person, as a rather significant Brigadier was playing for our opponents.

The match itself passed very agreeably. 77 Regiment managed the decent score of 172 (Raven 0, bowled first ball trying to hit it into the elms) and the opposition had made exactly the same when their last wicket fell to a brilliant catch at mid-on (not made by Raven). Everyone was pleased and excited by this sporting finish; the Brigadier, having made 63, was particularly happy, and so Lewis Pugh was particularly happy. After the game was over, there were 'informal drinks' by the Pavilion, of which non-commissioned ranks among the players were invited to partake, in order to demonstrate to the Brigadier what a true democrat was Lewis Pugh and how suitable for higher command in the egalitarian military climate which then obtained. So all was going as merry as a marriage with everyone present – except with me, who was

103

desperate to get away. I had arranged to dine with some woman at The Bustard, a lonely and lovely little inn which was set on the edge of the Ranges and provided imaginative meals for a few shillings. In order to meet my guest in the pub at 7.45 I must leave Rolleston at 7.30; it was now 7.10, and I was still unbathed and unchanged; yet I could not leave the party before the Brigadier, who was getting very jolly and showed no sign of moving.

In these tricky circumstances, I applied to my friend Second Lieutenant John Carson Parker (later just Carson).

'I've got a date,' I said, 'so I'm going to bolt through the copse and round to the Mess that way. If anyone asks where I am, tell him I've been urgently called to the telephone.'

'No one's come to call you.'

'They won't have been watching. Nobody will think of that – if you put your heart into the job.'

'They'll expect you back when you've finished.'

'Make it seem terribly serious, the sort of thing which would keep me for a long time. You might even hint that somebody was dying.'

'I shall do no such thing,' said John C-P righteously. 'It's bad luck to say that unless some one *is* dying, and the lie would be found out later on.'

'I only said "hint". No need to commit either of us to anything. You could say I had a sad look on my face when I went.'

'I've never known anyone look less sad. You look positively fatuous with self-satisfaction.'

This was probably true. The prospect of a good meal and a romp to follow gives all of us a bit of a gloss.

'For Christ's sake,' I said. 'It's what you make them *think* that counts. You hope to be an actor. God help you if you can't even pull this off.'

As I had hoped, he could not resist the challenge and undertook the task. I nipped behind the Pavilion, through the copse, into the Mess, in and out of a bath, and into a taxi by the Guard Room with seconds still to spare. One could do that sort of thing very swiftly when young, because one still thought women worth the effort. Though even then one was beginning to have doubts. When I arrived back at Rolleston that evening, I really could not imagine why I had put up with two hours of inane chatter about parties at Larkhill (my guest was a NAAFI manageress there, an improvement, however slight, on Mond's *galère* of the previous summer) simply to be allowed a ten minute fumble with stocking tops and damp bristle before being rather clumsily jerked off into one of my own handkerchieves…and this while standing up behind the NAAFI kitchens, as regulations forbade the admission of males into the NAAFI staffs quarters. But then if I had been allowed into her bed, I now reflected, it would probably have been much worse. If I'd done it ineptly (quite likely) I'd have felt a perfect bloody fool, and if I'd done it well she'd have wanted me to stay for another round. In either case I'd have been expected to listen to more inane chatter afterwards and possibly I'd have been required to say that I loved her. To *tristitia post coitum* would have been added *saeva indignatio*, for the difficulties of getting transport back to Rolleston after these delays would have been insuperable; I should have had to walk – a whole mile and a quarter. All in all, I congratulated myself, I had come off light with the loss of a handkerchief.

In my room John Carson Parker was waiting, along with Tony Hollis, now, like Conrad, a QC, in those days the most articulate and sardonic of all the anti-Pugh set.

'C-P's really gone and dished up the haggis,' Tony said.

'Dished up what?'

'It's your fault,' said C-P, 'you would insist that I did it.'

'Did *what*?'

'Tell that fib about your being called to the telephone.'

'So I *was* asked for?'

'Yes,' said Tony. 'I was introduced to the Brigadier because he'd been a childhood friend of my mother, God help the poor sod. Then it turned out that he'd had a dear little nephew at the OTS in Bangalore, and I was told to find you so that you could discourse on its delights to the jolly old uncle.'

'So Tony asked me where you were,' C-P took up the tale, 'and I said you'd been called to the telephone.'

'So I went back to the CO and the Brigger,' said Tony, 'and told them just that, whereupon there was a nasty little hush in the air (rather as if Baby had suddenly crapped himself while being shown to Granny for the first time) and then Pugh the Pong started to mizzle.'

'To mizzle?'

'To talk fery fin, like fis, wif his lips almost fhut. The upshot was that I was to get C-P over there p.d.q. to say his piece, about you and the telephone, in person.'

'Well?' I said to C-P after there had been silence for nearly a minute.

'I hardly know how to tell you this,' said C-P, and gurgled. 'You see, when I presented myself I'd made up my mind that I couldn't even hint at death or dying because such matters are not to be lightly spoken of. But I was determined to do my level best for you in any other way I could, so when the Pong said, "What's all this about Raven being wanted on the telephone?", I said, very seriously, "I'm afraid it's true, sir. Someone fetched him a few

105

minutes ago." I was scared he might take me up on the "someone" and want to know who, but his mind was working rather differently.

' "Doesn't Raven realise he's on parade?" he said.

' "Oh, not quite on parade," said the Brigadier, who seemed rather on your side.

' "Well, in the position of a host," said the Pong. "What do you know about all this, C-P?"

' "All I know, sir," I said, "is that he seemed very agitated. He muttered something like, 'Oh God, that again,' and took off very fast indeed."

' "Depend upon it, Pugh," said the Brigadier in a merry way, "it's either a dun or a woman. That's the trouble with being a subaltern: one is pestered morning, noon and night by Jews or women."

' "I wasn't," said the Pong.

' "I was once dunned on the Mess Lawn at Simla," said the Brigadier. "Fun to look back on but not so amusing at the time. God, it's marvellous being middle-aged," he said, and took a great suck at his glass, "no bloody Jews or women hanging about like vampire bats. Except the wife, of course, but she's just part of the bedroom furniture by now." '

'I'm beginning to like this Brigadier,' I said. 'Sporting type.'

'You won't be much in love with what's coming next,' said Tony with naked glee.

'I couldn't help it,' said C-P, 'it just slipped out.'

'What slipped out?'

'Well, the Pong wasn't very pleased with the Brigger's line of conversation, I suppose he thought it was setting a bad example; and at the same time he felt that though the Brigger wasn't at all put out by your absence, he couldn't just let it go at that; so what he tried to do was change the subject and close the whole matter, both in one go. "Just double over to the Mess, C-P," he said, firm but quite good-humoured, "and tell Raven not to take all night." And then to the Brigadier in a quick follow-on, "What about another drink, sir?" And the Brigger said, in a teasing way, "You are old enough, Lewis, to know that one never asks anyone to have 'another drink', even if he's had forty-nine already, but simply 'to have a drink'. Thank you very much, I don't mind if I do." It was then that it slipped out.'

'*What* slipped out?'

'Well, I was trying to kill time, you see – '

' – WHAT slipped out?'

'I shouldn't be in too much of a hurry to find out,' said Tony Hollis, 'not if I was you.'

106

'As I was saying,' said C-P, 'I was trying to kill time. I knew I shouldn't find you in the Mess, or that if I did you wouldn't thank me, so I was just trying to hang about, hoping that if it got late enough the Pong would think you weren't worth bothering about and not insist on my going to fetch you. And in order to have an excuse to hang about I busied myself with the matter of the Brigger's next drink. I beckoned to the waiter and said in my most smarmy way, "What will it be, sir?" "Pink gin and water." And I said, "Would you like to try a slight variation, sir? Peach bitters instead of angostura?" You know, I wanted to show the old place off a bit, show the Brigger that the 77th knew a thing or two, tirra lirra. But it was the most ghastly flop. Either his drink had suddenly turned sour on him – you know how it can on an empty stomach – or he was genuinely put out by the mention of peach bitters, but whichever it was he turned quite violent. "No I certainly would not," he said. "What's all this effeminate rubbish, peach bitters indeed, what's muck like that doing in your Mess?" So the Pong, remembering that I was Wines Member of the Mess Committee, said, "Well, C-P? What is this stuff doing here? This isn't the Ritz Bar, you know." He obviously thought it was rude of the Brigger to carry on like that when he was offered something special, and to judge from his tone he was trying to jolly the whole thing quietly off. But the Brigger wasn't on for being jollied off. "Answer up, boy," he yapped, "what do you want with that filth in your Mess? You'll be telling me next you sell scent." So I said, "Raven asked me to get it." "What did *he* want with it?" "He said he always liked a quiet glass of gin and peach bitters in the middle of the morning, sir. Sometimes he liked half a bottle of Champagne, he said, but since this Regiment was too dowdy to stock Champagne, Raven said – "

' – What in God's name were you thinking of?'

'I don't know,' wailed C-P. 'Once I'd started I just couldn't stop. I was kind of mesmerised by the awful look on the Brigger's face, and I heard myself going on and on and on.'

'Tell him the rest,' said Tony. 'You've got as far as "since this Regiment was too dowdy – "

' " – Since this Regiment was too dowdy to stock Champagne, Raven said," I said, "he would have to make do with what he could get, which was gin, and would I mind getting in a bottle of peach bitters, as angostura was such wretched stuff, strictly for clownish Majors, and if any snooping middle-class Artillery Officer complained about it, we could always annoy him by telling him they had a bottle in the Horse Gunners' Mess in Larkhill." "It strikes me," said the Brigger, clutching his glass so tight I thought it was going to shatter in his hand, "that I've heard this name Raven once too often for one evening. He sounds just the conceited sort of bloody young rotter who calls one 'Brigadier' instead of 'sir'. From the smell of him," said the Brigger (the drink had really hit his tripes by now), "that interminable telephone call is almost certainly from a bookie he's welshed on or a tart he's given a dose of clap. I want you to investigate Raven and his money, Pugh, and let me know, personally, what you find out." He swallowed his new drink in one and shook all over as if there'd been an earthquake in his belly. "And now, good night," he said, and stumped off followed by the Pong, who started to mizzle but then thought better of it, and shut his mouth up like a rat trap.'

In this subsequent event, Lewis Pugh was a brick. I think he thought that the Brigadier had carried on in a thoroughly disreputable fashion, and that all his boasting about his yeasty youth disqualified him from complaining about any extravagance of mine. What was in any case beyond question was that the Brigger had been a rotten guest, drinking too much and talking too big, then turning nasty and leaving in pretty poor style. All these considerations inclined Pugh to let me down as light as he could, though the Brigger's instruction to investigate me would have to be attended to in some sort. The course Colonel Lewis adopted was the mild one of writing to my parents and telling them he was slightly worried because I appeared to spend more money than most young Officers of my standing; but since he had yet to receive any complaints of me from tradesmen or others (he wrote) he was perfectly prepared to assume that I was in fact living within my means if they (my parents) would confirm that these (my means) included a certain amount of private money.

On receiving this letter, my parents for once behaved rather well. Up to a point, that is. My father wrote at once to the Pong and saved my face by informing him that I did indeed have some private money (technically true, since Granny Raven had left me £100 in the Post Office Savings Bank, to be mine when I was twenty-one), but that I was apt, like many young men, to be – well – rather too generous with it. If Pugh would gently caution me, my father would be most grateful. Gently cautioned by Pugh I then was – by Pugh at his best, who said that if ever I *should* be in trouble about money I should come immediately to him, and that provided I told the whole truth and told it promptly, he would see me through somehow. It was one of a Commanding Officer's duties, he told me – like preventing his young Officers from making rash or discreditable marriages.

So far so good – until I was written to by my mother. I was a bloody little fool, my mother said, showing myself off like this, but since the Colonel said there had been no complaints, she assumed that I had really got hold of some money. Where from, she wanted to know. I wrote that I had had a couple of very lucky bets at Salisbury Races. My mother wrote again to say that if I went on gambling like this I should certainly ruin myself, and she knew whom to blame for it all: my Grandfather in Cambridge (who had been a cavalryman and remained a keen race-goer ever since, never missing meetings at Newmarket or Huntingdon). He had encouraged me, hadn't he? Although I wrote at once to exonerate the old gentleman, my mother's perfectly sound instinct, that my grandfather was somehow at the bottom of my affluence, was not to be gainsaid. Once again, as I heard much later, she leapt to the telephone and bawled the poor old fellow out for his senile and interfering propensity to encourage me in my 'silly, independent habits'.

IX

LIGHT BLUE

But of that I only learned some nine months later, while dining with my Grandfather after I had come up to Cambridge as a freshman. I arrived in King's at the beginning of July, 1948; for the manner was, at that time, to encourage ex-soldiers to keep the Long Vacation Term which preceded the start of their first year proper at Michaelmas. In this way, it was thought, they would learn at leisure to exchange a military habit of thought for an academic one. In fact all they did was loaf around and drink too much...and occasionally play cricket in Long Vacation Matches got up by the College or the Crusaders.

In these days, I am told, most Colleges have trouble in raising a proper XI to play any game, even during Full Term. It is certainly known, by all club secretaries in the kingdom, that to make a fixture with a College team is to risk being grievously let down, very often without the smallest warning or the faintest offer of apology, since the young, in their widely proclaimed wisdom, consider that to keep appointments is servile and to apologise for breaking them is hypocritical. In 1948, however, King's had no difficulty in fielding a goodish XI in July and August, and a series of agreeable fixtures was arranged which included a game against one of the junior XIs at 'our sister College' at Eton. This would occur in late July, just before Eton broke up for the summer. We would hire a bus (which had recently become possible again despite continued rationing of petrol), arrive in time for an early luncheon, play till 7 p.m. and drift home by easy stages, at one of which we would dine by prior arrangement.

Since the day was intended to celebrate the Concordia Amicabilis between King's and Eton, we would normally be accompanied by a pair of senior dons, one of whom, in 1948, was Professor Frank (later Sir Frank) Adcock, the Ancient Historian. Aside from being a distinguished and eloquent scholar, 'Adders' was noted for his acumen as a code-breaker (1914, I fancy, rather than 1939), for academic intrigue of Machiavellian subtlety and nugatory import, for the rarity and sparseness of his entertainments, and for cheating at golf. He also patted a succulent undergraduate bottom from time to time, but never went further than that. Since he was an old acquaintance of my father, whose bottom he had pinched and whose golf ball he had trodden on twenty-five years before, during reading parties on the Norfolk coast, he summoned me to sit next to him in the bus.

'Your faver tells me you are extwavagant, dear boy,' was his opening service.

'I like to do things properly, sir, if I do them at all.'

'Very well: we must decide what things you can afford to do pwoperly on your allowance. I shall not be so impertinent as to ask you what this is: I shall merely hazard a guess that you have at your command, what wiv gwants, scholarships, et cetewa, et cetewa, some Four Hundred Pounds a year.'

Nosy old brute, he was dead right.

'On four hundred a year,' the Professor continued, 'you can afford Cwicket, Golf, Woyal Tennis and Fives wever Wugby or Eton. You cannot afford to hunt –'

' – I have no intention of hunting, sir –'

' – Don't interwupt. And you cannot afford to dine out more than fwee times a term. You can afford ale in Hall but not claret or burgundy, except on alternate Sundays and your birfday, and you can never drink Champagne unless it is somebody else's. Do I make myself plain?'

'Admirably plain, sir.'

'Nor can you smoke cigars,' said the Professor, 'indulge in Fine Editions, or Spode China, purchase Oil Paintings to decorate your wall, or keep a mistwess.' He nudged me roguishly. 'Ha, ha,' he ejaculated.

So the bit about a mistress was a joke. He then told me a story about an undergraduate who *had* kept a mistress, many years before. She had been, in sound tradition, a tobacconist's daughter, and the undergraduate had set her up in an apartment near the station. Being zealous for his good name, she insisted that he attended all his lectures and made a conscientious effort at all his exercises, and would never grant him her favours until she had seen his proses or whatever written out in a fair round hand, all ready to be punctually presented the next day. As a result of this and against all the betting, the undergraduate obtained First Class Honours in both parts of the Classical Tripos and was awarded a Fellowship of his College. Out of admiration and gratitude he now married the tobacconist's daughter; but since in those days a don who married, unless he was Head of a College, forfeited his Fellowship, they kept the marriage a secret. The young woman continued in her apartment near the station, while the new Fellow kept up the same routine which he had observed as an undergraduate, spending much of the day with his wife, as she now was, but dining and sleeping in College. She made him take the same pains with his work as she had demanded before his elevation, was so exigent in fact that eventually he became Master of his College.

Although it was now permitted to him to marry a wife and bring her to live in the Master's Lodge, he could not admit to having married years before and so to having breached the statutes. They therefore arranged a second marriage in the College Chapel, passing it off as their first. But alas, the tradesman's daughter had tradesmen's manners: from now on, instead of advancing his career by her secret exertions she jeopardised it by her public ineptitudes. The Master, who by now had his eye fixed on the Vice-Chancellorship, found the situation intolerable: he wanted his wife out of the way, yet such were the bonds of habit and affection that he could not bear to live without her.

So at last he put it about that his wife must go into another county to care for her ailing mother, and in fact sent her back to the apartment near the station – a manoeuvre which, to do the good woman full justice, she did not at all resent, indeed appeared, to the surprise of her husband, positively to welcome. Thus the years went on and the Master was at last inducted as Vice-Chancellor – only to be arrested, as he was escorted out of the Senate House by the Esquire Bedells after the ceremony, on a charge of bigamy: for whereas he thought he had married the same woman twice, he had in fact married, one at a time, two identical twin sisters, who had taken turn and turn about with him without revealing each other's existence. This deception, the Professor concluded, had been much easier to practice when he was absent from his 'wife' for long periods in each twenty-four hours, and hence the good humour with which she/they consented to be exiled from the Master's Lodge back to the apartment by the station.

'But sir,' I objected, 'it's only in Shakespeare or Menander that twins are absolutely identical; and even if these two had been, there must have been – well – observable differences in their intimate responses.'

'Quite wight, dear boy,' said the Professor. 'This is my test story for undergraduates new to my acquaintance. An undergraduate who believes it I write off as a cretin; an undergraduate who effects to believe it I designate a sycophant; but an undergraduate who, like you, raises rational or empirical objection I regard as being, *in posse* at least, an Intelligent and Honest Young Gentleman. Your only mistake was this: you should not have gone beyond the first part of your refutation, admirably decorated as it was with literary reference. By raising the question of intimate behaviour, you revealed yourself as "Knowing" without necessarily being correct. Have you sound biological warranty for what you say? Is it *impossible* that two twin sisters should conduct themselves indistinguishably under the same masculine stimulus?'

With such conjectures, and with many more tales (true ones now, or so he promised me) of dons who slept in coffins or rode tricycles or translated the whole of Shakespeare into Latin Iambic Trimeters or forgot to change their gear for two decades on end – with such matter did the adorable Professor Adcock (chubby and pink, bouncing about in his seat like a bungy children's ball) beguile the road to Windsor. What a splendid day I'm having, I thought, as we disembarked near College – little knowing what the afternoon had in store for me.

The first surprise which the afternoon sprung was the arrival of the Provost (of King's, not Eton).

There was, in the Cambridge of those days, a celebrated chauffeur called Mears, to whom the regulations about petrol rationing did not apparently apply and who would hire out himself and his Rolls Royce to take one anywhere from Trumpington to Timbuctoo. Him the Provost had engaged on impulse to ply from Cambridge to Eton that summer's day, and from his Rolls, looking seventy-five but in fact barely turned sixty, complete with wing collar, black boots, Master's gown and mortar board, the Provost now emerged to issue his celebrated benediction, 'Bless you, dear boys. Bless you one and all.'

While the cricketers stood in reverence, he doddered over the ground and across the middle of the wicket, disappeared behind a tree on the far side, coyly peeped out round it, gaily tossed his flowing grey locks, whisked back behind it, was still for a good ten minutes, then doddered back (fly parted to reveal much woolly white pant) by the same route, frequently pausing to acknowledge imaginary salutations or applause by waving his silver-topped cane in the air.

Two senior masters, who had been his contemporaries at King's, now took him in hand, and the match was allowed to continue. Our side, having lost the toss but been sent in to bat first, had made 35 runs for no wicket, the bowling was humdrum and the pitch was easy, the trees rustled and the doves murmured, the Pax Etoniana reigned over all...when this very English afternoon was suddenly disrupted by the following events, each one quite harmless by itself but the series quite appalling in its ultimate issue.

The first thing which happened was that a wicket fell.

I then walked in to bat.

As I was taking guard, Professor Adcock, who had been on some mission to the Library, came whizzing along from the direction of the School buildings and paused to watch me take my first ball.

Before this could be bowled, the Provost, who was walking round the ground with the two senior masters, came to a halt dead in front of the sight screen, started an oration about something or other with many gestures and even a certain amount of prancing, and either did not understand or would not heed his companions' admonition that he was standing behind the bowler's arm and thus obstructing the course of play.

The umpire at the bowler's end waved politely to the Provost in an attempt to move him on.

The Provost, who took this as a greeting, interrupted himself to wave back and then resumed his discourse.

A very presentable boy, who was fielding on the long on boundary, ran up to the Provost, took off his pretty cap, folded it, held it in front of him with both hands, and requested the Provost to walk a few steps to his left or his right and thus enable play to proceed.

The Provost handed his cane to one of the masters, seized the boy's two hands (and cap) in both of his own, and went on with his oration, which now turned out to be a speech from the *Iliad* in which Achilles laments the dead Patroclos.

The boy, who had been commendably bred, stood still and listened.

Professor Adcock, who was losing patience, cupped his hands round his mouth and called, 'Pway stand aside, Pwovost. You are impeding the pwotagonists.'

This the Provost ignored and went on pumping out Greek Hexameters.

I myself, having taken guard and being all keyed up to begin, said to the bowler and to the umpire at the bowling end, 'Never mind the Provost. Let's get on with it.'

The umpire assented and the bowler walked back.

The boy who was detained by the Provost, seeing that despite everything play was about to begin again, tried to back himself off, only to find that the Provost had him tight; all the boy's effort achieved was a slight movement of the pair of them which brought them from behind the boundary line and a foot or two on to the ground itself.

The two masters had meanwhile slunk away, trying to pretend that nothing was happening.

114

Professor Adcock, who was by now beside himself with annoyance at these irregularities, bounced up and down twice, then shot across the ground towards the Provost.

Since his route would take him some yards clear of the actual square, he was ignored by the players.

The bowler reached his mark, turned and began his run.

The Provost gushed with lachrymose Greek.

The boy with the pretty cap made no further attempt to escape.

The bowler bowled, a medium paced ball which was quite well up to me.

I put my foot down the wicket and struck the ball on the lift, hard and high, straight over the bowler's head.

Professor Adcock came up to the Provost from his flank, made to hustle him away from the sight screen, and startled him both into silence and into releasing the boy, who dropped his cap, turned adroitly and caught the ball with his left hand high over his head, his feet being perhaps a yard inside the boundary, a fair and splendid catch if ever there was.

But a catch that he should never have been able to make. If the Provost had not secured him, he would have been away at long on instead of being straight behind the bowler, and the ball would have sailed over the boundary for six. Or again, if Professor Adcock had not interfered, the Provost would have held the boy fast, and the ball would have passed over their heads by a clear yard – for six. Or yet again, if those two masters hadn't been so wet, they would have moved the Provost on, whether before or after he had secured the boy did not matter, and the ball would have gone unhindered – for six.

All this passed through my mind in the space of about one second, after which, maddened that such ill luck should have attended so seigneurial a stroke, 'CLITORIS,' I howled as I turned to walk away from the wicket.

There was a long and serious silence, not because I had been foul-tongued but because I had betrayed the code which we were all there to honour: I had shown bad sportsmanship.

Nor was that the end of my misfortunes. A little while later, as I sat down red in the face with shame and disappointment among the other members of my side, Professor Adcock came scooting up, tapped me on the shoulder and worried me away to one side. Then he informed me that the Provost, who was apt to interpret anything which might occur solely in relation to himself, was convinced that I had been swearing directly at him.

'It is imprudent,' said Adders, 'to call one's Provost by the name of a low physiological organ.'

'I didn't mean –'

'– Of course you didn't, dear boy. But he thinks you did.'

115

'How can I make him understand?'

'You can admit and apologise for your deleterious manners, but then explain that you were addressing fate and not the Provost of King's. If he believes you, he will hold your hand. If not, he will pretend to be deaf.'

In the event he did both. I muttered and stuttered for five minutes without receiving a word of reply or a single sigh of comprehension. At the end of my dismal recitation the Provost merely pressed my hand and then released it, which I took as a token of dismissal.

'So what does all that mean?' I said to Adders in the bus on the way home. Adders looked grave.

'It means,' he said, 'that he finds you personable and will take no immediate action; but also that you are by no means forgiven. You are under suspended sentence. Not an auspicious beginning to your career in the College.'

For a while at least I was careful to do nothing that might bring down the Damocleian sword on my head. I minded my book and my good fortune in being where I was, and in return was civilly treated, if somewhat obliquely regarded, by all the dons I had to do with. As the Dean of Discipline remarked a fortnight later: 'You seem to be settling in rather well – if only you would forget you were once an Officer.'

'Why should I? I'm not ashamed of it. Rather the reverse.'

'It's your manner. You march round the place as if you were expecting to be saluted.'

'Only by the college servants,' I smirked.

The Dean sighed.

'We do not distinguish here,' the Dean said, 'between ex-Officers and ex-Privates.'

'Do you mean, you actually accept ex-Privates?'

In those days that was my idea of a joke.

'Sooner or later,' the Dean said, 'you are going to annoy somebody here – not me, I think, but somebody – very much indeed. And then look out for trouble.'

How right he was to prove.

'This College,' the Dean continued, 'is the most tolerant in the kingdom. But like all highly tolerant institutions, or people, it can turn spiteful and vindictive over very minor misdemeanours if these offend against its particular fads. The fad here, with most of 'em, is equality. Think that one out. Now off you go and have a good time.'

I had come to him for a four-day Exeat, as I was going down to Charterhouse to play my first matches for the Friars. Bob Arrowsmith had invited me to stay with him in his lodgings in Pepperharrow Road, where we had pints of small ale for breakfast instead of tea or coffee.

'Rossall Wanderers today,' said Bob, and drained his tankard, 'watch out for Cyril Thackley.'

'What about him?'

'He's a cracking shit, that's what about him.'

Then we walked up Charterhouse Hill to Green.

Cyril Thackley was an Old Rossallian who had been a very fair cricketer as a schoolboy and had then, as an undergraduate player in the Cambridge of the early forties, achieved far higher place than he would have done in time of peace. For Thackley was a wartime Blue, and that just about summed the man up. He didn't smell right. Excused military service in order to read science, he stayed away from lectures and laboratories to play cricket, along with the conscientious objectors and sufferers from asthma, bed-wetting or flat feet who were likewise deferred or exempt. They were a rotten crowd and played the wretched sort of cricket one might have expected of them. I know, having watched it with my Grandfather at Fenner's in 1941 and '42.

'This lot needs a Drill Serjeant,' my Grandfather said, 'they can't even clean their pads properly.'

Nevertheless they were allowed to award themselves things which they called 'Blues' and to wear special haberdashery in celebration thereof, and on the strength of his, Thackley, who emerged from Cambridge three times 'capped' and with a bad third in the Natural Philosophy Tripos, had presumed to write a book about how to teach the game at school and university level. Thackley, in short, knew the lot.

To be strictly fair, he could bat to a very decent club standard and could well have kept wicket for a Minor County, if any such would have had him. This particular day on Green he was keeping for the Rossall Wanderers (who had lost the toss and been sent into the field) with accuracy and panache.

'Showing off,' said Bob, who was sitting with me by the scoreboard. 'You can always tell a really good wicketkeeper. He's the one you don't notice at all. As Pericles said of women, a wicketkeeper should be noticed neither for good nor ill.'

'I thought it was "spoken of neither for good nor ill".'

'Here comes Uncle Irvine. He'll tell us.'

But the Uncle said he could not remember, which was annoying as I knew I was right. I also knew he was holding out on me, as he did not approve of the confutation by the young of their elders. However, in all other ways he was exceedingly genial and very anxious to hear about King's.

117

'Have you come across Patrick Wilkinson yet?' he wanted to know.

Patrick (L P) Wilkinson was at that time Tutor of King's; he also taught and wrote about the Classics. He was, I had been told, an Old Carthusian, but beyond this I knew nothing more of him than I had learned from a five-minute courtesy call, most of which he had passed in instructing me how interesting I should find the black students from Africa and the white ones from the working class.

'Typical of Patrick,' said the Uncle when I told him this now. 'He's always had these left-wing hankerings and he's always tried to ram them straight down everybody else's throat. He's a good scholar, and he writes very perceptively about Latin poetry, but he's a ghastly Socialist bore. He *won't* leave it alone, you'll find. He wasn't just suggesting you should get to know the blacks and soon, he was telling you for your own good – which is Socialist lingo for commanding.'

A wicket fell: my turn to bat.

'I shall open a bottle of my Taylor '35 for you,' said Bob, 'if you can manage to annoy or discommode Cyril Thackley while you are out there.'

'How am I to do that?'

'My dear Shimon (*sic*),' said the Uncle, 'Remember your Tully [Cicero]. If you want to get best of shomebody, "*id quo superbit temnendum…*belittle that of which he has conceit."'

Which was what, more or less and by sheer accident, I did. For it chanced that the first three balls I received were all quickish deliveries, on a good length, just outside the leg stump. In each case I moved my left foot across in an effort to sweep the ball, in each case I missed it, and in each case I also blocked Thackley's view, so that he did not see, until too late, that the ball was turning very sharply to the leg. All three balls, then, went spurting past his left-hand glove to the boundary, which meant that he had given away 12 runs in byes inside three minutes, a very terrible thing to happen even to the most moderate of wicketkeepers. After the first boundary-bye he muttered, after the second he banged his gloves together, and after the third he came round the wicket to accost me.

'You may not know it,' he said, 'but in this class of cricket one does not deliberately mask the ball from the wicketkeeper.'

'I've played three perfectly fair strokes, and missed. What happened then was entirely your affair. If you're not happy, you could always try standing back.'

He mouthed and moved back behind the wicket. In those days wicketkeepers, particularly amateur ones, took great pride in *not* standing back except to the very fastest of bowling. I could hear Cyril grating away behind the stumps and muttering to himself about 'ignorance', a word he apparently used in its lower-class connotation of 'rudeness' or 'bad manners'. Then he lowered himself on to his hunkers to prepare for the next ball. So far from standing back, he nearly had his nose in my pocket.

The bowler sent down the next, a good length ball outside the off stump. I swished hopefully and got a very thin edge.

'How's that?' bawled Cyril, as he took the catch neatly in his gloves.

'Not,' rapped George Geary, who was umpiring at the bowler's end. 'Over ball.'

Perhaps it was such a thin edge that George didn't hear the snick, or perhaps he felt that he owed me something from the occasion when he had so harshly shattered my dream of playing for the Southern Schools at Lord's. In either case, there I still was, and there, by the Laws of Cricket, I was fully entitled to stay.

Not in Cyril's view. Before proceeding to the other end, he stuck his face into mine and said, 'A gentleman would have walked.'

'And so I would have,' I said disingenuously, 'if you hadn't appealed so quickly. As it was, you asked for a decision and got it, leaving me no choice but to abide by it.'

'So you admit you were out,' he snarled. 'It's not to late to go.'

'Yes it is. It would make George Geary look a perfect bloody fool, if I walked out now after he'd given me "not".'

'Rotten sportsmanship.'

'Look,' I said, 'I've been given out often enough when I wasn't and gone with a good grace. Now, just for once, it's worked the other way, and I'm damn well going to make the best of it. Principle of rough justice.'

The statement was morally sound (or so I have always considered) but factually misleading; for whenever I had been given out and thought I wasn't, I had gone with the worst possible grace and on one occasion I had thrown my bat through the (closed) Pavilion window.

Cyril went very red.

'If a gentleman knows he's out, he goes whatever the circumstances,' he said, and stalked away to the other end.

It was now clear to me that I had an excellent chance of drinking Bob's Taylor '35 that evening; but in order to clinch the matter Thackley must be goaded into some gesture clearly visible from the boundary. A red face and muttered insult, audible by me alone, were not enough. But Thackley was now out of close range and perhaps already cooling off; whatever action I took must be immediate and also effective over a distance of nearly thirty yards.

Seeing the batsman at the other end leave the first ball of the new over, 'WAIT,' I called very loudly as soon as the ball was in Thackley's gloves.

The next ball was also left.

'WAIT,' I shouted as Thackley gathered the ball, cleanly but with a conceited flourish.

By God's grace, the batsman played forward to the next and missed it.

'WAIT,' I yelled as soon as the ball was past him.

And Thackley, falling victim, as it were, to my propaganda, coming to believe that he might, as the loud call of 'WAIT' implied that he might, fumble the ball and give away a run, or if not believing it at least beginning to be nervous on that score – Thackley, I say, worn down by the repetition of the infuriating monosyllable, did indeed fumble the ball and give away a run, which brought me to this end.

'Another bye,' I said.

'*DAMN YOU*,' bellowed Thackley in a voice that carried to Godalming or at any rate to Bob and the Uncle on the boundary, '*DAMN YOU TO HELL*.'

Bob was as good as, indeed much better than, his word. He was so pleased that he produced the reigning Prince of all Port Wines – Taylor 1927.

The next occasion on which I drank Taylor '27 was in King's, at Founder's Feast on December 6 of this same year. I shall presently give some account of that festivity, for I suspect that Founder's Feast is now no longer what it was, and besides, some very important things happened to me at that particular one. First, however, and as a necessary preface, I must go back to some events of the preceding autumn.

Running true to the form of which Uncle Irvine had warned me, our Old Carthusian Tutor, Patrick Wilkinson, had indeed behaved like a 'ghastly Socialist bore'. I remain to this day very fond of Patrick, of whom I have grateful memories and whom, both as author and teacher, I have always enjoyed and respected; but there can be, I fear, no doubt about it: Patrick when his pink hat was on could nag a man into his coffin.

'Your Buttery bill,' he said to me in mid-November, 'is well over sixty pounds already. How can you hope to pay it?'

'That's my business,' I said.

'Don't be insolent.'

'I'm not being insolent, Tutor. The bill will fall due early next January. Correct?'

He nodded.

'By that time, Tutor, I shall be twenty-one. Of age. Entitled and expected to run my own money affairs. A task that will be all the easier for me as I shall have come into a legacy.'

Patrick's mouth drooped in displeasure. I don't know which he disliked more – the idea of my inheriting money or the plain fact that he had just been very soundly drubbed on points. In the matter of money he, of course, was to have the last laugh: my 'legacy' was Granny Raven's £100 in the Post Office Saving Bank; and my finances would be in incurable disorder before the next May was out. But that was still some months away and in any case Patrick could not be aware of it. For all he knew, I might be about to inherit tens of thousands. Undeniably humiliated on the one front, then, he changed his axis and attacked on another.

'I notice,' he said, 'that you spend all your time with old public school boys – and most of it with Etonians. I did indicate to you, when you arrived last summer, that you might find other and more interesting company.'

'A matter of taste,' I said.

'It makes for bad feeling in the College,' said Patrick, 'if there is a set of rich young men who lead a privileged and luxurious life – who *conspicuously* lead such a life – and ignore those who are worse off than themselves.'

'We don't ignore anybody and are perfectly civil to everybody. It's just that there are some people whom we do not seek out.'

'Exactly. You do not ask them to your parties and so on. They feel left out.'

'If one is to ask the entire College to one's parties, you would have even more cause for complaint about the size of one's Buttery bill.'

'The refreshments could be of a humbler kind and thus more widely distributed. What I really deprecate is the style of your entertainments… champagne being delivered to your rooms by the crate. It is that sort of thing which causes resentment.'

'Could you mean "envy", Tutor?'

'Justifiable resentment. A legitimate sense of grievance.'

'There was a time when both "resentment" and "grievance" were considered to be ugly words denoting mean and ugly reactions. Now, you tell me, they are "justifiable" and "legitimate". You will be telling me next, Tutor, that they are positively virtuous.'

'You must understand. This College will tolerate almost anything except assumptions of social superiority.'

I remembered the warning which the Dean of Discipline had given me the previous August. Like all tolerant institutions, he had said, King's had its fads against which one offended at one's peril. 'The fad here, with most of 'em, is equality.' And, earlier in our conversation, 'Sooner or later you are going to annoy somebody here very much indeed.' Now it had happened: I had offended against the fad of equality and had annoyed Patrick Wilkinson, to judge from the look of him, to a point not far short of actual rage. Ah well, I thought: in for a penny in for a pony [£25], a saying current among the smart set at the time.

'No one is assuming superiority,' I said, 'it is simply a matter of realities. Either one has the money to spend on these things or one has not.'

How often was I to remember these words and blush at them when I looked back from the shiftless penury of my future to the fraudulent affluence of my past. It is typical of the generous spirit which, at bottom, informed all Patrick's actions (however tiresome) that he never, at any stage of my subsequent financial disintegration, threw this remark back in my face.

'*If* one has such money,' he said now, 'it should be spent on other more worthwhile things than champagne and smoked salmon. It should be spent, at any rate, without vulgar public display. Perhaps it should not be spent at all. There is every hope that a Socialist Government will sooner or later see to that.'

'If there's one thing I loathe,' I said, 'it is Socialism. "A" and "B" getting together to decide what "C" should do about "x". Interference and spite disguised and excused by sanctimonious drivel.'

I thought so then and I think so now.

'You,' said Patrick, 'are a thoroughly selfish young man.'

He was right then and he is right now, though, alas, I am no longer young.

'There are two kinds of selfishness,' I said, 'doing what one wants to do; and making other people do what one wants to do, or wants *them* to do. The first kind, relatively harmless and venial, is mine. The second, self-righteous and dictatorial, is the driving force behind all forms of tyranny, the smelliest of which are Nazism and Communism – with Socialism a very close third.'

How long we would have gone on bickering in this imbecile fashion, I do not know. At this stage, however, Noël Annan, the Assistant Tutor, came in to drop off a file, and I was able to escape.

I walked down to the Cam to think over my discussion with Patrick. One thing was certain, I thought: whatever the rights or wrongs of his moral and social criticisms, his initial and financial enquiries were dead on target; as far as money went I was going to be found wanting. Granny Raven's hundred quid (plus thirty odd in accumulated interest) was already heavily mortgaged against my twenty-first birthday on December 28. True, there would also be substantial presents, and what with one thing and another I should definitely be able to settle the current term's College account as well as the tradesmen; but after that the prospects for 1949 were exceedingly bleak, offering a choice between amendment of life and abuse of credit, the latter of which could lead only to humiliation and even expulsion.

While I was pondering the choice and opting for abuse of credit (after all, something might turn up), my name was called from behind and Noël Annan came spinning up on his bicycle.

'What on earth,' he said, dismounting with the grace of a ballet dancer and the aplomb of a High Court Judge, 'what on earth have you done to Patrick? He is fizzing, my dear, but fizzing with fury.'

I told him what had passed.

'As to money,' said Noël, 'I never discuss it…my own or anybody else's. Your money, like your choice of friends, is of course a personal matter. But when we come to this question of ostentation, Patrick has a point. Oh dear me, yes: Patrick has a point.'

'Because Patrick is steward, shall there be no more cakes and ale?'

'Cakes and ale in plenty, my dear; but not rare vintages, prodigally consumed in a spirit of exhibition.'

'More discreetly consumed then?'

'Although there are no sumptuary laws here, Simon, there is a certain degree of sumptuary custom. You see, however much discretion you practise in the consumption of delicacies, *some* people, e.g. the College servants and the clerks who make up the accounts, are bound to know what you are up to. They are faced with the spectacle of a young man one half their age who spends on an evening's entertainment more money than they can earn in a month.'

'The wine is in the cellar. It has to be drunk.'

'And so it will be. At College Feasts, or by the elders of the College, men furnished with ability and some reputation, in whom the servants expect and even respect a certain amplitude of habit. My point is that they do not expect it in you, and it is unmannerly of you to thrust your extravagance in their faces. Hence the "sumptuary custom" which I mentioned just now. It does not operate by rule. It does not enjoin on you, as an undergraduate, that you shall have one bottle, no more, of this, and of that you shall have none at all. It is, let us say, a quiet prayer for decency and moderation.'

I was impressed by this, though I had forgotten it long before my next visit to the College Buttery.

'And of course,' said Noël, 'if you really want to revel in expensive luxuries, you can always go out to do so. Restaurants and so on.'

'Thus surely offending the servants *there*.'

'No. They do not know you and you do not know them. Not seriously. But the servants and clerks of the College do know you, and will for three years, perhaps much longer. They are *of* the College as surely as you are, though in a different way. They are part of the family. They must be treated with a kindness and respect that match their loyalty and love.'

'All right,' I said. 'I'll try to cut down on gin and champers.'

I wish I had.

'You might also try passing the word, with the reasons I have given, among your friends. Talking of whom, let me make a suggestion. Although I said just now that your choice of friends is entirely a personal matter, I nevertheless opine that it would be politic in you, after this morning's work, to please Patrick and get him back on your side by occasional association with the – er – less upper crust members of the College, or perhaps with one of the – er – Africans. What about Nikkai Urnandi, from the Gold Coast? Yes,' Noël said, tilting his face to the heavens as if giving thanks for his inspiration, 'Nikkai Urnandi is just the ticket. He has a passion for Trollope, like you; he's very nice looking in his way; and he is, I vouch for it, a thoroughly amusing fellow to talk to. Besides,' said Noël, as he remounted his bike with the elegance of a guardee and the precision of a gymnast, 'Nikkai is a gentleman in his own country and has quite a generous allowance, so you will probably find him preferable to some skulking son of toil with a Brumagen accent.'

If I first spoke to Nikkai Urnandi in furtherance of Noël's suggested policy of pleasing Patrick, I very soon came to relish his company entirely for its own sake. He once told me that there had been among his ancestors a famous professional storyteller who had lost his head for talking his way into one Royal bed too many. Nikkai certainly inherited his gift, though he did not use it to obtain the entrée to high class beds as these were open to him already. Of all the tales he told me, walking by the river or drinking coffee or on the way to or from lectures, the following has always been my favourite, not only for its substance but also because it was the indirect cause, as you will see, of my making some meetings which were to have an important effect on my immediate future and indeed on my whole life.

'My bedmaker says,' said Nikkai one winter's evening, 'that these coal fires we have are going to be replaced by gas during the summer, so that this is the last winter of coal in King's. "Aiaia, aiai," I told her, "I like your English coal fires." But she is very happy, she says, as she will no longer have to clean out the grates, which is her most hated task.

'What is so dreadful about the grates?' I asked. 'To clean out a grate is surely better than to empty the washing basins and the chamber pots?'

' "Oh, they can keep the jerries as long as they like," she said, "I don't mind a little piddle. I always amuse myself by imagining the cocks it came out of.

124

Young Mr Bruce's downstairs," she said, "it's as clear as a mountain stream. Just think of that spurting out of his lovely strong young doings. Yum, yumety-yum." '

'Well, this recalled to me the sad story of Joy my lady Jollif the wife of an English man of business in Lagos some while back. Aiaia, aiai, the Jollifs are now shamed and gone, and if you listen you will learn why; but five years ago they were a power in our land, for my lor' Jollif was a mighty merchant and bounteous with his gain – of which he lavished much gold on the Gold Coast Cricket Club, whereof he was called the Captain, though the season had now long passed when he could actually disport himself upon the pitch.

'Now as you know, my dear friend, we blacks can make good cricketers, but somehow there is not the same love of the game among us in Gold Coast as there is, say, in Cape Town or Port of Spain. So the people who were playing for the Gold Coast Cricket Club were mostly white. But of course all the ground staff and the bearers in the Pavilion were Africans, and so was the Club Scorer – who was I, Nikkai Urnandi. For I had been selected by the Headmaster from among all the boys of my school at the behest of my lor' Jollif, who had said to the Headmaster, "Find me one smart little nigger boy, to cast up the figures at our matches." So the Headmaster found me, and in return for a little money and my tiffin and my tea I would sit all day, when there was a match, in a little box at one end of the Pavilion, notching the scores of the cricketers. Sometimes the other side would bring a scorer who would sit and reckon with me and sometimes not; but I never lacked for company, as in the box was always Samuel Uziele, the groundsman's apprentice, who used to operate the scoring board, which was just above our box, with rows of handles which were always getting stuck.

' "Oil those handles, man," I used to say to Samuel, "and they will no longer be sticking."

' "O foolish little one-pubic-hair," Samuel would say, "there is no oil to spare for such trifles. It is consumed by the Roller, with which we prevent this ground from turning to dust and flying away beneath our very eyes. And what is not consumed thus is for me to sell in the market, bringing me money to take my pleasure among the women in the Street of Love."

'Samuel was only a year and a half older than I, but he vaunted himself a man of the world and my Mentor, and when he was pleased with me he would tell me tales of the women he had in the whorehouses...and other tales such as this:

' "You know that my mother is long since dead, little one-pubic-hair, and that I have a step-mother. This morning, since the spirits had stolen her wits and she knew no shame, she came to me as I lay on my couch and said,

125

"Samuel, your father is both a feeble and a jealous old man. But now he is gone to the market. Sweet Samuel, make me feel that I am a woman." '

' "Well, little Nikkai, my stepmother is still young and juicy, but I had made love to my pillow not ten minutes before, and this I told her.

' "You must be waiting perhaps one half-hour, mother," I said, "before the sap will be rising once more." '

' "Aiai, my sweet son, we do not have half an hour. Your father will not linger in the market. Aiai, aiaia. But I am older and wiser than thou, and I have thought of a shift to achieve my delight. Thus and thus." '

' "Then she sat down on a stool, lifted her robe and spread her hams to show her lotus, the lips whereof she did lewdly part with her fingers." '

' "Rise from your bed, Samuel my son," she cooed, "rise and make water upon me." '

' "So I rose and stood before her and being full of piss from the long night I let forth a mighty steaming jet straight into the shaft where she stores her sweet syrup. And she did moan and frot and fart, she did wriggle and jiggle and shudder and judder and shake. Thus and thus did she achieve her delight." '

Nikkai leaned forward to attend to the obsolescent fire.

'Yes, oh yes,' he said, 'I shall miss these fires of coal.

'Such then, Simon, were the tales with which Samuel did beguile the hours in the box, true or false I know not, but making my horn stand so stiff it nearly lifted the scoring desk. Nor did such merry talk make for prompt figures. Many were the times when my lor' would call from his seat beside my lady, "Scoreboard, scoreboard," because Samuel, in the midst of his bawdy discourse, had let the score mount by ten or even twenty runs without changing the numbers. Then, when my lor' shouted at him, he would lean out of the box and say, "Truly I am grovelling, my dread lord and master, but the handles do be sticking again." After which he would change the numbers and laugh and begin yet another tale of lust and infamy.

'Now of all the people in Samuel's tales – Rachel the fat whore, whose navel was more succulent than many a women's oyster, or Deirdre her maid whose nose was perished from the pox, or Parmula the seventy year old doxy with no legs, only stumps, who did as much business as any woman in the stews – of all these people, I say, my favourite was Samuel's stepmother, about whom he had some new lewdness to retail at almost every match. So one day, when we had been long in our box and Samuel was all but parched of stories, I cried out to him, "Come, Samuel, is there news of your stepmother?" And he replied, "Aiaia, you have reminded me. Such news, O one-pubic-hair, such news. Listen and learn.

' "My stepmother," Samuel said, "has invented a new device, or perhaps she has read of it in books, for I cannot feel she is the first woman in the world to discover it. She sits in a rocking chair and thrusts two large marbles through the mossy gate into her Cavern of Delights, first one, then the other. And as she rocks in the chair the two marbles roll slowly up and down, clicking together and inching apart, and thus affording, she says, the most wondrous sensation she has ever experienced – though not quite as violent as that which overcome her on the morning when I piped my piss into her nest."

' "Oh Samuel," I entreated, "tell me that story again, for I never tire of hearing it."

'So Samuel began with the well loved words, "One morning, when the spirits had stolen her wits and she knew no shame…", and I listened and made some shift to mark down the runs and balls of the cricketers, and little did either of us know that my lady Jollif (who, as I have said, was called Joy and though of a certain age was much younger than his lordship) was approaching the box from behind, having been sent by her husband to find out why no new runs had gone up on the board for nearly fifteen minutes. My lor' had a mighty crapula and did not feel up to shouting, which hurt his head, and as the Gold Coast XI was in the field he did not know any man in the Pavilion well enough to send him on this mission, and so he had commanded his wife. And even now, as Samuel described his stepmother's antics on the stool in his bedroom, she was standing on the steps that led to our box and listening to every word.

As Samuel concluded his tale, she burst into the box and said, "Simply too lust-making. I always thought I was missing out on something and now I know what. You're sure you're not exaggerating – about all that frotting and farting and juddering and stuff?"

' "No, no, ladyship," said Samuel. "She did heave like an earthquake and squeal like a banshee loose from the pit."

'I think Samuel rather hoped for an invitation to demonstrate there and then, but Joy my lady Jollif for all her heat, and for all she had revelled in lechery with half the blacks in Gold Coast was too discreet to take her pleasure in a scoring box with the entire Gold Coast team looking on from the field. Instead she whisked her husband home and refused to let him go to the closet till he had nearly burst asunder, then ordered him to do to her what Samuel did to his stepmother.

' "Here's your last chance," she said. "If you can't even manage *this*, then I'll call in the kitchen boy." '

'How do you know all this?' I enquired.

'My dear friend, that is such a question you should never ask of a storyteller. It simply is not done. Let us say that Samuel knew one of the servants, who was listening outside the door. Thus and thus. So the poor old peer person did his best, but it was a sorry dribble, bringing his lady no delight. And worse than that. My lor' Jollif had so much gin and whisky hanging about his kidneys that his staling was toxic and did cause her ladyship's noble fesses to turn every colour in the Atlas, and never again could she romp in riggishness and make the four-buttocked beast with the men of Gold Coast, for shame that all the hairs had fallen from her crotch, leaving her mound of joy as bald as a sucking pig. Such misfortunes of her lord and herself, and the embarrassment of knowing the tale thereof had been bruited throughout Gold Coast, did cause them soon after to despair and depart. And yet let us note that no amount of previous scandal, about her cavortings and his imbibings, had brought this to pass. So true is it, my dear friend, that we human beings can endure, can rather enjoy, to be seen as wicked or debauched, but we cannot stay among people once they have seen us to be absurd. Obloquy we can withstand, but never mockery. Thus and thus. Such is the moral and melancholy tale of Joy my lady Jollif, and such fate may God keep from you and from me, my dear friend, and from all that are dear to us.'

And what, you well may ask, has all or any of this to do with the promised account of the Founder's Feast of 1948? Well, I said I must make a preface to this account, and so I have done. Had Patrick Wilkinson not tried my patience, and had I not answered back and angered him, Noël Annan would not have spoken to me as he did, and I should not have sought out Nikkai Urnandi. Had I not consorted with Nikkai, I should not have heard the tale of 'Joy my lady Jollif,' and I should not have been able to tell it, as I did, at Founder's Feast, with such very far-reaching consequences. But I must not anticipate. Thus and thus, as Nikkai might have said. One thing at a time, and first to the commencement of the Feast.

X

ROYAL PURPLE

The founder's feast of December 6, 1948, at King's College of Our Lady and St Nicholas in Cambridge, commonly known as King's *tout court*, began with a sung Grace in Greek. When the Choristers and Choral Scholars had finished it (all ten minutes of it), there followed a spoken Grace in Latin, a cumbrous and euphuistic piece complete with detailed encomia of our Royal Founder and the more substantial of the College Benefactors. After this we all sat down at last and were served with Turtle Soup and Sherry.

I was sitting at the bottom of one table next to J E (John) Raven, son of Canon C E Raven, who was Master of Christ's College and present Vice-Chancellor of the University, but was more famous, perhaps, for his works of popular theology, in which he praised austerity with the condescending unction of a man who has twice married wealth. While eponymous we were not related, though I often found it convenient to hint at distant cousinhood with the Vice-Chancellor when opening new accounts with tradesmen.

John Raven, who had come from Trinity that Michaelmas at the age of thirty-three, was a profound Platonist and also a shrewd Scholar of Greek pre-Socratic philosophy; he was, furthermore, a botanist of international distinction, having recently unmasked some German rotter who had been planting things where they never grew before and then claiming to have discovered them there; and on top of all this he was prominent as Pacifist, Puritan and Prude. (He tried very hard not to be the last of these, but was defeated both by his genes and his enlarged moral sense, which sometimes seemed to have been force-fed by his upbringing as remorselessly as the liver of a Strasbourg goose.)

Since I received tutorials from John, since I went to his dry but admirable lectures and was by way of being his friend (not a close one, but certainly a friend rather than a mere acquaintance), I knew all this very well, and it was exceedingly silly of me to behave as I did later on and am now about to relate. For it wasn't as if John were being stuffy or disapproving, were wet-blanketing the occasion or grizzling about the extravagance of the refreshments in a world of want, etc, etc, as other Puritans might have done (and were doing in several parts of the Hall). Nor did he come on heavy with those of us near him who were making pigs of ourselves; nor did he try to limit the supply of wine at his end of the table. No: he was entirely genial and tolerant in every possible way, and why I should have tried to get a rise out of him, I cannot say for the life of me.

It came about in this wise.

After the Soup and Sherry had been followed by fish with a delicious Montrachet; after the Choir had sung a string of glees in celebration of food and drink and the lighter aspect of love; after we had devoured fat goose washed down by a seigneurial Chambolle-Musigny; after the Quiristers had melodiously reminded us of the transience of pleasure ('Thus passeth in the passing of a day/Of human life the leaf the bud, the flowre') and urged us to desport ourselves while the going was still good ('Gather the Rose of Love whilst yet is time/Whilst loving thou mayst loved be with equal crime'); after the Pudding and the Yquem and the Port and the Bordeaux; after the Loyal Toast (drunk by many of us, I am proud to say, in bumpers); after a final and exquisite elegy by the Choir on the melancholy conclusion of fleshly delights

> For gone she is, the prettiest lass,
> That ever trod on toe.
> For why? She was her own foe
> And brought about her overthrow
> By being far too free of her
> Hey-nonny-nonny
> Hey-nonny-nonny
> Hey-nonny-nonny
> NO...

after all of this, John Raven said: 'I wonder what Nikkai Urnandi and the other Africans are making of the occasion.'

And I, flown with insolence and wine, replied: 'I can't answer for the others but Nikkai will love it. He's the jolliest thing out in any colour. You'll never guess what he was telling me the other day...', and then launched into

130

Nikkai's story of 'Joy my lady Jollif', beginning, as he had done, with the preface about his bedmaker's fantasies, though I knew very well the distaste and the disgust, the real pain, with which John would hear it.

In fact he heard very little of it.

'That's enough,' he said quite mildly, before the bedder's speech had really got off the ground.

But I was not to be stopped. I now skipped to the first scene in the scoring box (thus completely losing continuity, but what did I care about that after the Sherry, the Montrachet, the Chambolle-Musigny, etc, etc?) and launched into Samuel Uziele's story of his step-mother. As she sat down on the stool, 'You really must stop this,' said John gravely, 'or I shall have to ask you to leave the table.'

So I stopped. And I sulked. And when we were dismissed, a few minutes later, with instructions to rotate round the rooms of certain dons who were kindly putting up yet further potations, I resolved that I would boycott John's rooms, though he had expressed, as we rose, a very civil hope that he would see me there.

No, I said to myself: he can't talk like that to me, he can't interrupt *my* witty stories and expect to be forgiven in five minutes flat. I shall not go to his rooms, and this will be *noticed* and reckoned up against him. Simon Raven refused to go to John Raven's rooms, the word will go round, because John got all priggish at dinner. Quite right, Simon, everyone will say... In those days, you see, I thought I was quite something.

So I went first to an impromptu concert that was being given by Donald Beves, the Vice-Provost. Fat, good-natured Donald, who was named by some imbecile a few years back as the 'Fourth Man' in the Burgess-Maclean-Philby brou-ha-ha, had got himself up as a Victorian after-dinner entertainer and was standing by a potted palm singing,

> "Daddy's on the Engine;
> Don't be afraid:
> Daddy knows what he is doing,"
> Cried the little maid.
> "Daddy's on the Engine,
> So nothing need you fear:
> Everything's all, because
> MY DADDY'S THE ENGINEER."

After joining in three rousing choruses of this and hearing Donald's Unique Rendition, as Given before Her Gracious Majesty Victoria Queen of

England and Empress of India, of 'One Night as I sat at the Organ', I began to wonder where I should go next. According to the schedule, which was issued to prevent overcrowding in any one don's rooms, freshmen from 'M' to 'Z' were meant to go first to Mr J E Raven, then to the Clerical Dean, then (if I remember correctly) to Mr Boris Orde the College Organist, and lastly to the Tutor. I had prohibited myself from going to John, and pride and pique still sustained me in the embargo; but I could not yet go to the Clerical Dean, as this would violate the schedule and upset the old fusspot. Donald's concert was now concluding with Don Juan's descent into Hades: so where should I go when the defiant fellow was finally engulfed?

'I don't think I can be bothered to go to John Raven's,' said somebody near me to somebody else, 'he always looks so *accusing* and he'll probably offer one beer.'

The speaker was someone whom I very slightly knew, called Peter Dixon, now in his second year. (Second year men 'A' to 'L' were meant to go to John Raven's rooms first and mix with first year 'M' to 'Z'.) But while I was acquainted with Peter, I had never before seen the man to whom he was talking. This was a long-haired and heavily spectacled number, who carried his torso at a cant (about 15 degrees forward) which pushed his buttocks right back, till you could almost set a glass on top of them, and his nose right forward in a permanent attitude of close enquiry and wry (perhaps lewd) speculation.

'Good point,' this person now said to Peter, 'let's go to your rooms instead.'

'We always go to my rooms,' Peter said.

'We can't go to mine – now can we? – when they're halfway to Fenner's.'

'I know we can't. But I'm sick of being a sort of unpaid Mother Gin Sling.'

'Are you calling me mean?'

'No. I'm just hinting, ever so delicately, that you might like to bring a bottle along, because you finished the last one before lunch.'

'All right,' said the stranger, after a pause during which he seemed to be shivering quite violently despite the warmth of the room, 'I'll go to the Buttery, and I'll buy some fucking gin, and then we'll drink it in your rooms till it's time to go to wherever we're meant to go after John Raven.'

He moved off, buttocks swaying imperiously like the stern of a man of war under canvas.

'Do you mind if I come with you?' I said to Peter. 'I'm not keen on John Raven either.'

'You're welcome,' said Peter. 'There's some wine if Muir can't find any gin.'

'Muir…? The chap you just sent to the Buttery?'

'I only hope it's still open.'

'If he's called Muir – '

' – Temple Muir – '

' – Or even Temple Muir,' I said pedantically, 'he's under M to Z. Second year M to Z are meant to go first to the Tutor. But he seems to think he's on the same schedule as you.'

'I know. Dickie doesn't bother much with schedules. Anyway, I didn't disillusion him because I was very keen he should get the gin. In fact he's quite generous, but you have to know just when and how to operate him.'

On our way to Peter's rooms, Peter told me how he had learned, during their four years together at Uppingham, to 'operate' Dickie (Temple) Muir.

'It's all a question of making him feel guilty,' Peter said. 'It's quite untrue, what I said, about his finishing the last bottle before lunch; and he knows it as well as I do. But if you accuse Muir, however unjustly, he will feel guilty because you will have reminded him, by the very act of impugning him, that other and truer and more damaging accusations might well have been laid against him. Guilt is never far from the surface in Dickie: all you have to do is summon it up, and then he will do whatever you ask in reparation.'

'What else should I know of him?'

'He was in the Rifle Brigade during the War, and he's Captain of the College Squash Team.' Peter giggled. 'He gets a special ration of petrol for his car to take the Squash Team away to matches.'

In those days an undergraduate who kept a car at Cambridge was one of a tiny and most delectable elite. This Temple Muir was clearly somebody and a half. My opinion of Dickie rose even higher when he arrived in Peter's rooms ten minutes later, bringing not only two bottles of gin but also a bold, handsome, spring-footed, sandy-haired don, about as old as the century, whom he announced as 'Dadie Rylands.'

This, then, was the legendary George Humphrey Wills Rylands, the poet, the beauty, the wit, the actor, the sage (one of the most notable lecturers in English Literature at either university), the toast of the twenties and the ornament of the forties. I nearly fell on my knees. Instead I shook hands, mumbled my name and perspired copiously.

We discussed the speeches at the Feast. Noël Annan had put on a witty performance, replying on behalf of the College to the guest who had proposed it.

'But I fear Moley rather overdid it,' Dadie said. 'When he said of the Provost, "Age cannot wither him nor custom stale/His infinite variety", it will not have escaped many present that this observation was made, in Shakespeare's text, by Mark Anthony about his leman, to wit Cleopatra. The Provost, flighty as he is and knows himself to be, may not care for the comparison, if only because Cleopatra's story is not, in the end, a story of success.

'The Provost,' continued Dadie, 'for all the unworldly airs he gives himself, is very keen on success. He comes of a middle class Puritan family who believed strongly in effort and reward. He was very put out when he was not made Professor of Greek, indeed he thought it must be a punishment for something. But what for, he asked himself. His life had been blameless, his appetites and diversions moderate. Was it because he had – well – *tendencies*? Hardly, because he had never indulged them, or not to the right true end, or if he had he could have counted the occasions on the fingers of one hand. Of course there *was* a little rumour about Maynard Keynes and another about Rupert Brooke, the latter of which was the more credible as the Provost was often heard to complain of the ugliness of Rupert's legs; but all that, to paraphrase Webster, was in another era, and besides the whore was dead. Surely God had not withheld the Professorship of Greek simply because he had, in his hot youth, been very occasionally shameless of a summer's afternoon? But then again, if it wasn't this, what was it?'

Dadie paused, sipped his drink, leant forward breathlessly.

'Well, what it was, of course, and what he always really knew it was, was nothing to do with a punishment for past moral iniquity but quite simply the result of present academic inadequacy. The Provost was not elected Regius Professor of Greek because as a scholar he was neither accurate nor profound, indeed he was merely trivial. But how to disguise this provoking truth from himself and from the world? Answer: assume the mantle of age. For if you look and behave as if you are eighty years old, no one will blame you for not being elected to Professorships, everyone will say, "What bad luck it didn't fall vacant a few years ago – he'd have got it then all right." He *wouldn't* have got it, of course, then or ever, but the English tradition enjoins charity and respect for the aged, regardless of their achievements or the lack of them, and it is easy to mistake this general respect for the particular respect which one would accord someone who truly might have been a Professor had vacancies fallen differently, and to mistake this in turn for the respect due to one who actually had been a Professor in his day. Thus the Provost, when he realised the election for the Professorship would go against him, aged himself overnight, in an attempt to conjure the idea if not the reality of a Professorship for the embellishment of his career.

'But unfortunately it didn't turn out quite like that. The world, instead of seeing the Provost as a worshipful old gentleman who might have been or even had been a Professor, saw him as a case of premature senility and began to doubt whether he was even fit to be Provost. In order to charm the world out of this unkindness, the Provost cultivated what he hoped would be endearing eccentricities. If he could persuade everyone that he did not really belong to his own era but was in habit, mind and spirit a contemporary of Bentley or Porson, then it would be said (he hoped) not that he was a doddering old idiot but that he was a rare and picturesque survivor from a bygone etcetera, etcetera.

'And indeed to the Americans, who incline to naivety in such matters, that is what he is. They cherish him when he goes there and they worship him when they come here. They accept him in his self-appointed role to the extent that to them it is a venerable reality. It is left to the cynical eyes of Europe to see that it is fact only rather a clumsy impersonation.

'The truth is,' said Dadie, 'that the Provost is just an old ham. He's always been putting on acts of some sort or another – this sere and hoary old production is only the last of a long line – and he's always hammed them. One summer before the war Arthur Marshall and I went with him to Monte Carlo, for he has a passion for Roulette. But while the passion is genuine, the accompanying acts were not only false and self-indulgent, they were played with an absolutely shame-making absence of talent or charm. Arthur and I did not know where to look. On our first night there we spoke to an Englishman who suggested we should join him at one of the Chemin-de-Fer tables where they needed three more people to make up a quorum. Now, the Provost doesn't play Chemin-de-Fer, for the sufficient reasons that he doesn't like card games, doesn't care for the comparatively high stake, and in any case hankers after the long odds offered at Roulette. But instead of saying just this, he launched into a long and righteous tirade about how his conscience forbade him to play Chemmy because he could not bear the idea of winning money off ordinary private people.

' "Roulette is pardonable," he said, "because one wins from a huge, wealthy and faceless organisation, i.e. from the Corporation that owns the Casino. But at the Chemin-de-Fer tables individual persons are trying to *cut each other's throats* and paying the Casino a percentage for giving them the opportunity."

'The Englishman then pointed out that anyone who played Chemmy was, after all, over twenty-one and presumably went into it fully aware of the perils. One need not, therefore, feel guilty about anyone else's losses any more than anyone else would feel pity for one's own.

' "But look there," said the Provost, pointing to the table we were being asked to join, "look at that tender young lady," he said, indicating a raddled hag as tough as an alligator who was sitting behind a rampart of plaques a yard and a half high, "how could one bear to win from so frail and innocent a creature, thus bringing her to destitution and perchance to a life of shame." '

'Could he have been joking?' asked Dickie.

'Not a trace of irony anywhere. He was putting on an act as the sporty old gentleman with high moral principles and a soft heart. In fact he's as hard as nails. He waits until he sees you are having a losing run and then deliberately backs the numbers which you don't.

'Then there was another kind of performance when it was time to come home. He kept pretending he was trying to escape us and go back to Monte Carlo – all feyness and quaint-old-fogey fun. Our part was to chase him along the platform and coax him back into the carriage. We played along at Nice and Cannes, but then we started to get fed up, and at St Raphael we took no notice whatever. So he got back into the train of his own accord when the whistle blew and sulked the whole way to Paris.'

Dickie, who was something of a gambler, had listened with interest. Peter, who was a Scot and very Scottish about such matters, was beginning to be restless, and now put on a gramophone record – one of the old 78s, a song of Monteverdi.

'Such a charming opera,' said Dadie. 'We were thinking of having it at the Arts Theatre in the spring, but unfortunately the only week that the Company's free is the one that's booked for the Greek Play. *Oedipus Rex*,' he said, rather aggressively as though one of us were about to deny it, 'I'm playing Oedipus and Joyce Carey's coming down to play Jocasta.'

'Joyce Carey?' I said. 'Surely, she's the one who plays genteel tea women for Noël Coward?'

This did not go down well.

'Joyce is a fine tragic actor,' Dadie said sternly. 'We were hoping to engage Bobby Helpman for Creon, but he's busy.'

'This *is* in English?'

'English this time, Greek next,' said Dadie. 'Alternate years. You should know that by now.'

'Just so long as Joyce Carey isn't going to talk Greek,' said Dickie, and went into fits of laughter.

'It is time you all learned,' said Dadie, 'that there are subjects about which to be frivolous and subjects about which to be serious. The Drama is very much a subject about which to be serious.' He paused, then unexpectedly giggled. 'The trouble is,' he said, 'that Drama ceases to be serious as soon as it becomes stagy. And since the Provost is to produce *Oedipus Rex*, nothing in the universe can prevent its becoming stagy. He will keep on and on demanding more and more "passion" until one is screaming at the top of one's voice and waving one's four limbs about like a rogue windmill.'

He paused to consider this picture and then became thoughtful.

'It would appear,' he said, 'that I've been very much running the Provost down this evening. In some ways it serves him right: it is an essential part of your education that you be taught to recognise the techniques of faking, whether in life or art. But there is one thing I very much wish to impress upon you all. So long as we have this Provost or someone like him as Head of the College, then absurd as he may be in many respects, we are nevertheless *safe*. Our values will be preserved. Festivals like this one will be properly celebrated. Honourable connections will be respected and maintained. It will continue to be recognised that it is better to give a place to an amusing or beautiful boy who will only get a third class degree (or may perhaps even fail) than to give it to some boring swot who might manage a second with the wind behind him. There will be diversity, and a certain amount of wealth. Wide interests will be encouraged as much as specialised studies; there will be tolerance and civility; in a word, there will be civilisation. The present Provost stands for and guarantees all of this.

'But there is a new kind of man who will surely come to us in time. I'm not sure how soon; I suspect in about twenty years; but sooner or later come he will. This new sort of man will be a scientist, or possibly a practitioner of what I believe are called "social studies"; he will be a philistine and a prig; he will be left wing; he will wish to repudiate the past and to disown its monuments; he will be determined, as he will put it, to "cauterise" or "disinfect" the present, that is to sever all the old and well loved links, with people, with families, with institutions, so that the spirit which now obtains, having had its lifelines blocked or wrenched away, will die for want of nourishment. He will destroy and expel and pervert. For all I know, he may even let in women.'

In these circumstances and by the most frivolous accident (simply because of the stupid tantrum which caused me to boycott John Raven's rooms that evening) did I first meet and speak with the undergraduate who became and has remained my favourite person of all, and the don who was to be the principal influence on my behaviour (when it was sensible) and on my thought (when it was sound) during the next four years. Our discussion that evening went on for very much longer, most of it being a monologue by Dadie on this topic and on that; but on none was he more percipient than he had been in his forecast of the future fate of King's College of Our Lady and St Nicholas in Cambridge, commonly known as King's.

After Christmas I applied for a part in *Oedipus Rex* and was very properly rejected. But the mere act of application gave me some kind of toehold in theatrical circles – a toehold which became a definite stance when, a year or two later, I was employed by *The Cambridge Review* to write the weekly drama column. It was therefore a matter of course that I should be present at the festival cricket match between the Amateur Dramatic Club and the Marlowe Society which was played on Parker's Piece during the May Week of 1950, at the end of my second academic year.

If the cricket was undistinguished, the crowd in and near the Pavilion was (by our standards) positively star-studded. Literary and dramatic lions prowled and swished their tales, hungry for applause or spoiling to strike. Christopher Layton, who had played Prince Hal back in March, sparred with John Barton (Sir Toby Belch in the 1949 production of *Twelfth Night*). Peter Hall (a pretty, gangling Hamlet the previous autumn) denounced Julian Slade for the tinkling banality of the songs in his operetta, *Lady May*, the current musical attraction. Toby Robertson (still a tyro) rolled in the grass like a puppy with Michael Birkett; and Peter Wood, the iconoclastic Producer, snarled in warning at Milton Grundy, the Editor of *Granta*.

Suddenly the fauna tensed, were silent, looked in awe towards the road, where the King of the Forest (Noël Annan, no less, a sizzling Pope in the latest Webster production) was descending from Mears' Rolls Royce with an entourage – Maurice Bowra of Wadham College, Oxford, and two Conservative Members of Parliament, Mr Robert Boothby and Captain Malcolm Bullock.

Of Warden Bowra I have already said something in these pages, while Bob Boothby is well enough known, to the kind of person who may read this book, to need no introduction from me. Malcolm Bullock, however, is at once sufficiently obscure yet sufficiently intriguing to merit a word of explanation.

Of shadowy origin and indifferent education (the malicious said he had been to Brighton College, though he himself claimed to have had a private tutor), he first came to notice as an Officer of Foot Guards in the 1914 War, an event which made his fortune for him. Badly wounded at the Front, he was posted on an extra-Regimental tour of duty as Assistant Military Attaché in the British Embassy in Paris, an appointment that gave him ample opportunity, which he did not neglect, to enlarge his social scope. By the time he had come up to and gone down from Trinity College, Cambridge, he was considered eligible in the highest places, so eligible that he was permitted to marry the Lady Victoria Stanley, daughter of the Earl of Derby, who presented him with the cast-iron Conservative constituency of Crosby which in those days lay in his lordship's gift. A faithful husband and a fond father, he grieved in manly fashion when Lady Victoria was killed out hunting, and soon afterward sought discreet consolation, from members of his own sex. This predilection, rather dangerous in those days, he camouflaged cannily enough to be regularly received at Buckingham Palace and repeatedly returned to the Commons; and when I first met him, on the occasion which I am describing in the summer of 1950, he had either just become or was just about to become the Father of the House...the House in which he had uttered scarcely a score of words in as many years. For although he was in private a superb raconteur, telling his stories with perfection of phrase and rhythm, he could make no way as a public orator. Nor could he write to any effect, a great pity this, as he failed in all his attempts to transfer to the page the marvellous and manifold anecdotes of the famous and the infamous which he had collected throughout thirty years in the most august circles. When he died in the sixties his tales died with him, so that I am most privileged to have heard many of them while we sat and watched the cricket that afternoon on Parker's Piece.

He began by teasing Bob Boothby with a succulent selection of Boothby stories, to repeat which here would, I think, be straining even Bob's sense of sportsmanship too far. He went on to make a satirical choice of hymns for Noël Annan's forthcoming wedding ('Perverse and foolish oft I strayed') and to quote, extensively, the more injurious reviews of Maurice Bowra's recent book on Epic Poetry. Having then embarrassed my friend, Francis Haskell, by speculating about his activities during his National Service as a Sergeant in the Army Education Corps ('Did the boys call you "Sergeant" – or "Sarge"?'), he went on to congratulate me on winning the Member's English Essay Prize with the remark, 'It goes, I apprehend, to the undergraduate with the largest member.' With this stroke he had at last finished with present company, and he now soared away to grander regions, whence he condescended to let fall a description of dinner with the reigning Duke of Wellington at Stratfield Saye.

'We drove down together from London. He was very excited as he had discovered some new stuff called Froom, which I took to be a kind of hairdressing or unguent of great efficacy in certain amorous contexts. He never actually told me what it was, but kept saying, "You'll see, you'll see, and you'll be delighted at the economy," and with that I had to rest satisfied.

'As we drove up to the house, we knocked over a pheasant. No, "knocked over" is not the phrase: we absolutely crushed the poor beast under the off-side wheel. He insisted that the remains be scraped off the drive and then, rather surprisingly, told his man to put them in the boot. A little later we passed a nettle patch, whereupon he became very thoughtful and asked me to remind him to have a word with the Head Gardener after tea.

'So we arrived and had tea, and I reminded him about the Head Gardener, and off he went to see him while I unpacked. Just as I'd finished he knocked on my door.

"Time for a stroll before it gets dark," he said, unplugging the electric fire.

' "Don't turn it off," I said, "I'm freezing." And I plugged it in again.

' "I'm afraid we have to be very careful of the wiring," he said, switching it off once more. "We mustn't let the system be overloaded. Anyway, this thing shouldn't be here at all. And with that he picked up the fire and carried it out of the room. "You'll soon get warm," he said, "we're going blackberrying."

'And into the woods we went, with me carrying the basket and the Iron Duchess wielding a sort of shepherd's crook to hook down the brambles.

' "There aren't any left," I said, when we reached the bushes. "Rubbish," he said, putting up his crook and dragging down a branch covered in tiny little red and green berries, "these will do very well." And I was made to help him pick a basketful of wizened nasties, with an occasional berry that actually was black but had grown rotten and plopped all over my fingers.

' "Time for a rest," he said. "You won't mind not having a bath? The boiler uses too much coal, so I'm having it replaced with a much smaller one. But to make up we've got some real treats for dinner tonight. I hope you're hungry." "Hungry and cold," I said. "Can I have a fire of wood or coal in my room?" "Coal fires are illegal in this part of the world," he said, "pollution." "Wood then?" "The Head Gardener's got the key to the Wood Shed and he's busy with that patch of nettles we saw. But I'll tell them to bring you up an extra blanket, though I rather think they're all damp. The airing cupboard's not much use, you see, while the boiler's not working."

'In the end, I went down to dinner feeling like Scott of the Antarctic...and was very heartened to see what looked like a champagne bottle, wrapped in a napkin.

' "Have some Froom," said the Iron Duchess, "a florin a bottle and every bit as good as real bubbly. You have to hide the label though, as so many people have silly snobbish ideas."

'Froom tasted like fizzy white lemonade with an after flavour of semolina.

' "I'm afraid that I have silly snobbish ideas," I said. "Can I have some whisky or a dry martini?"

' "Sorry, Malcolm, it would take too long. We've got to be at table in two minutes flat in order not to spoil the first course."

'This at least sounded hopeful, so I gave up any idea of an aperitif and wondered what the first course would be. Not caviar, because that can wait as long as you like; it must be something cooked and still hot, a lobster soufflé perhaps, or quenelles of some kind.

'In fact it turned out to be a boiled egg each.

' "You see why we had to be so punctual," he said, "they get hard if you leave them." Mine was hard, as hard as granite, in any case. So was his. "Little

140

mistake in the kitchens," he said, "Never mind, the next course will make up for it."

'The next course came in under a vast canopy and was announced as pheasant.

' "It isn't yet in season," I said.

' "That doesn't matter if you run over them by accident, like we did," said my host, "and it's a great lot of nonsense about having to hang them. The Germans eat 'em fresh, so why shouldn't we?"

' "Because they're as tough as a squaddy's boots," I said, "except, in this case, for the bits the wheels went over, which taste like minced gizzard."

'I tried a mouthful of what I took to be spinach. They can't have got *that* wrong, I thought. It was like mashed sewage.

' "One of the good things about the war," said His Grace, "was all those interesting discoveries about vegetables. You'd never guess – would you? – that this delicious purée is made of those nettles I spotted this afternoon. I heard about eating them on the wireless in 1942."

'After which, as I need hardly tell you, we had blackberry fool. Then an invalid's tawny Port, from the Chemist.

' "Douro," he drivelled, holding up the bottle, "one of the family titles, you know. Deuced good name, deuced good stuff." '

'What sort of breakfast did the Iron Duchess put up?' I enquired.

'The Duke of Wellington to you,' said Noël Annan briskly. 'You must understand that one does not talk with familiarity of those, whether they be dukes or bed-makers, whom one does not know. If you are not careful, you will grow up to be like Goronwy Rees.'

'Who is Goronwy Rees?'

'A third XI writer,' said Maurice Bowra, 'and a first string shit. He was the model for the juvenile lead in Elizabeth Bowen's *The Death of the Heart*. She had an affair with him, you know, and he behaved quite poisonously. Eddie in the book is really rather a charitable version.'

'It would be fun,' said Francis, 'to have a lady novelist for a mistress.'

'Now's your chance,' said Bob Boothby, as Dadie Rylands came up with a large, blonde lady and a saturnine, hollow-cheeked gentleman, on whose hair was a suspicion of Brylcreme.

'Mrs Philipps,' said Dadie to Francis and myself, 'better known to you both as Rosamund Lehmann; and Mr John Sparrow.'

'We were talking of Goronwy Rees,' said Noël.

'He has just published a novel,' said Rosamund, 'about spies during the war. It is called *Where No Wounds Were*, and it is a peculiarly dreadful work.'

'Why?'

'It is without love.'

'Goronwy may not be very strong on love,' said Maurice Bowra, 'but he ought to know a bit about spies by now.'

'If I am not badly mistaken,' said John Sparrow, 'there will be trouble in that quarter before long.'

'Trouble for Goronwy?'

'Trouble at least for some of his friends.'

'Guy was down here some months back,' said Noël, 'he was slightly less drunk than usual.'

'But even more dirty,' Dadie sighed. 'And talking of all that crowd, I had dinner in London last month with Wicked Ant. Only of course he isn't wicked any more, he's terribly respectable and so highly thought of in the art world that I can hardly believe it's true.'

'I don't know what you see in that left wing mob,' said Sparrow. 'If they're sincere they're no better than cut-throats, and if they're insincere they're the meanest kind of opportunists.'

'Poor John – he will oversimplify,' breathed Rosamund.

'Wicked Ant at any rate,' said Dadie, 'is a man of industry and purpose.'

'But exactly what purpose,' said Maurice darkly, 'we have yet to find out.'

An innings now closed, giving Dadie and Noël their cue to go among their fellow-actors. Bowra waddled off with Sparrow and Boothby, Francis started to worship Rosamund, and I was propelled by Malcolm Bullock across Parker's Piece towards the Roman Catholic Cathedral.

'I cannot resist this building,' he said, 'a real banquet of ugliness.'

Once we were inside, however, he paid it little enough attention, but concentrated instead on stories about John Sparrow.

'Of course you know that he edited Donne while still at Winchester,' Malcolm said, 'and later was a Fellow of All Souls. He became a brilliant, brilliant barrister as well as an eminent legal scholar, and will almost certainly be Warden of All Souls when the present incumbent goes – which will be at any second now.'

'Any competition for the post?'

'Considerable competition, there always is. But Sparrow will get it because he is determined to have it. When Sparrow is determined he always gets his way. Look at what happened when the war started. They came to Sparrow and offered him quite a high position in the expanded Army Legal Department. Yes, yes, cried patriotic Sparrow, I'd love to do my bit and Military Law is just my dish, but I have one little request: when my Commission is drawn, can I be gazetted into the Coldstream Guards? He wanted, you see, to dress up as a Guardee. But what on earth, they said, is the point of being commissioned into the Coldstream Guards (as if they didn't know) if you're to be working in the Army Legal Department? That's my biz, says Sparrow. It's also ours, said they, because we would have to arrange it and what you ask is just not on. The Regimental Lieutenant-Colonel of the Coldstream would have a fit if we went to him begging combatant Commissions for legal advisers. If that's your attitude, huffs Sparrow, you can count me out. It's a Guards' Commission for me, or nothing.

'Now it happened that they very much wanted Sparrow, because when all was said and done he really knew his stuff and had a considerable presence in Court, should they ever need him in one. So some senior chappie in the Army Legal Department goes cringing along Bird-Cage Walk and grovels into the office of the Regimental Lieutenant-Colonel of the Coldstream Guards – and of course is thrown straight out into the Park. Please, please, they now say to Sparrow: we can't manage the Guards, but we love you very much and we think we can fix you up with a Commission as a Hussar. Won't that do? Well, for a minute or two Sparrow's mouth waters at the thought of riding boots and spurs, but no, he remains firm: it must be the Guards; it's what he's always dreamed about ever since he first saw pairs of Guardsmen walking out in Kensington Gardens with scarlet coats and swagger canes and Nanny told him what they were.

'And in the end, through sheer determination, Sparrow wins the battle. He just won't budge, and they need him more and more desperately, so the head of the Legal Department nobbles a Field Marshal to thump the table in Bird-Cage Walk, and our Trusty and Well Beloved John Sparrow, Esquire, becomes an Officer of the Guard. Whereupon he joins the Guards' Club – for how can they decently stop him? – in which he sits to this day, writing letters to his intellectual and pacifist friends on Guards' Club paper, and annoying elderly Generals with his theories about Lady Chatterley's anus.'

An evening or two later, I was asked to dinner by E M (Morgan) Forster (an Honorary and resident Fellow of King's) to meet his friends J R (Joe) Ackerley, at that time Library Editor of *The Listener*, and Christopher Isherwood.

Now, I am rather embarrassed to be dropping names like this. I do not wish to give the impression that I passed my entire time as an undergraduate hob-nobbing with famous novelists and fashionable dons. The fact remains that I was, for a time at least, taken up by some of the more glittering Fellows of King's and other Colleges, and that I did, during that time, meet and talk with certain distinguished and even powerful men and women who visited Cambridge, as the guests of Dadie and others, to take a look at the oncoming form. I did indeed see E M Forster and Christopher Isherwood plain, and they did stop and speak with me, and I did answer them again. This being the case, it occurs to me that what we said, or at any rate what *they* said, may be of more interest to any reader who is still with me than an account of the progress of my classical studies or of my political development (nil) or of what my precocious friends said about Kant while we walked in the Fens. Ah, you may say, but this book is advertised as being Memoirs of a Cricketer: certainly Kant and the Classics have no place in it – but neither has E M Forster. Well, I should reply, even the most dedicated cricketers cannot be playing the game every day and talking about it forever; of if they can, I for one would have small wish to read their Memoirs.

So back to Morgan Forster's dinner party. I am told, and I partly believe, that Morgan was quite generous in the way of private charity: in matters of entertainment, however, he was the meanest man that ever drew breath, compared with whom Professor Adcock was Lord Bountiful. The dinner which Morgan had ordered for us that evening was the cheapest to be had from the College kitchens; the wines – all the one bottle of them – were thin, pale and sour. Since Isherwood and Ackerley were convivial men the evening promised very drearily, and indeed was only rescued by a ruse of Isherwood, who pretended he had forgotten to bring his 'present for Morgan' over from his guest room, went off to get it, and came back with three bottles of Champagne, one of Port and one of Cognac, which he had, of course, bought from the College Buttery. We all knew this because Christopher, perhaps deliberately, had carried the bottles back in a packing case prominently labelled TO THE BUTTERY, KING'S COLLEGE. Ackerley and I exchanged winks, while Morgan gently simpered. Christopher opened the first bottle, which we drank with the grey-green 'shape' served to us as dessert, and thereafter, despite the absence of savoury, cheese, fruit and even coffee, the evening began to revive.

As I remember, Christopher was spouting about the American Dream, particularly that version of it which was current in Los Angeles. He came at length to the story of a young weightlifter or muscleman of his acquaintance, who spent his entire life 'working out' in gymnasia and developing more and more hideous and congested lumps of gristle on his biceps and shoulders. The two other things about this creature were, first, that he had an extremely gentle presence and temperament, and, second, that he had excellent degrees in Literature and Philosophy, on the strength of which he could have had a prestigious job in the Groves of Academe for the mere asking. Why, then, did he not ask? 'Because,' he once told Christopher, 'I am sick.'

The significance of this tale, said Christopher, was that what the youth was in fact seeking through his endless exercises was the beauty, the strength and the immortality of the Gods. In short his, the American, dream was to live for ever. The reason why he described himself as 'sick' was that while he was intelligent enough to know that the dream was an absurd delusion he yet continued to pursue it.

'You refer to the "beauty" of the Gods,' said Joe. 'But if these mounds of sinew he keeps sprouting are as unsightly as you say, how can he imagine he is achieving divine beauty?'

'I have already told you,' said Christopher, 'that he knows his quest to be illusory and despises himself for persisting in it. And so he is punishing and satirising himself. It is perfectly possible to follow a regimen, in Californian gymnasia, which does indeed make for a correctly proportioned and beautiful physique as well as for strength. He, so far from following such a regimen, is deliberately making a freak of himself. Why? Because he knows that the great American Dream premise, the assumption that physical immortality will one day be made possible by the medical profession, is just so much rubbish. And yet, in a way, he wants to believe it. Angry with himself for sharing the folly of the West Coast rabble, he purposely deforms himself, thus symbolising by distortion of his body the distorted and diseased thoughts of the mind which lies within it.'

'Where does dear old sex come into all this?' enquired Joe.

'The American Dream promises an eternity of abundant and deeply fulfilling sexual activity – another load of old rubbish, if ever there was one. Our muscle boy, as a protest against such imbecility, is making himself sexually repulsive.'

Morgan quietly put the Port and one bottle of Champagne away in a cupboard.

'Why are they so afraid of death?' I asked.

'Because death is an insult to American know-how. They can move mountains and put girdles round the earth: and can they not live longer than a hundred years? Can they not keep the mechanisms of the flesh in sound running order for more than three paltry generations? No, they cannot, and it's a goddamn disgrace. Every American citizen is entitled, not just to eternal life, but to eternal youth and eternal happiness.'

' "Eternal" means without beginning or end,' said Morgan mousily, 'you should revert to the word "Immortal" – something that, having been born, cannot die.'

145

'Thank you, dear Morgan. Now we come to the interesting question: why are they so desirous that their immortality should be *physical*? Only a few years ago they were prepared to settle for immortality of the *spirit* – '

' – If a spirit is immortal, it must also, by definition, be eternal,' nattered Morgan. 'Spirits are not born. Spirits – should they exist – would be of coeternal being with their creator.'

'Thank you, *dear* Morgan. Let me recast the question as follows: why are the Americans no longer content to live on in the spirit? Why do they hanker to do so in the flesh? In the old days, there were any number of sects that were liberally subsidised by their proselytes to cater for the needs of the spirit, to promise and to ensure its happy continuance hereafter and forever. Now many of these sects are derelict and bankrupt, outmoded by the gymnasia, which undertake to preserve physical form and gloss against the day – the day which is surely, they tell each other, at hand – when the medical profession will have conquered physical death. Now why have they rejected the spirit? Why is *physical* survival so important to them?'

'Because they've rumbled the great Christian lie,' said Joe, 'they've realised, at last, that there is neither soul nor spirit. All they have, all any of us has, is this bag of bones and lights we call the body. So they want to make it eternal.'

'Immortal,' Morgan said.

'And are doomed to disappointment,' Joe went on, winking at me once more, 'because a body can no more be immortal than this bottle can remain for ever charged with liquor. But luckily, though we cannot renew or exchange our vile bodies, we can always find fresh, sweet bottles of cordial when the old are taken from us by the Ferryman.'

And with this he went to Morgan's cupboard and retrieved the Champagne and the Port.

'Heart's ease, heart's ease,' he proclaimed, raising them on high, then rapidly opened them both.

Morgan looked cross but was too timid to prevent him. Christopher began a new speech, about Americans and their mothers this time. Apparently the swearword 'motherfucker' was so popular in America quite simply because any American worth his salt wanted to fuck *his* mother. Morgan went rather prim. Joe said he'd never wanted to fuck his mother. Morgan muttered something *sotto voce* about Joe's dog. I went out for a pee and was very soon joined by Joe.

'The thing about Morgan,' said Joe, 'is that he's just an old auntie. He is mean, coy, prudish (although he purports to be of Rabelaisian tolerance) and very, very spiteful.'

I agreed that there had recently been many amusing instances of all the personal defects he had catalogued.

'Ah, dear boy, how rich your life down here,' said Joe. 'In London I miss all this. I adore Morganiana, yet I am wholly deprived of such – except when I spend a day or two here.'

So there and then, as we buttoned our flies, we made a bargain. I would supply Joe with occasional 'Morganiana', i.e. deleterious items about the shabbier aspects of Morgan's conduct, while Joe would supply me with occasional work for *The Listener*. In those days reviews in this journal (except for the fortnightly novel review) were printed unsigned and paid for unhandsomely; but at least, I thought, it would be some kind of beginning. In fact it was a jolly good one, for which I have been most grateful to Joe ever since; for while we were both as good as our word, Joe was much better: whereas I could only supply Morgan stories up to the time I left Cambridge, Joe supplied me with work, when I needed it, for long afterwards, and twice let me have a three months' stint at the fatly paid and fully signed novel column.

Our bargain concluded, we returned to Morgan's rooms, where Joe began a story about how he once slept with Ivor Novello, who smelt of fish when sexually excited and was seriously underhung.

XI

FULL CIRCLE

About a year and a half before all this, Dickie Muir had asked me to play fifth and last string for the College Squash Racquets Team in a match against Eton. As Peter Dixon had affirmed would be the case, a special petrol allowance was duly made available, and off we went to Windsor, where I hoped that my abominable conduct on the cricket field had by now been forgotten. Forgotten or not, it was not raised against me, although one of the boys in their Squash side was the one with the pretty cap who had caught me on the boundary and was now, being their last string, my opponent.

This time our situations were reversed. I was playing quite well, though I say it myself, while he was utterly out of form. Very soon the Court was mauve with his astonishing language. Compared with the ferocious hatred with which he now cursed the ball, the walls, his racket and himself, my performance at the cricket match had been but an innocent bleat. And yet he had seemed so impeccably mannered on that day when he doffed his cap to address the Provost. How had the change come about? Or was it simply that he, like myself, could not bear playing badly, and that when he did, then despite his breeding he lost all control of his temper?

Certainly he began to make himself agreeable again the moment our game was over. He did not resent defeat, I concluded, he merely detested, while actually playing, the incompetence he had then displayed. He had been, I told myself, mortified by the sheer ugliness of his botched strokes, by the hideous feeling which went up his arm when he scuffed the ball with the frame of the racket. His bad temper had, at root, been a matter of aesthetics.

'I'm afraid not,' said Nigel Forbes Adam, a senior boy and a friend of Dickie, when I proposed this theory at tea. 'It is a matter of face. He cannot

148

bear to look silly. If he feels that he is, he gets in a furious bate – and of course looks sillier still.'

'At least he doesn't keep it up,' I said. 'He was as civil as you like the minute we got out of the Court.'

'He'd cooled down and worked out that the only way to make you forget what a bad figure he'd cut was to present a good one now. You know who he is, of course?'

'I know his name.'

'That won't help you. His mother married again, so that when the scandal occurred she was called Q— and not, as he still is, P—.'

'His mother was Mrs Q—?'

'If ever such a one there was. Makes you think. Everyone thought the world of her. Thought butter wouldn't melt in her armpits. Then the husband died, she became a brave little widow, after a suitable interval she marries again, very properly, to provide a father for her dear little son, all just what you'd expect from one of her family and background – until hey presto, she turns into a galloping Messalina and shags with queues of guardsmen in the park. So I think,' said Nigel, 'there is some excuse for P—'s being uneven in temper.'

'Does he show any signs of going the same way?' Dickie asked.

'He don't entertain queues of guardsmen, if that's what you mean. In fact over all *that* he's a dark horse. He hasn't wanted for proposals, as you can well imagine, but up till now there's not a breath against him, not in that line. But a chap who has a mother that suddenly breaks out like a pornographic Grand Opera…one does rather wonder what might happen.'

A year or so later P— was to run amok in the scent department of a famous Kensington store, causing over £3,000 worth of damage in three minutes…after which he was permanently retired from the world and confined in circumstances which gave great sadness to those that remembered the bright boy who had courted the Provost on the boundary or even the foul-mouthed ephebe in the Squash Court. But my reason for telling this gruesome tale lies less in the tale itself than in the occasion on which its chief protagonists were discussed, that of my first meeting with Nigel Forbes Adam, whom I have known ever since. Dickie stood godfather to his first son, I to his second, and to this day the three of us watch cricket at Lord's every summer.

We also watch it up in Yorkshire, where Nigel has a house near Selby, convenient for the Test Match at Leeds. The first time I went up there to stay must have been in 1952, by which year Nigel had left Eton, done his National Service as an Hussar, and been for some months up at King's. As I remember, it was very early autumn; and one morning Nigel's mother, Irene, came flitting over the dewy grass, like the goddess Iris 'as she skimmed the teeming ocean', waving a telegram in the air, 'My dears, it's from Ronald Storrs. He and Lady Storrs are arriving tomorrow.'

In many cases, of which that of Sir Ronald Storrs is typical, I have been extremely unlucky in my brief encounters with great or famous men. The memories which I have brought away from such encounters are far too often trivial or even worthless. I once had luncheon with Jean Genet in Athens, and the only remark of his which I can remember is, '*On ne peut pas manger correctement en Athénes*' – true enough, as far as it goes, but neither witty nor profound. When I saw Evelyn Waugh plain, on a summer's afternoon in Heywood Hill's bookshop, all he did was to repeat to the assistant, like some mechanical toy, 'Isn't it hot in your shop, isn't it hot in your shop'; as indeed it was, but it needed no sage come from Somerset to tell us that. Of the occasion I had dinner with Patrick White in Sydney all I can remember is the way in which Mr White rebuked an obstreperous guest, 'I shouldn't have asked you. I should have known better. Queens Means Scenes.' This is a bit above the average; it concludes in rhyme, and the circumstances in which the remark was made were mildly dramatic; but I still think I should have got rather more from a meeting with the author of *Voss*.

I'm afraid it is the same with Ronald Storrs. Author of *Orientations*, big wheel in the Horatian Society, Statesman, Mage of the Middle East, Manipulator of T E Lawrence – surely such a one must have said or done something memorable during the thirty-six hours he passed with me at Skipwith Hall? No, he didn't; or rather, yes, he did, as I still actually remember it, but not the sort of thing which important men should be 'memorable' for.

He discovered that I had been at Charterhouse, as he had, and drank down, rather quickly, several glasses of Nigel's (absent) father's admirable Port in celebration; he then discovered that I had been a Saunderite, as he had, and promptly drank several more to toast this extraordinary coincidence; and then, finally and fatally, he discovered that I had been reading the Classics at Cambridge, a feat which pleased him so much that he woofed a huge bumper in its honour. After this he became flamboyant, then grandiose, then petulant, then incoherent, at which stage Nigel, who was rather diffidently presiding over the table in his father's stead, at last found the courage to put the stopper in the decanter and on Sir Ronald, and ushered the gentlemen into the drawing room...where Lady Storrs, who was a harpy at the best of times, seized shrilly and vengefully upon her knight and propelled him with beak and talons up the stairs to bed.

The next day Lord Anglesea came to luncheon. Both the Storrs positively grovelled before this amiable young nobleman, introduction to whom worked a total cure on Sir Ronald's crapula, which had been very evident (face like a road map and eyes like tapioca) all through the morning. Of Anglesea I remember little save an unusual combination of courtesy and candour, the latter of which, in certain situations, marched rather uneasily with the former. When, for instance, Sir Ronald bowed himself up to Anglesea in the garden after luncheon and all but curtseyed while presenting my lord marquess with an inscribed copy of *Orientations*, I observed a glint of satirical merriment in his lordship's eye which was not to be quenched, despite the manifest cordiality and respect with which he, the aspirant historian, received this gift from his distinguished senior. His eyes said, 'Although you are a man of great experience and some fascination, you are really the most appalling old toady', and I had the impression that he was hard put to it not to rehearse the words aloud; for certainly, some ten seconds after accepting the book, he broke into a peal of laughter, quite inexplicable to me except on the surmise that he was relieving the strain of withholding his honest opinion of Sir Ronald and his sycophantic manner of presentation. Notwithstanding an element of wariness, the gusto of the laugh was quite Chaucerian, and so put me in mind of a Chaucerian image to describe the whole phenomenon: thus did a man who wished to defecate find at least temporary relief by letting a vigorous but carefully controlled fart. Something had to be done: but were it overdone, my lord, like the farter, were quite undone.

Lord Anglesea I have never seen since, but with Sir Ronald I had some correspondence, as he was kind enough to propose me for membership of the Horatian Society. This met once a year to dine and listen to encomia of Horace in the form of toasts proposed by Horatians both professional and amateur. All this happened, then as now, in the Dining Room of the House of Lords, where the food was like that served in a decaying Railway Hotel and boisterous waitresses used to make the most tremendous racket from the kitchen all through the speeches. Old friends turned up from time to time, Patrick Wilkinson as an Officer of the Society, Noël Annan and Robert Birley to address it; but my principal memory is not of any person or persons present on any particular occasion but of a kind of collective perversity displayed by the Society at large and in the following fashion.

When the food in their Lordships' House had become all but inedible, the Honorary Secretary secured a promise from one of the Livery Companies that we might use its premises and its facilities for our dinner the following year. For once the food and drink were quite delicious; but such was the snobbery of the Horatians that after the change of venue had been announced the number of subscribers dropped to less than half the average. Those lucky few who did dine, in (I think) the Cordwainers' Hall, were peremptorily informed, even as they sat digesting their sumptuous yet delicate repast, that the Annual Dinner would revert next year to the Lords…where the usual number assembled twelve months later to eat the usual hogs' wallop.

To the Horatian Dinner which was addressed by Robert Birley I invited Bob Arrowsmith; and on the occasion when Noël Annan spoke I asked Francis Haskell. Two things of note occurred at the latter party: Noël made a brilliant but depressing speech, in which he deplored but declared inevitable the passing of the Classical Tradition; and later on Noël, Francis and myself reenacted, for our own pleasure but somewhat to the scandal of Horatians who overheard us, THE BUMPER BOB BOOTHBY DISASTER of 1951:

Dadie Rylands had been invited to give one of the big annual lectures in London, to the British Academy if my memory serves me; and if it doesn't serve me in this detail, it does very clearly in everything else which occurred.

Dadie very kindly invited Francis and myself along with Noël and Mrs (Gabriele) Annan, to accompany him to London in Mears' Rolls Royce for the occasion. We were to picnic on Royston Heath, have tea in the United Universities Club, and hear the lecture: after which Noël and Gabriele would attend some family function, while Dadie, Francis and myself would dine with Bob Boothby and Maurice Bowra, who would both be at the lecture.

All went swimmingly. The picnic was a minor triumph for Gabriele, Mears' Rolls purred punctually into London, the United Universities Club provided commodious lavatories if not much of a tea, and the lecture was a major triumph for Dadie. Then there was a cocktail party to celebrate, at which I met both Rose Macaulay and Ivy Compton Burnett, the former of whom was very jolly with Francis and me, while the latter was quite strikingly not. Bob and Maurice duly appeared to congratulate Dadie, though Bob himself had had to cut the lecture as something of major importance to the nation had required his attention. He would now, however, make amends by inviting all of us to White's, an institution, he reminded us, paramount among its kind, and one to which by no means anybody, in fact almost nobody, and certainly none of us except of course for him, could ever aspire to be elected. So to White's we all five went, Dadie elated by gin and success, Francis and I elated by gin and Rose Macaulay, Warden Bowra elated by his own brilliance, and Bob Boothby by his own importance – and also by a new suit which he was wearing for the first time, he told us, and by the new car in which he drove us. He had been allowed to jump a long queue to get it, he said, because he was so important; it was (baruuuum, baruuuuum) the finest and fastest model going, and it was taking us (honk, honk) to the finest and most exclusive gentlemen's club in London, in England and therefore in the World.

At dinner everyone got more elated, except, perhaps, Maurice, whose personality was always pretty voluble but seldom more or less so. There was Champagne to celebrate Dadie's lecture and to give Bob the opportunity of telling us how excellent and how expensive it was, the finest Champagne, in the finest club, in the finest capital, etc, etc. When we had had too many bottles of it, and a good many other things beside, we climbed into Bob's new car to drive across the river and inspect the work in progress on the site of The Festival of Britain, a trip for which we just had time before we rejoined Noël, Gabriele, Mears and Mears' Rolls at the appointed rendezvous − the Athenaeum.

At first we were denied admission to the site − but then the Gate Keeper recognised Bob Boothby and bowed us through. When we drove up near the buildings some late workers also recognised him and raised quite a satisfying 'Hoorah for Bob Boothby'. As we departed the Gate-Keeper threw up a smart military salute − to Bob Boothby. As we drove towards the Athenaeum Bob himself took up the topic − of Bob Boothby: how he had been cheered and saluted, how he was dressed in his new and splendid suit and was driving in his new and peerless car, and how privileged we were to be driving with him, Maurice Bowra in the elegant new-style cup-seat in the front, Francis, Dadie and I on the luxurious foamy triple bench at the back...until, as Bob reached a crescendo of self-applause, there was suddenly that well known choking noise and one of us in the back (never ask me who) was sick all over Boothby's new suit and Boothby's new car and Boothby's quacking head, as neat an instance of hubris and nemesis as ever I heard of.

By the time of the bumper Boothby frolic my blithe days at Cambridge were − or so it seemed − fast running out. Money had long since done so. Although I managed to keep going somehow by a series of disgraceful shifts, I was reaping a bitter and well earned harvest from my prodigality of two years before; and had it not been for the forebearance, even the charity, of those who, like Patrick Wilkinson, had warned me and been snubbed for their pains, I should long ago have been sent down. But now there was a sudden and surprising twist in my affairs. However badly I had behaved, I had always worked quite hard; and at the end of my third year the College decided that I showed promise enough as a scholar to be invited to stay on as a post-graduate Student and to submit a thesis in competition for a Fellowship.

This generous decision was made by the College Council at the beginning of the Long Vacation Term of 1951 and was communicated to me by one of

the Fellows in the course of the annual cricket match against the College
Servants. Pleased, proud and touched, flushed with the additional pleasure of
having just taken two wickets, I vowed there and then to abandon my
dissipated courses and cling wholly to learning, a vow which I kept pretty well
for the remainder of the Long Vacation. But by now I was being regularly
employed by Joe Ackerley and others to write reviews for the weekly journals;
by October of 1951 I had begun to be infatuated with a vision of myself as
an urbane and affluent man of letters; and to realise the vision I put aside my
thesis and started to write a novel (which was indeed to be published but not
until thirty years later). By March of 1952 my thesis had not advanced by a
single paragraph, though even then perhaps, had I put my heart into it, I might
have made up enough ground by July to convince the Council that my
Studentship should be renewed. But finding the drudgery of research
intolerable, I went instead to Italy to join Francis Haskell, who was using his
own opportunities and resources to better purpose than myself and was even
then assiduously laying the foundations of his fascinating first book, *Patrons
and Painters*.

When I returned to Cambridge in the late April of 1952, every kind of
writing was large upon the wall. My academic career was closed, my literary
career had not yet, in any real sense, begun; money, which, through the
kindness of certain Fellows of King's, had been got right a few months back,
was now, through my extravagance in Italy, a ghastly problem again. 'What
shall I do,' I said to James Prior, whom I chanced to encounter at Fenner's
where the University was playing the Free Foresters, 'whatever shall I do?'

James had taken his degree (a First in Estate Management) a year ago and
was up on a visit.

'Count your blessings,' he said. 'You weren't cut out for a don. You haven't
that sort of mind – or that sort of grit. To become a don, leave alone to remain
one, you have to have a very high tolerance of boredom. Boring research, as
you've found for yourself already, boring colleagues, and boring pupils. Not
your kettle.'

'Still, there would have been advantages. Lovely rooms, dainty dinners
inside them, the College cellars...

'How long do you suppose all that's going to last?'

'It's seen the Labour Government out.'

'There'll be other Labour Governments. More thorough. *Socialist*
Governments. Those buggers never stop, you know. They never say, "Right,
that's settled, now let everyone enjoy himself." Oh no. They go sniffing round
for something else to interfere with. And sooner or later they're going to sniff

out fruity dons who are having "dainty dinners" in their "lovely rooms". Count yourself lucky that they won't be sniffing out you.'

'All right. I'm lucky to be going. But where shall I go?'

'You say you want to be a writer, a novelist. So go and find yourself something to write about. What do you know as yet? Where have you been?'

'Italy. France. India.'

'Not a bad start. But if you're going to spend your life writing novels, you'll need more capital, so to speak, than six months in India as a Cadet and odd weeks in France and Italy. So travel.'

'What with?'

'Your two feet. If you're too soft for that, if you want to go first class, why not rejoin the Army? They're dishing out Regular Commissions to graduates who formerly held Emergency Commissions, as we did. And they're throwing in a few years seniority with them. If you can get some decent sort of Regiment to take you on, you'll go scudding round the world in comfort if not in luxury.'

'I might get shot.'

'That'd settle all your problems.'

'But James, all those beastly manoeuvres and exercises and things in the rain.'

'You'll get no wetter than you already are. For Christ's sake. Do you expect your friends to get up a subscription of five thou a year so that you can travel round the world *en prince* and without lifting a finger?'

Then Marc Boxer came up, wearing his crimson velvet jacket. I introduced him to James, who eyed him with misgiving.

'James says I've got to go and be a soldier,' I said.

' "So I said, I will 'list for a lancer," ' camped Marc, ' "O who would not sleep with the brave?" '

'Thank you very much, but I shall sleep in the Officers' Mess.'

'You old *Fascist*, darling,' said Marc. 'I think I see something by the pavvy. Those white flannels, so rise-making. So ta-ta for now, Mummy's poppet,' and to James, 'bye-bye, Jamiekins.'

With that Marc (who often joins Dickie and Nigel and me in the Pavilion at Lord's, where his behaviour is rather more staid than it was at Fenner's thirty years ago) went skipping on his way.

'Who was that?' said James.

'I told you. Marc Boxer.'

'I meant, what does he do? He must think himself pretty special to put on an act like that.'

'He draws very clever cartoons.'

155

'Need he be quite so…well…*errrr.*'

'He tells me he's turning normal at the beginning of next academic year. Being queer is no longer fashionable, he says, or it won't be by Michaelmas. Heterosexuality is going to be all the rage – and so, he predicts, is Socialism.'

'There you are. What was I telling you? You take my advice. You'll be safe from Socialism in the Army, for as long as anyone is, and you'll be somewhere privileged with syces and doolibearers and barra pegs and things like that.'

'Those are all in India. We don't go there any more – or had you forgotten?'

'Well, there's still Africa and Hong Kong and Singapore and God knows what. You go off with the Army and get a good look at all that. If you follow your usual form, you'll be kicked out in four or five years, and then will be the time to come home and start writing novels.'

And so once more I went for a soldier, though I was not finally gazetted until May of 1953. My previous Commission had been in the Oxfordshire and Buckinghamshire Light Infantry (the 43rd); but they, though they accepted me as a Regular during the winter, later found that they had no room, and I was passed on to the King's Shropshire Light Infantry (Housman's '53rd') instead. At that time this was a jolly, *louche*, discernibly amateur, above all *bachelor* sort of a Regiment which couldn't have suited me better. But even the KSLI had occasionally to go through stern motions for the look of the thing; and a few days after I joined I was sent off to the Tactical Wing of the School of Infantry at Warminster, to undergo a ferocious refresher course in the techniques required of a junior commander of foot soldiers.

Chief Instructor at Warminster was Lieutenant-Colonel John Mogg (later CGS) of the 43rd, throughout his career a keen if light-hearted cricketer. When the Light Infantry Cricket Week came round that June he procured two days' special leave for himself and for me, so that we might play for the Light Infantry against the Greenjackets at Oxford. The occasion was the height of the Light Infantry Social year, Field Marshals and Generals were thick as confetti, and it was rather important to me that I should make a good impression or at any rate not a bad one. But unfortunately there was a joker in the pack. Keeping for the Greenjackets was an old Cambridge chum of mine called Mark Watney, who never took the field without a flask of gin and lime juice in his hip pocket.

When John Mogg and I walked out to open the batting for the Light Infantry, 'Hallo, darling,' said Mark Watney, whose idiom and mannerisms, when it suited his purpose, were very similar to those of Marc Boxer, 'and who's that adorable cuddly old girl who's come in with you?'

'That,' I said, 'is Colonel Mogg, my Chief Instructor at Warminster. I do not want him to think that I am a poofter or that I have poofter friends.'

'But darling, no one ever thought you were a poofter. You were quite the butchest thing on King's Parade. If you like, I'll tell Mrs Mogg that myself. Hey, Moggy,' he called down the wicket.

I should explain that Mark enjoyed considerable licence as he was no longer a serving Officer and had always been considered, even when he was serving, to be a privileged jester. The Greenjackets, an extremely broadminded crowd, were therefore quite happy to put up with this sort of thing indefinitely; but I doubted whether this were true of John Mogg...who mercifully did not hear Mark's call.

'For Christ's sake,' I said, 'do you want to get me drummed out?'

'Oh sweetheart, you have come on heavy since you joined the Colours,' said Mark while I was taking guard. 'I do not think it at all kind or nice. You are no longer the Simon that Mummy loves. For all our sakes I think it is my duty to get you thrown out.'

'PLAY,' called the Umpire.

There was only one thing for it. With Mark in his present mood – to say nothing of the gin and lime juice in his hip pocket – I could expect no quarter. I must get off the scene as fast as I could and yield my place at the wicket to some other butt. At the first ball, which was dead straight, I swished as wildly as you like – and was rewarded with an enormous six and applause from all over the ground, applause happily loud enough to drown Mark's comment, 'If you go on showing off like that, you silly minx, your prick will drop right off.'

Exactly the same thing happened to the second ball. Even louder applause doused Mark's next insult, 'She thinks she's Victor Trumper in drag.'

My luck couldn't last. The third ball shattered my wicket. Which was just as well: I escaped from Mark Watney before he made any too injurious and public revelation about my Cambridge past, and at the same time I was congratulated by General Paget, Colonel-in-Chief of the 43rd, on getting the Light Infantry innings off to such an exciting start.

'That's what I like to see,' he said, 'attack, and then again attack. Some Frog chappie once said something of the kind, only he called it "*audace*". Who's that nice-looking wicketkeeper you were talking to? Friend of yours?'

'I played cricket against him at Cambridge, sir.'

In those days I was too green to call Generals 'General'.

'Name of what?'

'Watney, sir.'

'Anything to do with the brewers?'

'A distant relation, I think.'

'Well he certainly enjoys the product.'

For Mark was now taking a long swig at his flask between overs.

'He always does that when he's keeping wicket, sir.'

'Does he, by Jove? Damned bad manners, and so one of those Riflemen ought to tell him. Besides, they've only been out there ten minutes, so he oughtn't to be needing it. That boy's heading for a bad end.'

You would not have thought so from his performance on the field that day. For it was Mark who (between copious draughts of gin and lime) made two brilliant stumpings from the leg side; it was Mark, nimble Mark, who flung himself on his face to catch John Mogg when he was well set at 40; and it was Mark, blithe and beautiful Mark, who made 53 runs in sixteen minutes, flickering down the wicket to drive like some bright spirit among the shadows that fell across the green while the bells tolled curfew from the city. Today has been Mark's day, everybody said amid the tinkling glasses in the marquee. What a pity he is not going the right way, said General Paget, to enjoy many more like it.

And of course the General was right, as Generals (popular opinion not withstanding) usually are. Not so many summers later Mark Watney was to be dead of drink and disappointment, shot by his own hand.

So began my time as a regular soldier, of which I have already written in these pages. It lasted until 1957 and the scenes which were described at the beginning of this book.

Apart from a brief exordium, then, these Memoirs began with cricketing (and associated) events which took place in 1957; then went back, stage by stage, to 1938; then turned in time, and have now come forward to within easy hailing distance of 1957 once more.

1957 was to prove the great turning point in my life. It was then that I ceased at last to flit vainly and shadily from School to scandal to Army to Cambridge to Grub Street to penury and back to the Army again; it was then that I realised that I had arrived at my last chance: there was now only one thing left to do, and I must do it with my might, or perish. So I settled to my desk to write my way back into a decent and solvent existence, and for several years I had no time for cricket. No time, that is, to play; but I found time, before long, to watch occasionally, at Canterbury or at Dover or, as a special holiday from my task, at Lord's; and always it seemed to me to be the most beautiful and intricate and thrilling of all games, just as it had beneath the Surrey pines, when I was eleven, or on some Fenland green with Dickie in the Long Vacation of 1949, or on the ludicrous afternoon at Brunswick when only two overs were bowled.

So during those early and grinding years of my career as an author it was from watching cricket that I looked for my repose. Later, much later, I was to play once again, with what good friends and kind fortune I shall perhaps write hereafter, should any care to read of these things and if God should still lend my hand the skill to conjure them.

June, 1979 to February, 1981

Deal; Dieppe; Hove; Cannes;
La Garde Freinet.

SIMON RAVEN

MORNING STAR

This first volume in Simon Raven's *First-born of Egypt* saga opens with the christening of the Marquess Canteloupe's son and heir, Sarum of Old Sarum. The ceremony, attended by the godparents and the real father, Fielding Gray, is not without drama.

The christening introduces a bizarre cast of eccentric characters and complicated relationships. In *Morning Star* we meet the brilliant but troublesome teenager Marius Stern. Marius' increasingly outrageous behaviour has him constantly on the verge of expulsion from prep school. When his parents are kidnapped, apparently without reason, events take a turn for the worse.

THE FACE OF THE WATERS

This is the second volume of Simon Raven's *First-born of Egypt* series. Marius Stern, the wayward son of Gregory Stern, has survived earlier escapades and is safely back at prep school – assisted by his father's generous contribution to the school's new shooting-range. Fielding Gray and Jeremy Morrison are returning home via Venice, where they encounter the friar, Piero, an ex-male whore and a figure from a shared but distant past.

Back in England, at the Wiltshire family home, Lord Canteloupe is restless. He finds his calm disturbed by events: the arrival of Piero; Jeremy's father's threat to saddle his son with the responsibility of the family estate; and the dramatic resistance of Gregory Stern to attempted blackmail.

SIMON RAVEN

BEFORE THE COCK CROW

This is the third volume in Simon Raven's *First-born of Egypt* saga. The story opens with Lord Canteloupe's strange toast to 'absent friends'. His wife Baby has recently died and Canteloupe has been left her retarded son, Lord Sarum of Old Sarum. This child is not his, but has been conceived by Major Fielding Gray. In Italy there is an illegitimate child with a legitimate claim to the estate, whom Canteloupe wants silenced.

The plot also sees young Marius Stern and his school friend, Tessa Malcolm, drawn into Milo Hedley's schemes and into a dramatic finale orchestrated by Raisley Conyngham, Milo's teacher.

NEW SEED FOR OLD

The fourth in the *First-born of Egypt* series has Lord Canteloupe wanting a satisfactory heir so that his dynasty may continue. Unfortunately, Lord Canteloupe is impotent and his existing heir, little Tully Sarum, is not of sound mind.

His wife Theodosia is prepared to do her duty when a suitable partner is found. Finding the man and the occasion proves somewhat tricky, however, and it is not until Lord Canteloupe goes up to Lord's for the first match of the season that progress is made.

'Raven's unique vision of our times – classes battling, corruption raging, ideas flashing – is not only valid, but valuable. He spins webs of chance, intrigue and wit to ensnare civilised values and trap the truth'
– *Mail On Sunday*

SIMON RAVEN

BLOOD OF MY BONE

In this fifth volume of Simon Raven's *First-born of Egypt* series, the death of the Provost of Lancaster College, Cambridge, is a catalyst for a series of disgraceful doings in the continuing saga of the Canteloupes and their circle.

Marius, under-age father of the new Lady Canteloupe's dutifully produced heir to the family estate, is warned against the malign influence of Raisley Conyngham. Classics teacher at Lancaster, Conyngham is well aware of the sway he has over Marius, who has already revealed himself a keen student of 'the refinements of hell'. With fate intervening, the stage is set for another deliciously wicked instalment.

'Raven is one of our best and funniest storytellers'
— *Times Educational Supplement*

IN THE IMAGE OF GOD

The sixth in the *First-born of Egypt* series sees Raisley Conyngham, Classics teacher at Lancaster College, Cambridge, exert a powerful influence over Marius Stern. His young pupil, however, is no defenceless victim.

Marius has a ruthless streak and an ability to sidestep tests and traps that are laid for him. Which is just as well because everybody is after something from him…

'Raven's world of upper- and upper-middle-class mores, or amores more like, is outrageous and funny, elegant and sharp'
— *The Times*

OTHER TITLES BY SIMON RAVEN AVAILABLE DIRECT
FROM HOUSE OF STRATUS

Quantity		£	$(US)	€
☐	BIRD OF ILL OMEN	7.99	12.95	14.50
☐	BROTHER CAIN	7.99	12.95	14.50
☐	CLOSE OF PLAY	7.99	12.95	14.50
☐	DOCTORS WEAR SCARLET	7.99	12.95	14.50
☐	THE FORTUNES OF FINGEL	7.99	12.95	14.50
☐	AN INCH OF FORTUNE	7.99	12.95	14.50
☐	THE ROSES OF PICARDIE	7.99	12.95	14.50
☐	SEPTEMBER CASTLE	7.99	12.95	14.50
THE FIRST-BORN OF EGYPT SERIES				
☐	MORNING STAR	7.99	12.95	14.50
☐	THE FACE OF THE WATERS	7.99	12.95	14.50
☐	BEFORE THE COCK CROW	7.99	12.95	14.50
☐	NEW SEED FOR OLD	7.99	12.95	14.50
☐	BLOOD OF MY BONE	7.99	12.95	14.50
☐	IN THE IMAGE OF GOD	7.99	12.95	14.50
☐	THE TROUBADOUR	7.99	12.95	14.50

ALL HOUSE OF STRATUS BOOKS ARE AVAILABLE FROM GOOD BOOKSHOPS
OR DIRECT FROM THE PUBLISHER:

Internet: www.houseofstratus.com including synopses and features.

Email: sales@houseofstratus.com
            info@houseofstratus.com
            (please quote author, title and credit card details.)

Tel: Order Line
            0800 169 1780 (UK)
            International
            +44 (0) 1845 527700 (UK)

Fax: +44 (0) 1845 527711 (UK)
            (please quote author, title and credit card details.)

Send to: House of Stratus Sales Department
            Thirsk Industrial Park
            York Road, Thirsk
            North Yorkshire, YO7 3BX
            UK

PAYMENT

Please tick currency you wish to use:

☐ £ (Sterling)   ☐ $ (US)   ☐ € (Euros)

Allow for shipping costs charged per order plus an amount per book as set out in the tables below:

CURRENCY/DESTINATION

	£(Sterling)	$(US)	€ (Euros)
Cost per order			
UK	1.50	2.25	2.50
Europe	3.00	4.50	5.00
North America	3.00	3.50	5.00
Rest of World	3.00	4.50	5.00
Additional cost per book			
UK	0.50	0.75	0.85
Europe	1.00	1.50	1.70
North America	1.00	1.00	1.70
Rest of World	1.50	2.25	3.00

**PLEASE SEND CHEQUE OR INTERNATIONAL MONEY ORDER
payable to: HOUSE OF STRATUS LTD or card payment as indicated**

STERLING EXAMPLE

Cost of book(s):. . . . . Example: 3 x books at £6.99 each: £20.97

Cost of order:. . . . . Example: £1.50 (Delivery to UK address)

Additional cost per book:. . . . . Example: 3 x £0.50: £1.50

Order total including shipping:. Example: £23.97

VISA, MASTERCARD, SWITCH, AMEX:

☐ ☐ ☐ ☐ ☐ ☐ ☐ ☐ ☐ ☐ ☐ ☐ ☐ ☐ ☐ ☐ ☐ ☐ ☐ ☐

Issue number (Switch only):

☐ ☐ ☐

Start Date: **Expiry Date:**

☐ ☐ / ☐ ☐   ☐ ☐ / ☐ ☐

Signature: _____

NAME: _____

ADDRESS: _____

COUNTRY: _____

ZIP/POSTCODE: _____

Please allow 28 days for delivery. Despatch normally within 48 hours.

Prices subject to change without notice.
Please tick box if you do not wish to receive any additional information. ☐

House of Stratus publishes many other titles in this genre; please check our website
(**www.houseofstratus.com**) for more details.